*Goodbyes and Stories*

The Texas Pan American Series

# Goodbyes and Stories

by Juan Carlos Onetti
Translated by Daniel Balderston

University of Texas Press, Austin

Copyright © 1990 by the University of Texas Press
All rights reserved
Printed in the United States of America

First Edition, 1990

Requests for permission to reproduce material from this work should be sent to
Permissions, University of Texas Press, Box 7819, Austin, Texas 78713-7819.

Published with the assistance of the Kayden Translation Committee.

The Texas Pan American Series is published with the assistance of a revolving publication fund established by the Pan American Sulphur Company.

♾ The paper used in this publication meets the minimum requirements of American National Standard for Information Sciences—Permanence of Paper for Printed
Library Materials, ANSI Z39.48-1984.

**Library of Congress Cataloging-in-Publication Data**
Onetti, Juan Carlos, 1909–
    [Short stories. English. Selections]
    Goodbyes and stories / by Juan Carlos Onetti ; translated by
Daniel Balderston. — 1st ed.
        p.      cm. — (The Texas Pan American series)
    ISBN 0-292-72743-7 (alk. paper). — ISBN 0-292-72746-1 (pbk. :
alk. paper)
    I. Balderston, Daniel, 1952–   .  II. Title.  III. Series.
PQ8519.O59A6   1990
863—dc20                                                    89-39745
                                                              CIP

# Contents

# Introduction

Juan Carlos Onetti, the most important Uruguayan writer of this century, was born in Montevideo in 1909. He has spent much of his life as a writer in Argentina and more recently in Spain, yet his writing is distinctly the product of the cosmopolitan little country of his birth. Onetti grew up during the great social experiment that turned Uruguay for a time into the "Switzerland of South America," with some of the most impressive public institutions on the continent; his writing, however, dates from the period of Uruguay's stagnation and slow decline. Onetti has always rejected the idea that literature should express political commitment. He has said: "The writer does not carry out any task of social importance" and "Literature should never be 'committed.'" Yet in 1974 Onetti was arrested and jailed by the military government; his subsequent experience in exile in Spain and the grim situation of his compatriots at home is the theme of his story "Presencia" (1978).

Onetti's career as a writer began with the composition of several stories in Buenos Aires in 1933. His first major published work was the novella *El pozo* (The well) in 1939, a disturbing memoir of frustrated love and avid desire, which already contains, as the Uruguayan critic Angel Rama has pointed out, the essential elements of Onetti's narrative fiction: desire, deceit, disillusionment. In the 1940s Onetti wrote several other novels, notably *Tierra de nadie* (No-man's-land, 1941), an urban novel set in Buenos Aires important for introducing Larsen, one of the central characters of Onetti's fictional world, and for experimentation with the identification of characters not by name but by motifs or characteristics ("the man in the middle chair," "the woman with the yellow hair," and so on), to a bedeviling degree of complexity. It is not until 1950 that Onetti's career as a novelist coalesces, however, with the publication of *La vida breve*, available in English translation as *A Brief Life*.

*A Brief Life* is the first of the many works in the saga of Santa
Maria, an imaginary small town on the banks of the River Plate. In
the novel a frustrated scriptwriter in Buenos Aires named Brausen
elaborates a fictional situation involving a corruptible Santa Maria
doctor, Diaz Grey, and a female patient who comes to him for morphine, Elena Sala. Brausen chooses Santa Maria as his setting because he had "been happy there years ago," a phrase that implies
that Santa Maria has (at least initially) some independent existence
outside of his imagination. Late in the novel, Diaz Grey is forced to
flee Santa Maria at the very moment that Brausen, for reasons of his
own, is forced to flee Buenos Aires; their paths cross, but Brausen
does not recognize his creation. When Brausen finds himself in
Santa Maria at last, he finds a statue in the center of the main
square; later works will reveal that this is a statue of Brausen himself and that the square is also named after the founder. And the
people of Santa Maria invoke Brausen's name in vain, in much the
same way we might take the name of God.

The Santa Maria cycle is continued in several other novels: *Para
una tumba sin nombre* (Toward a nameless grave, 1959), *El astillero*
(The shipyard, 1961), *Juntacadáveres* (Corpse-gatherer, 1964), *La
muerte y la niña* (Death and the girl, 1973), and most recently *Dejemos hablar al viento* (Let the wind speak, 1979), in which the characters take revenge on their author. The major characters of the
cycle appear also in some of Onetti's shorter fictional works, including a number of the stories included here. They include the doctor,
Diaz Grey; Jorge Malabia, a young man from a prominent Santa Maria family, whose failures in life and love are chronicled in detail;
Larsen, or Juntacadáveres, the sordid underworld figure from Buenos
Aires who opens Santa Maria's first brothel in *Juntacadáveres*; the
old journalist Lanza; Petrus, the industrialist and developer; and
various pharmacists, journalists, police chiefs, bartenders, prosti-
tutes, funeral directors, and other well-known characters in the town.

The town itself is located by the River Plate or one of its tribu-
taries, and despite the quantity of critical ink that has been spilled
on the subject, it matters little whether it is located on the Argentine or the Uruguayan bank of the river. It is a town which, though
never prosperous, is now in a state of perpetual decline, and its
prominent citizens are in danger of being displaced by upstart immigrants, particularly those from the industrious Swiss colony on the
outskirts. Though Larsen and others make a valiant effort to save
one of the shipyards in *El astillero*, even the activities of the port are
in decline, and the only easy money seems to be made by specula-
tion and trading in contraband.

The characters in this world live in a state of expectation, always imagining a world where things will work out better than they tend to in reality. They also cling to memories which, though emblematic of their failures, at least prove that they have lived. Torn between past and future, they prove unable to accept things (or themselves) as they are, and are almost frenzied in their feverish imagination and obsessive memories.

As might be expected, much has been made of Onetti's debts to Faulkner. Indeed, in the filmed interview with Onetti by Jorge Ruffinelli and Julio Jaimes, Faulkner's picture hangs above the head of Onetti's bed in the position where a crucifix might traditionally hang, and Onetti's lone book of essays and chronicles is entitled *Homenaje a William Faulkner y otros ensayos* (Homage to William Faulkner and other essays, 1975). Faulkner no doubt lent Onetti the idea of an imaginary place with a density of its own, which would nonetheless never fully overcome its fragmentary and decaying form. Similarly, it is easy to recognize in Onetti some of Faulkner's familiar themes, and even traces of his convoluted baroque style. It is no secret that Faulkner was widely read in Spanish America in the forties, and found a superb translator in Borges; in Onetti's career, the reading of Faulkner helped consolidate features already present in his earlier fiction and facilitated the full elaboration of the imaginary city of Santa Maria.

I have spoken up to now mostly of the Santa Maria cycle, yet the mature Onetti after 1950 is also the author of a number of fictional works independent of that cycle. Most notable among these are the novella *Los adioses*, here translated as *Goodbyes*, and the recent novella *Cuando entonces* (Back then, 1987). A number of the short stories are also unrelated to the larger cycle. As will become obvious to the reader of this volume, however, Onetti's thematic and stylistic concerns are fairly consistent, whether or not the particular work is set in Santa Maria. It is also worth noting that all of Onetti's fiction leaves the reader at a loss, never quite telling the whole story, so an acquaintance with the full Santa Maria cycle is not necessary for the adequate appreciation of the fragments of it, just as the autonomous (non–Santa Maria) works tantalize more than they explain.

A word or two must be said in closing about the misogyny of Onetti's fictional world. In that world women are desired, possessed, and remembered but rarely exist as beings with any interiority or depth of their own. An objection might be made that the women are also more trouble than they are worth, but much the same could be said of the men. Onetti in his pessimism perhaps dwells more than the contemporary reader might care on the imperfections of women, but his larger subject is human imperfection and the striving for perfectibility. Though dark and sometimes gloomy, his fiction delivers insights into the nature of imagination, or what may come to the same thing—self-deceit.

One interesting aspect of these stories is the curious lack of inwardness in Onetti's presentation of character. Though the stories as a group focus on human emotion, the emotion is distanced, as if the narrator were numb. Human feelings—whether hate or love or anger—are like glancing blows. The emotions are not dealt with directly, contributing to the atmosphere of powerlessness and lack of control.

*Goodbyes*, first published in 1954, is one of the best examples of these features of Onetti's fiction. This story of a former basketball player and his women is carefully presented to us through a series of narrators whose blindness is as notable as their insights. Comparable to Henry James's *Turn of the Screw* or José Bianco's *Sombras suele vestir* (Shadow play) for its masterful narrative ambiguities, it envelops the reader in a quest for truths that are never quite accessible. Apropos of *Goodbyes*, Onetti has had considerable fun at the expense of one of his critics, Wolfgang Luchting, who has proposed a "solution" to the enigmas of the novella. Onetti, in a brief note called "Another Half Turn of the Screw" ("'Media vuelta' de tuerca"), has written that Luchting's "solution" does not seem to him the "definitive" one but that it is not his task to provide this. As in James and Bianco, the reader is very much the villain of the piece, but I will say no more so as not to give too much away.

The novella is set in the hills near Córdoba, Argentina (the name of the provincial capital is seven letters long according to the narrator); the town known as a resort and a refuge for sufferers from tuberculosis is no doubt Cosquín, used later by Manuel Puig as the setting for part of his *Heartbreak Tango* (*Boquitas pintadas*). The topos of consumption, the "belle dame sans merci," is given a twist here by the fact that the shopkeeper, our narrator, is himself a recovered consumptive, who stakes his reputation on a prediction of the fate of the new arrival. One conclusion that can be drawn from his story is that more important than the truth is an understanding of how we arrive at what we think is truth.

The stories included here are chosen from the volume *Cuentos completos* (Complete stories, 1974), a volume that is of course not a complete collection of Onetti's stories. A number of his pseudonymous stories have recently been collected in *Cuentos secretos*, 1986; a wonderful collection of late stories, *Presencia y otros cuentos* (Presence and other stories), was also published in 1986.

"A Dream Come True" ("Un sueño realizado") was first published in 1941 in the Buenos Aires newspaper *La Nación*. The setting—a theater in a small town—may anticipate the Sotano Repertory Theater in Santa Maria in "Hell Most Feared." This haunting story is the most accomplished of Onetti's early short fiction.

"Esbjerg by the Sea" ("Esbjerg, en la costa") was also published in *La Nación*, in 1946. Set in Buenos Aires, it tells the story of the yearning for Europe by a Danish immigrant (Esbjerg is on the western coast of Jutland) and is important in the literature of the River Plate region for showing the darker side of the immigrant experience.

"The House on the Sand" ("La casa en la arena") appeared in *La Nación* in 1949. It marks the first appearance of the Santa Maria doctor Diaz Grey, here (as in *La vida breve*, published in the following year) involved in writing illegal prescriptions for morphine. The "Rusty" of my translation was originally named "Colorado"; I have changed the name to avoid turning the story into a Western, especially since the nickname seems to refer to the color of the character's hair.

"The Photograph Album" ("El álbum") appeared in the Argentine periodical *Sur* in 1953. It is narrated by Jorge Malabia, a major figure in the Santa Maria saga, who tells here of his sexual initiation. Malabia and his friend Tito Perotti were later Diaz Grey's informants in the masterful novella *Para una tumba sin nombre* (Toward a nameless grave, 1959), and the further development of Malabia's sexual experience is important to the story of *Juntacadáveres*.

"Hell Most Feared" ("El infierno tan temido") appeared in the Argentine literary journal *Ficción* in 1957. The title of this story comes from a famous seventeenth-century poem, the devotional sonnet "No me mueve, mi Dios, para quererte," probably written in colonial Mexico. The full text of the sonnet reads:

> *No me mueve, mi Dios, para quererte,*
> *el cielo que me tienes prometido;*
> *ni me mueve el infierno tan temido*
> *para dejar por eso de ofenderte.*
>
> *Tú me mueves, Señor; muéveme el verte*
> *clavado en una cruz y escarnecido;*
> *muéveme el ver tu cuerpo tan herido;*
> *muévenme tus afrentas y tu muerte.*

> *Muéveme, en fin, tu amor, en tal manera*
> *que aunque no hubiera cielo, yo te amara,*
> *y aunque no hubiera infierno, te temiera.*
>    *No tienes que me dar porque te quiera;*
> *porque aunque cuanto espero no esperara,*
> *lo mismo que te quiero te quisiera.*

*[It is not the heaven you have promised me that moves me, my God, to love you; nor does hell most feared move me to stop offending you for that reason. You move me, Lord; it moves me to see you nailed on a cross and mocked; it moves me to see your body so wounded; your humiliation and death move me. Finally, your love moves me, to such an extent that even if there were no heaven I would love you, and even if there were no hell I would fear you. You don't have to give me reasons to love you; because even if I did not expect what I do expect, I would love you the same as I do love you.]*

The full ironies of the reference can only be appreciated after a couple of readings of the story. Set in Santa Maria, it relates only tangentially to the central characters in the rest of the Santa Maria series, though the old journalist Lanza makes appearances in a number of the other works.

"The Image of Misfortune" ("La cara de la desgracia") was the title story of a collection published in 1960. Dedicated to Dorothea Muhr, Onetti's fourth wife, this is one of the most intense of Onetti's stories; it has been called a masterpiece of Uruguayan literature. Independent of the Santa Maria cycle, it nonetheless uses a beach resort setting reminiscent of "The House on the Sand" and part of *A Brief Life*. The delicate counterpoint of the intertwined stories—the narrator's feeling that he is the keeper of his brother (who committed suicide a month before) and his obsession with the girl on the bicycle—culminates in a haunting ending as ambiguous as that of *Goodbyes*.

"Sad as She" ("Tan triste como ella") was the title story of a collection published in 1963. This astonishingly grim story is set in Santa Maria, though the only indication of that is the location of the house in Villa Petrus, the area near the town developed by old Petrus (a central figure in *The Shipyard*). I have taken a small liberty with the vegetation in the garden, replacing one thorny bush (the "cina-cina" of the original) with an unrelated thorny bush known to North American horticulture, the pyracantha.

"New Year's Eve" ("Justo el treintaiuno") appeared in the Uruguayan periodical *Marcha* in 1964. Under the same title, it later appeared as the eight chapter of the novel *Dejemos hablar al viento* (Let the wind speak) in 1979. The title derives from a tango written in 1930 by Enrique Santos Discépolo about a man who clears out his apartment and abandons his lover, "the crazy Englishwoman," on the last day of the year, the day before she was planning to run out on him. The narrative situation in the story resembles the song to some extent, though the ending is different. Discépolo's comment on the tango "Justo el 31" seems oddly appropriate to Onetti's fiction. Discépolo said the typical Buenos Aires male is reserved in expressing his emotions and feelings; "He tries to mislead when he speaks. He is afraid of being made fun of."

"The Stolen Bride" ("La novia robada") appeared in *Papeles: Revista del Ateneo de Caracas* in 1968. Josefina Ludmer has written at length about the relations of this story to Faulkner's "A Rose for Emily." The brothel mentioned in the story is central to the novel *Juntacadáveres*, and a number of the characters in the story, including the druggist Barthé, the playboy Marcos Bergner, and his uncle, Father Bergner, are important in the story of the brothel. In this story Onetti employs an epigram which may serve to define the force of much of his fiction: "Words are more powerful than deeds."

The close of the last story seems to mark a sort of farewell to Santa Maria, but it is only the first of a series of such farewells. Onetti has seemingly concluded the Santa Maria cycle several times: in *La muerte y la niña* (Death and the girl, 1973), in *Dejemos hablar al viento* (Let the wind speak, 1979), and in the story "Presencia" (1978, published in book form in 1986). Djelal Kadir writes of *La muerte y la niña* that it "seals off the world of Santa Maria and its myth definitively." However, Onetti's more recent work reveals that there can be no definitive end to Santa Maria, that it is instead caught in a lingering decline reminiscent of the slow death in *Goodbyes*. No sweet sorrow, this parting.

To conclude, I will cite a few words from Onetti's requiem for Faulkner (1962): "He defines what we understand as an artist: a man capable of accepting that people, especially those closely related to him . . . will go to hell, as long as the smell of burning flesh will not impede him from doing his work. And a man who . . . ultimately does not take his work seriously."

The reader who desires to read more of Onetti in English has available two of the Santa Maria novels: *A Brief Life*, a fluent translation of *La vida breve* by Hortense Carpentier (New York: Grossman, 1976), and *The Shipyard*, translated by Rachel Caffyn from *El astillero* (New York: Scribner's, 1961). Two books on Onetti are available in English: Djelal Kadir's *Juan Carlos Onetti* (Boston: Twayne, 1977) is better than most of the books in the Twayne World Authors Series, yet is constrained by the formulas governing the series. Mark Millington's *Reading Onetti* (Liverpool: Francis Cairns, 1985) is a sophisticated recent study of Onetti's textuality. The most important work on Onetti to date is Josefina Ludmer's *Onetti: Los procesos de construcción del relato* (Buenos Aires: Editorial Sudamericana, 1977), a brilliant psychoanalytic study that focuses on *La vida breve, Para una tumba sin nombre*, and "La novia robada." There is, of course, a great deal of other critical writing on Onetti in Spanish.

Daniel Balderston

*Goodbyes and Stories*

*For Idea Vilariño*

# Goodbyes

I would rather not have seen the man, the first time he came into the store, except for his hands: slow, fearful and clumsy, moving without confidence, long and not yet tanned, begging pardon for their disinterested behavior. He asked a few questions and drank a bottle of beer, standing at the darkest end of the counter, his face turned—past a foreground of sandals, the calendar, sausages turned white by the years—toward the outside, toward the setting sun and the violet crest of the mountains, while waiting for the bus that would take him to the door of the old hotel.

I would rather not have seen more than his hands; it would have been enough to see them when I gave him change for a hundred-peso note and the fingers held the bills tight, tried to put them in straight, and then, all at once, decisively squashed them into a flattened ball that he stuffed shamefully into a coat pocket; those movements on the wood of the counter (full of gashes, full in turn of grease and grime) would have sufficed for me to know that he was not going to be cured, that he did not know where to summon the resolve to be cured.

In general, it is enough for me to see them, and I do not remember having erred; I always made my prophecies before learning the opinion of Castro or Gunz, the doctors who live in the town, without any other information, without needing anything more than to see them enter the store with their suitcases, with their various portions of shame and of hope, of pretense and of daring.

The orderly knows that I do not err; when he comes to eat or to play cards, he always asks me questions about the new faces, makes fun of Castro and Gunz. Perhaps he only flatters me, perhaps he respects me because I have lived here for fifteen years and for twelve have gotten by with three-fourths of a lung; I cannot say why I guess right, but I know that it is not because of that. I look at them, some-

times I just listen to them; the orderly would not understand it, perhaps I do not understand it completely myself: I guess at the importance of what they said and of what they came looking for, and I
compare the one with the other.

When this man arrived on the bus from the city, the orderly was
eating at a table next to the grate by the window; I felt his eyes following me, trying to discover my diagnosis. The man entered with a
suitcase and a raincoat: tall, with broad, stooped shoulders, greeting
us without smiling because his smile was not going to be believed
and had become useless or counterproductive a long time before,
years before he got sick. I looked at him again when he was drinking
his beer, turned toward the road and the mountains, and I observed
his hands when he handled the bills on the counter, right beneath
my eyes. He did not pay upon leaving but instead stopped and came
from the corner, slowly, an unselfconscious enemy of pity, incredulous, in order to pay me and to put the bills away with those young
fingers numbed by the impossibility of holding onto things. He went
back to his beer and to the deliberate position facing the road, in order
not to see anything, not wanting anything except not to be with us, as
if those of us in shirtsleeves, almost still, in the shadow of the de-
parting spring day, constituted a clearer symbol, less easily avoided
than the mountains starting to blend into the color of the sky.

"Incredulous," I would have said to the orderly if the orderly were
capable of understanding. "Incredulous," I repeated to myself that
night, alone. That's it: precisely incredulous, with an incredulity he
has been creating himself, because of his savage resolution not to lie
to himself. And in that incredulity, an easily contained desperation,
limited, spontaneously and absolutely, to the cause that brought it
about and that feeds it, a desperation to which he is already accustomed, which he knows by heart. It is not that he believes that it is
impossible for him to be cured but that he does not believe in the
value, in the importance, of being cured.

He was about forty and his gestures were unrestrained, revealing a
certain immaturity. When he went out to catch the bus, the orderly
stopped looking at me, raised his glass of wine, and turned toward
the window.

"And this one? Will he depart walking or feet first? If he is sick
and goes to the hotel, Gunz will see him. I will have to ask him."

He said it in jest or perhaps he thought to guarantee that he would
be asked to give any possible shots. I would have liked to sit down
and drink wine with him and tell him something of what I had seen
and guessed. I had time: the bus had not brought any passengers and it
was the hour at which meals were being planned in all the little houses

in the mountains. I wanted to talk and the orderly was inviting me, smiling over the glass and the plate. But I did not come out from behind the counter; I started dusting some cans and hardly spoke.

"Yes, he has a touch of it, there's no doubt. But it's not too bad, he's not lost. And yet, he's not going to be cured."

"Why won't he be cured if he can? Because Gunz will kill him?"

I laughed too. It would have been simple to tell him that the man would not be cured because he did not want to be cured; the orderly and I had known lots of people like that.

I shrugged my shoulders and kept on dusting.

"I have said what I think," I stated.

Later I began seeing him come from the hotel in one bus and wait for another one in front of the store, the bus to the city; he almost never came in, was always dressed in the clothes in which he arrived, always wearing a tie and a hat, different, unmistakable, without knickers, without sandals, without the brightly colored shirts and handkerchiefs which the others wore. He would come after lunch, in the suit he had used in Buenos Aires, stubborn, maintaining his aura of solitude, ignoring the whirls of dust, the heat and the cold, indifferent to his bodily well-being: protecting himself from the acceptance of his sickness and separation with clothes, a hat, and some dusty shoes.

I found out from the orderly that he went to the city to mail two letters on those days when there was a train to the capital, and then he went from the post office to a cafe opposite the cathedral, where he sat in the window and drank a beer. I imagined him, solitary and idle, looking at the church just as he looked at the mountains from the store, without accepting that they had any meaning, almost as if to annihilate them, bent on deforming stones, columns, shaded steps. Dedicated with an old, sweet tenacity to persuade or bribe what he was looking at, so that everything would give sense to the slight desperation he had displayed to me in the store, he displayed distress without knowing it or without the possibility of dissembling if he had known it.

He made the almost hour-long trip to the city in order not to mail his letters at the store, which is also a postal station, and he did it by virtue or fault of the same rigid, obsessive disposition not to admit, faithful to the naive game of being not here but there, the game whose rules decree that the effects are infinitely more important than the causes and that the latter can be substituted, perfected, forgotten.

He was not in the hotel, did not live in the town. Gunz had not advised him to go to the sanitarium; all of this could be erased so long as he did not come to the store to mail his letters, so long as he slid them across the rubber pad in the window of the post office in the city. The interruption was obliterated if, instead of giving me his letters as did everyone else in the town, he watched them be canceled and stamped with a date, handled by a monotonous and anonymous hand lost in the buttoned cuff of a uniform, a changeable hand not linked to any face, to any pair of eyes that might hint that they understood and deduced. The present could be avoided if he saw the seal striking the envelopes, printing on them, next to the two or three words of a name, the seven letters of the name of a provincial capital, a city which can be visited on business.

But sometimes when he returned from the city, he came into the store to have another beer. That happened on the afternoons of failure, when the woman's name he had written on the envelope grew incomprehensible, suddenly, at the decisive moment when the seal rose and fell with a sound of softness and resilience. Then the name did not denote anyone and it confronted him, intricate and malignant on the rubber pad, to suggest to him that perhaps the separation and the feverish lines were true.

I would see him fill the glass and empty it in silence, showing his profile, his elbows on the counter, fighting the idea that not even the past can be preserved unchanged, that the dullest ears must listen to the sound of the sand the past scrapes away, in order to descend, draw away, change, stay alive. He would leave before getting drunk and would walk to the hotel.

But the letters sent him from the capital came to me at the store, and I sent them to him with the Levy boy, who acted as mailman even though he did not get paid a salary from the post office but instead received a few pesos from the hotel, the sanitarium, and me. Perhaps the man believed that I was sufficiently interested in people and situations to open the envelopes and pry into the various ways people have of managing to say the same things. Perhaps for this reason also, he went to mail his letters in the city, and perhaps it was not just because of impatience that after a few weeks he began to come to the store about noon, soon after the bus driver threw me the thin, wrinkled sack of mail.

He had to show up, preferred to come out of the corner where the salami and the calendar were and force me to talk, without trying to convince me, without hiding his disinterest in the variant spellings of the patrician last names, showing politely that the only thing he wanted was to make me remember his name in order to avoid asking me every time if there was a letter for him.

At first he received four or five a week, but very soon I was able to eliminate those envelopes which brought letters of friendship or business and interest myself only in those which arrived regularly, written in the same hand. There were two types of envelopes, some with blue ink, others typed; he tried to distinguish them with a quick, severe glance, before putting them in his pocket, before going back to his dark corner, restoring his profile to its place in front of the picturesque sheet of the calendar, blurred by flies and smoke, and going on drinking his beer with the same presence of mind as on the days when I had not given him any letters.

Doctor Gunz had told him not to take walks, but he only took the bus to return to the hotel when he had one of the typed envelopes in his pocket. And not because of an urgent need to read the letter, but because of the need to shut himself in his room, lying on the bed with his eyes fixed on the ceiling, or coming and going from the window to the door, alone with his vehemence, with his obsession, with his fear of hope, with the letter still in his pocket or clutched in his other hand or lying on the green blotter on the table, next to the three books and the pitcher of water he never used.

What mattered to him were the two kinds of letters. One was written in a woman's hand—blue, wide, round, with the capital letter like a musical sign, and the double z's like number 3's. The envelopes which made him obey Gunz and take the bus were also visibly from a woman—long and brown, almost always with a pronounced crease in the middle, written on an old typewriter with dirty, uneven type.

We were in the middle of spring, disconcerted by furtive, weak sunshine, by cool nights, by useless showers. The orderly went up to the hotel every day, with his practiced, bold smile, his jokes, and his briefcase full of vials; the maids came down to the store frequently to get provisions for the hotel's pantry or to buy ribbons or perfumes, whatever could not wait for the weekly trip to the city. They spoke about the man because for many weeks, even though other travelers arrived, he kept on being "the new one"; the orderly spoke also, because he needed to flatter me and he had understood that the man interested me. He lived in the garage off the store, doing nothing but giving shots and putting his money in a bank in the city; he was alone, and when solitude bothers us we are capable of all the base acts necessary to assure ourselves company: eyes and ears to pay attention to us. I speak of them, the others, not of myself.

They would come and chat; and little by little I began to see him—tall, stooped over, with a surprisingly broad frame, in his shoulders—slow but not cautious, poised between special forms of timidity and of pride, eating by himself in the hotel dining room, always near a window, always with his head turned toward the indifference of mountains and hours, fleeing his condition, the faces and conversations that would make him remember.

I began seeing him in the lobby by the little covered tables of the bar, looking at a book or a newspaper, bored and patient, admitting, superstitiously, that it was enough to show himself, empty and without memory, for two or four hours a day to the guests in the hotel, in order to be free, unconnected to them or to what linked them. So, idle in a wicker armchair, his legs stretched out, forcing his lips to hold a slight smile expressing benevolence and homesickness, he lost interest in the abnormally quick or long paces of the others, in their false voices, in the offensive perfumes in which they seemed to drench themselves, as if they were convinced that the frenzy of aromas was sufficient for each of them to keep the secret that united them all, that grouped them as if in a tribe.

Among them and apart from them, two or four hours a day, seeming to believe that he had transformed his incredulity into a habit and a definite ally, and for whom a careful comedy of carelessness sufficed to keep him linked to everything that had existed before the date of a diagnosis.

I never found out whether I came to feel fond of him; sometimes, playing, I let myself be tempted by the thought that it would never be possible for me to understand him. There he was, unknown, in the bar of the hotel, his back to the scale modestly located in a corner by the staircase, sure that he would never have occasion to use it, indifferent to the metallic sounds and the comments the others made when they stepped on it to read the needle. There he was, on the grounds of the hotel before and after lunch—immediately before and after coming to the store and asking me wordlessly for the letter that awaited him—walking until he reached the river, until he drew near the rounded white rocks of the riverbed and the miserable ribbon of water that wound its stubborn, luminous way through them; looking at and kicking against the five columns of the bridge; descending through brambles and reddish patches of bare earth to reach the hotel dump and kick around cardboard cartons, bottles, the remains of vegetables, cotton balls, yellow paper.

I kept on seeing him come into the store every day at noon, in his gray city suit, his hat pushed back, giving me a brief, dull fiction of a greeting. And when he went into his corner to drink a beer, with or without letters in his pocket, I insisted on examining his eyes, on guessing the strength and quality of the rancor that could be discovered in the bottom of them: a domesticated rancor, made patient, decisively altered. He turned his head to erase me; he looked at the stubble and the paths in the mountains, the ultimate whiteness of the little houses under the vertical sun.

One night at the beginning of November, the orderly came into the store and sat down to challenge me with a smile. I served him wine and his usual plate of cheese and salami; I killed sleeping flies, turning my back to him and whistling.

"So you don't know about it?" the orderly finally began. "It's unbelievable. You remember the guy, don't you? It seems that he's leaving the hotel; it seems he got tired of so much talk or that he doesn't have anything left to say, because one afternoon he met up with the Gomeza blonds on the terrace and he had to say hello, making a mistake, of course, because he is careful never to be right and always says "Good afternoon" in the morning or "Good evening" in the afternoon. So that everyone will know how absentminded he is, because he does it with pleasure, so that people will know that he does not think about those he greets or know what is happening around him."

Sometimes he broke off to chew the visible mixture of salami and cheese, other times he chewed while talking; it occurred to me that the orderly's cool, stubborn hatred could not have come from the other's refusal to have the shots recommended by Gunz, that at its origin was an incomprehensible humiliation, a secret offense.

"He is leaving the hotel. He must have run out of things to say, because once he talked about the rain with the waiter in the dining room or asked the maid how late there is hot water. He still hasn't said goodbye, hasn't gotten up the nerve to ask for the bill or explain, if there is anyone interested in listening to his explanations. And already nobody talks to him, or if they do, it is in jest, to guess whether he will nod or shake his head, with that wooden face of his, his eyes of a sleeping fish."

I laughed a little, to make him happy, to show that I was listening to him; I kept on swinging the flyswatter; I did not ask any questions.

"The thing about the eyes of a sleeping fish was something I heard from Reina, the tall maid," the orderly admitted. "He still hasn't said goodbye. But one afternoon instead of going to inspect the garbage dump, he went up the mountain to speak with Andrade and rented the chalet of the Portuguese girls. He must not know what happened in the chalet. Since he doesn't talk to anyone, who could warn him?"

"It doesn't matter," I said. "If he's already sick . . ."

"That goes without saying. I don't say it because of the possibility of infection. But, in any case, a house where three sisters died, with the cousin that makes four. . . . all at twenty-five. It's strange."

"She wasn't a cousin of the Ferreyras," I said, yawning. "Besides, he won't see twenty-five again."

The orderly started laughing as if I had made fun of someone. While I was pulling the blinds, I imagined the man going up the mountain to interrupt Andrade's nap; introducing his long, idle body—like a contradiction, almost like a desecration—in the gloom of the business of sales and commissions; interesting himself in opportunities, prices, and details of construction in his low, monotonous voice; letting himself be cheated; drawing his eyes across the huge, whimsical map of the mountains hanging on a wall, crisscrossed (in an absurd attempt to establish order) by thick white lines that corresponded to streets and avenues never built, by curving, jumbled blue and red arrows which prophesied bus routes where tires would never be worn out going up and down past the imaginary names. The man looked at the pins with colored markers marking on the map the approximate locations of the houses Andrade had been asked to rent or sell, trying to discover a glimmer of warning, of promise, filtered through the dust that covered them.

And Andrade, sweaty, smiling, offering him, cautiously at first, then later enthusiastically and almost insistently, the Ferreyras' little house with its four rooms, the furniture covered in light cretonne, the touches of faded grace created by the girls to have something to do together, worked on by alternate pairs of hands.

It was strange that the man had decided on the Ferreyras' house, not only because it had three rooms too many or because from the porch he would be forced to view almost the same landscape he traversed every afternoon: the bridge over the stones of the dry riverbed, the garbage dump of the hotel.

"Would you have thought that the guy had enough money to rent that house?" the orderly asked before going to bed. "Without counting the fact that Andrade must have overcharged him."

But he soon convinced us that he could spend still more money, because the weeks went by and he stayed in the hotel, going every afternoon, from lunchtime until the evening, to shut himself up in the little house in the mountains or to rest on the porch, his head pointed to the place where the river cut almost straight through the bridge and the foothills.

"Who's to say if maybe he wasn't in love with one of the Portuguese girls?" the orderly commented. "Probably with the second oldest, who was as talkative as he is. The other day he bought about half a dozen bottles at the hotel and had them taken up to the chalet. Now we know why he shuts himself up there. Besides, he could have bought them from you."

Until one day he came to the store before the bus brought the mail and did not come up to the counter or ask for a beer. He leaned against the tree, outside, his hands in his pants pockets, his legs stretched out, for the first time without a hat or tie.

The woman got off the bus, her back toward me, slow, round without being fat, slowly extending a strong leg until reaching the ground; they embraced and he drew away to help the attendant who was getting the luggage down off the roof of the bus. They smiled at one another and kissed again; they came into the store, and since she did not want to sit down, they asked for soft drinks at the bright end of the counter, looking into each other's eyes. The man conversed with a dizzy constancy, caressing the woman's forearm during the brief pauses, conjuring up whole paragraphs between them, believing that the mountains of words altered the sight of his thinner face, that something important could be saved as long as she did not ask the predictable questions.

Under the sunglasses, the woman's mouth opened effortlessly after almost every one of the man's sentences, always repeating the same formula of happiness. She smiled at me twice when I waited on them, thanking me for nonexistent favors, exaggerating the value of my friendship or my sympathy.

"No," he said, "it is necessary; there's no advantage in that. It's not because of the money, although I would prefer not to use that money. At the hotel I have a doctor also, everything that's necessary."

She insisted for a while, whispering without conviction; she must have been sure of being able to dismantle any of the man's projects and that it was impossible for him to overcome her remote objections, her coolness. He moved away from the counter and went out to the shadow of the tree to convince Leiva to take them to the hotel in his car; Leiva was waiting for the bus from the sanitarium to pick up two women who were going to the city. He ended up agreeing; perhaps the man offered him more money than the trip was worth; perhaps he thought that the women would have to wait for him at the store until he returned.

The woman in the dark glasses addressed her brief, precise smiles toward me.

"How do you find him?" she asked. I realized that he had spoken of me in his letters, that he must have lied about conversations and friendship.

She had time to tell me, with a fresh, jubilant voice, as if the news improved matters:

"You must have seen his name in the papers, perhaps you remember. He was the best basketball player, they all say, an international star. He played against the Americans, he went to Chile with the all-star team, the last year."

The last year must have been the one in which they realized that the thing had begun. Without joy, but excited, I was able to explain to myself the breadth of his shoulders and the excess of humiliation with which he bent them now, that tamed rancor in his eyes, born not only from the loss of his health, of a certain kind of life, of a woman, but, above all, from the loss of certainty, of the right to be proud. His life had been based on his body: in a certain way, he had been his body.

I accepted a new form of pity; I supposed him weaker, more ravaged, younger. I began to see him in elongated pictures in the newspaper *El Gráfico*, in short pants and a white numbered jersey, surrounded by men dressed the same way, smiling or turning his eyes away with the mixture of boredom and modesty appropriate for opera singers and heroes. A youth among youths, his head shining and just combed, displaying, even in the vulgar format of the late editions, the healthy shine of his skin, the smooth, oily glow of energy, virile, inexhaustible. I saw him stooping down, with his head turned to offer a three-fourths profile to the flashbulb, the five fingers of one hand pretending to rest on a ball or protect it; I saw him also in a dark room, examining by himself without understanding the flexible plate of the first X-ray, surrounded by trophies and souvenirs, loving cups, pennants, pictures of the head tables of banquets. I could see him run, jump, and squat down, sweaty, credulous, and happy, on courts whitened by violent lights, sure of being that long and half-naked body, convinced of the eternity of each period of twenty minutes and that the name the crowd called out with gratitude and exigency served to express him, denoted something real and lasting.

While the woman in the sunglasses was there, neither the handwritten nor the typed brown envelopes arrived. They lived in the hotel, and the man did not return to the garbage dump or to the Ferreyras' chalet; they walked around with arms linked, rented horses and little coaches, went up and down the mountains, smiled in turn, rigidly posing, against picturesque backdrops, to take pictures with the Leica she had brought with her on a shoulder strap.

"It's like a honeymoon," the orderly would say, appeased. "What the guy lacked was the woman—you can see that he can't stand to

live apart from her. Now he's a different man; they invited me to
have a drink with them in the hotel, and the guy asked me questions
about a thousand different aspects of the town. The sickness does
not worry them; they cannot be together without holding hands;
they kiss even when there are people around. If she could stay (she is
leaving this weekend), then I would bet you anything that the guy
would get better. Don't you see that, when they come at noon to
have an aperitif?"

The orderly was right and it was impossible for me to say anything by way of dissent; and yet, nonetheless, I did not come to believe or even to know what kind of belief was at stake, what artifice I
added to what I saw, what absurd, unpleasant hope kept me from
being moved, from accepting the happiness they built every day before my eyes, with the insistence of their hands among the glasses,
with the sound of the voices proposing and commenting on projects.

When she left, the man went back to visiting the house he had
rented, sometimes going there in the morning with a bundle of
things for lunch and not appearing until the evening, sitting at his
corner table in the hotel, withdrawn and laconic, hastening to reconstruct the walls of separation he had demolished fourteen days before, obliterating all trace of intimacy with his gray, discreetly disconsolate look.

And the letters started coming again also, two days after the
woman's departure, the envelopes with wide, sincere letters and
those written on a typewriter with an old ribbon coming in pairs
once more.

So we remained, the man and I, virtual strangers just as we were
at first. Once in a while he would come in the afternoon and settle
down at the corner of the counter to repeat his profile over a bottle of
beer—once again in his severe city suit, tie, and hat—to join me in
the habitual, never declared duel: he, struggling to make me disappear, to erase the testimony of defeat and misfortune I persisted in
giving; I, struggling for the dubious victory of convincing him that
all of this was true—the sickness, the separation, the end. He would
come in looking me in the eye, with a hint of a smile which saved
him from having to say hello, and stopped looking at me as soon as
he received the letters; he put them in his suit pocket, trying not to
hurry or fumble, his head and body still, pretending that they had
nothing to do with the five fingers that handled the envelopes.
Sometimes he asked for beer, other times he thanked me and left;
then he really did smile, and with that smile and that voice of gratitude, he only tried to reassure me, to say that I was not responsible
for what the letters said.

"Gunz finds him worse," the orderly recounted. "That is to say, that he does not improve. Stationary. You know that sometimes we are happy if we achieve a stable condition. But in other cases it is the opposite: the organism weakens. And how is he going to get better? I assure you that he rented the house only in order to be able to get drunk without being seen. He ought to go to the sanitarium; if I had Gunz's responsibility, the guy would already be flat on his back twenty-four hours a day. Gunz ought to give him a good scare."

To frighten the man, I thought, it would be necessary to invent another world, other beings, other dangers. Death was not enough; the type of fright he showed in his eyes and in the movements of his hands could not be increased by the idea of death or soothed by plans for treatment.

So there we were, as at the beginning, when the town began filling up and dozens of men and women, with colored ponchos and caps on, with riding pants and dark glasses, scattered through the mountains, the roads, the hotels, the bars with dance floors, even the store itself. It was a good year: the same crowd I had seen arrive fifteen times, bigger, noisier, more excited each time; and the man vanished into it. The orderly and the maids from the hotel stopped bringing me news; they lost sight of him; and even I myself, occupied with tending the store, gave him the letters unthinkingly, indifferently. But not altogether. Because the imagined duel continued, and at night, when the store emptied out or there was only one group of men and women who had taken refuge there to have a last drink—because they were on vacation, because the room was dirty and sordid, because the wine from the cask astonished them by how bad and harsh it was, because they would never have dared to go into a place like this in Buenos Aires—I devoted myself to thinking about him, attributed to him the absurd decision to take advantage of the invasion of tourists to hide from me, felt myself responsible for the fulfillment of his destiny, compelled to be as cruel as necessary to avoid modifying the prophecy, sure that it was enough for me to remember it and remember my spontaneous curse in order for him to continue to draw nearer the catastrophe.

A little before the end of the year, he stopped using the bus to take his letters to the city; he went on foot from the hotel, and sometimes I saw him pass by, having made no concessions in his dress to the place or the weather, oppressed and absentminded, as far from us as if he had never come to the town, one arm rigid, independent of the movement of walking, his hand buried in the coat pocket where I knew he kept the letter he had just written, clinging to the letter with misgivings and a need for confidence, as if it were impossible to foresee the form, the pain, and the consequences of his wounds.

The idea was the orderly's, but not completely; and I think, besides, that he did not believe in it and proposed it to make fun, not of me or of the store, but of the idea itself. We were watching the cars passing by, seeing them shiny and towering, going in and out of the clouds of dust they stirred up on the road, when the maid burst out laughing and put her glass of anisette on the counter. Her name was Reina and it was said that she planned to marry the orderly.

"If that black car goes to the hotel," Reina said, "it'll be back soon. Did you see if it turned? Since Monday we don't have even a cranny. And we put up cots all over the place. We are not going to have anything until February."

Now she was serious and proud; she emptied the glass, pouting, looking me in the eyes, asking for admiration and envy.

"And the same thing is happening at the Royal," said the orderly. "I don't know where the people are going to fit. And they keep coming. Suffice it to say that at the Royal all the tables have been reserved for Christmas Eve and the thirty-first. If I were you I would clean this place up with cleanser, put in a radio, and have a big dance." The maid started laughing again, but it was only from excitement, a short little laugh over the handkerchief with which she wiped away the sweat and the anisette.

"Why not?" said the orderly then, putting on the face of an honest man. "I say it in all seriousness. Those two nights we're going to have a lot of people who cannot find a place to dance and get drunk in celebration. You know how they get."

He knew, because I had told him. Everyone, the healthy people and the others, those who were passing through the town and those who could still convince themselves they were passing through, they all let themselves be surprised by the holidays as if by a sudden shower in the open; those who lived in the hotels and in the monotonous red-and-white cabins, all of them assumed a special and tolerable form of madness on both holiday eves. The dates always came upon them by surprise, even though they made plans and calculations, even though they counted the days, even though they foresaw what they were going to feel and struggled to avoid the sensation, or abandoned themselves to the desire to anticipate it or to strengthen it, assuring it a higher degree of cruelty. Then they were like animals, dogs or horses; they mixed a tractable acceptance of their destiny and circumstance with rebellion and panic, with deceitful and

savage attempts at flight. I knew that on those two nights they were
going to show their fervent and expectant eyes, covered by censure
and of a hardened brightness, to the waiters and their table companions and to all those who could see them, to the remote summer sky
over the mountains, to the misty bathroom mirrors, and show them,
as if they believed in imperishable testimonies. I knew they would
be moaning soundlessly beneath the music, the cries, the explosions, pricking their ears toward supposed calls, from men or
women, from supposed kindred souls who would appear on the
other side of the forest, in Buenos Aires or in Rosario, at any name or
distance.

I was moving my head and shrugging my shoulders between the
orderly and the maid, pretending that I was trying to remember and
that there was not enough in my memory to convince me.

"You know they go slightly crazy," the orderly stated with precision, turning to the maid to convert her into an ally. "They want a
place to dance and drink a few bottles. Any hole as long as it's not
the one where they live."

At that moment, I no longer needed the orderly; I had made a decision and had resolved almost all of the details.

"Seriously," said Reina, while she opened her pocketbook in order
to put on lipstick. "If you set up more tables and clear a space for
them to dance . . . There will be music on the radio."

I was already much farther along; I was thinking about the Christmas tree—where to get it and how to decorate it. So I could look at
the orderly in friendship, forgetting the suspicion that he had proposed the dances to make fun of me and of the store: I could look at
him with a smile, remembering that he had said "any place as long
as it is not where they live," feeling myself capable of tolerating the
idea that he had more intelligence than what was strictly necessary
for breaking vials, giving shots, and taking the money to the bank
every Saturday.

She began to laugh again and commented enthusiastically on the
two evenings of dances at the store; the orderly told her a joke containing a proposition which did not put her in a compromising situation. Once again grave and humble, he repeated, "I say it in all seriousness. You can make lots of money."

So tables appeared and began filling up the room of the store,
some on loan, others made from boxes, boards, and sawhorses, and
I covered them all with colored paper. On the twenty-fourth, although it rained all afternoon and later on there were a few showers,
the room filled up, and each of the women had a kind word or a re-
juvenating gesture on seeing the pine tree covered with tinsel on the

counter. Despite the rain the radio worked all night; they danced all packed together, uncomfortable, showing that this was how they liked it, just as they like to drink from cups with cracked brims, to resign themselves to ordinary drinks and to the garlic on the meat. They danced, laughed, sang, and began to leave in the midst of the downpour, lifelong friends of mine.

And the night of the thirty-first was almost better; I had more people and even set up some tables outside. But halfway through the night, I began to feel tired, although the Levy boy was helping me. So when the orderly heard the horn, went out, and came to tell me with a smile, almost daring to pat me on the back, that the bus from the city was arriving with some passengers and full of groups who were coming to dance at the store, I put on an expression of surprise and happiness but began desiring with all my heart that the night would end.

Perhaps they were all drunk; at least I had sold enough for them to be. They sang and asked what time it was; at the table of some English people from the Brighton, in a corner, a woman began throwing streamers, first at the rest of the tables, then so they would hang from the garland of wire and paper flowers that hung across the room from the top of the Christmas tree to the window grate. She was thin, blond, sad, dressed in black, with a low neckline, a pearl necklace, a gold brooch over her heart, a nervous grin that bared her upper gums, a happy, disgusted, and fierce contraction that suddenly raised her lip and then slowly relaxed; it was a grin that simply happened on her face, with regularity, before and after drinking a bit of the mixture of white wine and rum which the fat, ruddy man who presided at the table had invented.

She would lean back on the kitchen stool, with the rolled-up streamer over her head, carefully observing the position of the garland, already sagging a lot, while the flowers seemed to wilt; then she suddenly would lean forward toward the table and her dress would hang down, almost revealing her bosom, the small, melancholy spheres, and the streamer would whistle as it stretched out. She never missed, although she was far away; the Levy boy and I had to push our way through the curtain of streamers with our trays, and the dancers touched them with their faces, turned around to wrap themselves in them while trying not to break them, turning very slowly, fooling the beat of the music.

We got through the commotion of midnight and I can only remember my headache, its irregular, constant palpitation, and surrounding it the people standing up raising glasses and cups, toasting, and embracing—a palpitation confused with the shooting someone

started in the mountains and which spread downhill to the Royal, to
the houses along the road, mixed with dogs' barking, with the con-
ceited voice of the announcer on the radio someone had turned
up till it howled. The thin Englishwoman, mounted on her stool,
held up by two men, was eating white grapes from a bunch I had not
sold her.

I cannot figure out if I had seen her before or if I discovered her at
that moment, leaning against the doorframe: a bit of skirt, a shoe,
one side of a suitcase poking out into the lamplight. Perhaps I did
not see her then either, at the moment when the New Year began,
and I only imagined, but do not *remember*, her still presence situ-
ated precisely between the jubilation and the night.

But I definitely remember her later, when some group decided to
leave and the rest were discovering that it was impossible for them
to stay on there in the store any longer, while outside there were
sounds of shouting and laughter, car doors slamming, the engines in
second gear climbing the hill toward the old hotel or the group of
houses at Los Pinos. Then I do remember her, not really her, not her
leg and her suitcase, but the staggering men who were going out,
turning one after another, as if struck dumb, as if the sexual organs
of the women who accompanied them had withered, to ask questions or make insincere invitations to what was a little beyond the
illuminated skirt, suitcase, and shoe.

Then we come to the moment when I stopped, behind the counter,
to look at her. Only the English people from the Brighton were left:
the two men smoking their pipes, the three women dispiritedly singing sweet, incomprehensible songs in chorus, the thinnest one emptying the last package of streamers. Now she was inside the store,
sitting next to the door, the suitcase between her shoes, a little hat
on her lap, her head raised to talk to the Levy boy who was fighting
to stay awake. She was wearing a tailor-made gray suit and white
gloves, and a dark pocketbook hung from her shoulder; I say all that
to be done once and for all with everything about her, with everything that was not her round face, shining from the heat, wavering
behind the streamers hanging from the wreath and beginning to be
stirred by the early morning air.

The Levy boy left her to wait on the English people and came to
tell me that they wanted their bill; I calculated the total and crossed
in front of her, without looking at her, avoiding putting her on her
guard, in order to be able to continue observing her from behind the
counter. But when I finished accompanying the English people to
their car, thanking them, rejecting their praise of my party, and talk-

ing with the oldest of them about whether or not that afternoon's weather would be favorable for fishing from the dam, I saw that the orderly was sitting next to her. I understood that he had taken advantage of the girl's position, when she got up a little to attract the eyes of the Levy boy and ask him for something; so the orderly had to content himself all the while with an expression that was not meant for him, that was directed toward someone else, in truth toward anyone at all. But this did not discourage him: he went on asking her questions, agreeing enthusiastically every time she murmured something, understanding this and everything else, what the girl was saying and what was beneath her words, connected with her past and her future.

I told the Levy boy to start closing up and straightening things a bit.

"Did the young lady ask you for anything?"

"No," he said, blinking, letting sleep and exhaustion invade him, letting his face fill up with freckles. "The thing is that she says that they were supposed to wait for her here, that she sent a telegram, that the train arrived late."

"Who was supposed to wait for her?" I asked. I was thinking that she was too young, that she was not sick, that there were three or four adjectives to define her and that they were contradictory.

"Do you want me to ask her?" said the Levy boy.

"Let her be. They'll come get her soon or we'll find room for her at the Royal or somewhere. But ask her if she's hungry or if she wants anything to drink."

While I was not looking, the boy went up to the table slowly and came back.

"She wants a beer, no ice, she's not hungry."

I moved the bottle around in the ice chest to chill it. "She is too young," I thought again, without understanding the meaning of that "too" or what undesirable thing she was being rescued from: not only her, but her youth. When I stood up straight, the orderly was leaning with his elbows on the counter, smiling at his hands, reticent, modest, and triumphant.

"Do you know?" he began, while I dried the bottle and examined the glass.

"Wait," I said to him, sure of the importance of not listening to him right away. I went to the table and opened the bottle; she thanked me with the same expression she had already directed toward the Levy boy and maintained next toward the orderly. But the face preserved enough of how it had appeared when it was in the shadow next to the door of the shop and perhaps of some traces of the trip by train and bus, and, if I was not imagining it, of what it was like when she was alone and in love.

I knew it as soon as the orderly asked "Do you know?"; or I had known it earlier and let myself be misled because she was too young . . . But I had no reason to boast in front of the orderly, so when I returned to the counter, playing with the bottle cap, I put up with his repeating the question and taking his time weighing a prefatory smile. When the Levy boy failed to close the blinds for the third time, I told him to go to sleep, that I would take care of closing up, and that he could come at noon to help me with the cleaning and get paid. All this over the shoulders of the orderly, with his arms crossed on the counter, with his party tie and a white carnation in his buttonhole—past the indelicately vulgar smile he continued to exude.

"Do you know?" I heard him say finally. "It's unbelievable. The girl sent a telegram saying that she was coming and asking them to wait for her here, at the bus stop, in the store. The train arrived more than two hours late, and they left. But they were not waiting for her. Can you guess who? Someone from the old hotel, who is also from the mountains. Did you guess? The guy. So that's how things are: a woman in the spring, this girl for the summer. And the best of it is that the guy has the telegram in the hotel and is having a party at the Ferreyras' chalet, getting drunk by himself. Because I went to the old hotel twice tonight, because of the old maid with the dog and because of the assistant bookkeeper, and the guy wasn't anywhere to be seen. Drunk in the chalet, I bet you. She wants someone to accompany her to the hotel. Since the telephone is in back, it didn't occur to her that she could call from here. Now think about it— what if the guy isn't there? It also could be that he has received the telegram and didn't want to come; he is capable of that."

"No telegram arrived; they always arrive two days late."

"Well," the orderly insisted, "it didn't come through here; they didn't bring it to you. But if it was special delivery, you know, sometimes they take advantage of the trip and deliver it directly."

"Why would it be special delivery?" I asked, almost furious. "To announce that she was coming? Did she say that she sent it special delivery? And why didn't you offer her the phone?"

"Yes," said the orderly, impatient and excusing himself. "But wait."

"Tell her to come in and call the hotel," I said, curious, placating myself. "The telegram won't get here for three days. Or better yet, let's call."

"Wait, please," he raised a hand and smiled once more. "Of course we'll call right away, and I can get a car at the Royal to take her, and if the guy isn't at the hotel, we can take her on to the chalet. But now, tell me, seriously, is she sick? Is she going to be cured? The lungs?" He was drunk, sustaining his excitement, opening his eyes wide with an intense, intelligent expression. "Or do you think that she has only come, after the one with the sunglasses, to be with him so he will not be bored? Tell me. So it turns out that he rented the chalet for this girl. Doesn't she seem a little too young to you?" He was drunker than I had thought, mocking, almost insolent, but I felt that the strongest thing was his unease, his confusion, and that he had chosen a multitude of things to hate in me.

"Let's call," I said, touching his arm.

Now she stood up next to the door, looking out, with firm legs and hands always gloved, white, clasped above her hips, as if she were stupid enough to be waiting for the telegram to arrive from one moment to the next at the old hotel and force the man to come down to get her. I went to the door and spoke to her, and she answered, never looking at me, her face pointed at the darkness, at the scarce, feeble lights in the mountains. It did not seem like a good idea to her to call the hotel at that hour; she asked that they take her there in a car or accompany her on foot or point the way. I partly closed the store while the orderly crossed to the Royal. When the orderly drove up in front of us in a little reddish car with an Oncativo license plate and the telephone rang and he went to answer it, I made the resolve not to think, fearful of finding the adjectives that corresponded to the girl and of making them fall, together with her, on top of the man who was sleeping in the hotel or in the little house. When the orderly approached and told me, "Don't wait for me, go ahead," that he had to go back to the Royal to give an injection to the blond named Lamas, who was getting worse, who was no longer conscious, I knew suddenly that the brown typed envelopes were from her and that the meek happiness of her face had been anticipated for me, at one time or another, by the incredulous sweetness of the profile of the former basketball player.

I knew this, many other things, and the inevitable end of the story when I put her suitcase on her lap and started the car up the road to the hotel. I did not try to look at her during the trip; with my eyes fixed on the light that wavered back and forth on the dirt road, I did not need to look at her to see her face, to convince myself that she was going to be—until death, on bright, crowded days and on nights similar to the one we were crossing—facing the self-assured, foolish, illusive approach of men, with the little nose that displayed its sinuous, innocent openings seemingly at random on her head, with the lower lip a little too thick, with the eyes flat and without convexity,

like simple sketches of eyes drawn with a brown pencil on a sheet of
lighter brown paper. But not facing only men, of course, those who
would come after the one we were approaching, those whom she
would doubtless make happy, without lying to them, without having
to force her goodness or her understanding, and who would leave
her, already condemned forevermore to confuse love with the memory of that serene face, of the corners of a smile that was always
there without springing from anything in her thoughts or in her
heart, the smile that simply expressed her organic serenity at being
alive, at coinciding with life. She was not only facing men, her face
round and without perfume, not trying to fight against the bumps of
the car, her face bouncing up and down like a scale, agreeing, with a
candid, obscene habit of agreeing, because men could only serve her
as symbols, landmarks, points of reference for an eventual, artful,
and diligent ordering of life. But rather, that her face confronted what
the men represented and honored; the face revealed itself as endlessly anxious, incapable of true surprises, transforming everything
immediately into memory, into remote experience. I thought of that
excited, alert, hungry face, taking everything in, while she drew her
knees apart for each definitive love and to give birth; I thought of the
hidden expression of her flat eyes before old age and death throes.

"Do you know him?" she asked. She had her elbows on her suitcase and was making her little hat spin around.

"He comes to the store."

"I know. How is he?"

"It would be better to ask the doctor. But he is going to be fine, in
a few minutes. You know."

"I know, already," she said again.

I turned right and we entered the grounds of the old hotel. She did
not let me carry her suitcase; she walked a little behind me, taking
long steps, her face lifted toward the stars, which were starting to
vanish. I spoke with the night watchman, and we stood waiting in
the hall, standing apart in silence; the night watchman pressed the
button of the telephone, and she slowly turned her patient, anxious
head, acquainting herself for the rest of her life with the distances,
the floor, the walls, the furniture of a place the man passed through
every day.

When he appeared on the staircase, thin, sleepless, in shirtsleeves,
with a dangerous tendency toward mockery, step by step, before
seeing the girl, before looking for her, anticipating her despair, their
swiftly achieved harmony, I made a gesture of greeting with my
hand and walked toward the door. She smiled, her head lifted toward

the man's excessive slowness, and did not turn when she thanked me, twice, aloud. From outside, through the curtain on the glass door, I saw the man stop, holding onto the railing, stooped over, his old, protective incredulity rendered grotesque and childish for a second. I stayed until I saw them on the staircase, embracing and motionless.

It will do no one any good, neither them nor me, to think, I resolved as I was returning in the car. The manager of the Royal was moving tables with the help of an employee. I sat down to chat and drink something.

"If it were the end of the year all year long, with only a year's work I wouldn't have to work again," the manager said, rapidly, showing that he had said it many times; he is fat, bald, pink, sad, young. "The blonde named Lamas apparently won't last the night; the orderly is with her and the two doctors. Right at the beginning of the year."

Someone had a window open on the second floor of the hotel. They were dancing and laughing; their voices suddenly lowered to a tone of goodbyes, of unequivocal confidences; dancing, they passed by the window, and the record was "La vie en rose," played on the accordion.

"We need a little more publicity and a little less regulation," said the manager. It did not matter what the subject, he spied on my face and my movements, as always, nervous and grateful. "Another beer, won't you? The hotel industry is very special; it cannot be managed like other businesses. Here, as you know very well, the matter of personnel is decisive."

The night had already become white, and the roosters crowed from their various stations on the mountainside. The dancers stopped and a woman sang "La vie en rose," which had been put on once more, in a gentle voice, in French.

"You can still put on one more good party for Three Kings' Day," I told the manager; the woman upstairs sang, putting a heavy stress on the beat, exaggerating the pauses, as if she were singing so that someone else could learn the song. "And if the weather is cooperative, you can be sure that the hotel will fill up every weekend."

"I think so too," answered the manager; they opened another bottle and I raised my glass.

"It's going to be a good year, be sure of that."

"All the odd-numbered years are good," he agreed.

In the early hours of the new odd-numbered year, the man left the old hotel; they found out the following day, in midmorning, when he appeared to fetch some clothes—not all, he did not vacate the room,

although he did not come to sleep there while the girl was in town—
and to arrange for them to bring food every day to the Ferreyras'
house.

So they left for the mountains soon after I stopped seeing them
embracing on the staircase, when the girl's body corrected her initial
anger to offer only those things which do not require a response: protection, patience, different kinds of concern. They must have gone
up to the room, but only for a moment, only because he needed to
get dressed and she wanted to look at the furniture he used. They
went out walking in the darkness and climbed the mountainside, he
with the girl's suitcase, holding her hand in order to guide her, half a
step ahead, proud and insistent, his impatience to arrive dissolved in
that sensation of power, of benign authority, enjoying it as if he had
stolen it, knowing that as soon as they closed the door of the house,
he was going to be despoiled again, without anything lasting to give,
without anything authentic besides an ancient and tamed despair.

The girl stayed less than a week, and I did not see them again on
any of those days, nor did anyone tell me of having seen them; in
reality, they existed for us only in the trip, every day at noon, of the
hotel employee who climbed the mountainside with the lunch basket and a newspaper under his arm. And they also existed for me in
the two letters that arrived, the envelopes in the blue, vigorous hand
that I put away at the bottom of the drawer of mail, separate from
the rest. And all that I could think of them—and for them, besides,
with the vague, superstitious desire to help them—was of the labori-
ous trip in the darkness, holding hands, silent, he a little ahead, warning her of the dangers with a squeeze of the fingers, his broad shoulders doubled as if to simulate the effort of dragging her, their heads
bent down toward the uneven, invisible ground, the sound of the first
birds over their shoulders, step by regular step, unhurriedly moving
over the wetness of the earth and grass, as if the house were at an
infinite height, as if time had stopped that first dawn of the year.

I did not see them again until the eve of Three Kings' Day; I could
not see them except walking with their heads down, linked by two
fingers, across and beyond a night in suspense, until the orderly came
over one afternoon from the Royal, put an elbow on the counter, and
murmured, without looking at me, with the pronunciation of one of
the Englishmen at the Brighton, "A cold beer, if you please."

He burst out laughing and patted me on the back. "So that's how
things are. He finally left his cave and they had lunch at the hotel;
she is leaving today. Maybe they couldn't stand any more being shut
up together. In any case, it looks like a suicide. I said that to Gunz

and he had to agree. And the guy let his bill at the hotel keep adding up, all week long. And, while we're at it, he does her a wrong too; it is not gentlemanly—he should not have taken her to the hotel, where everyone saw him live with the other one. Everyone knows that they have slept together in the chalet since she arrived. And she, as you might imagine, spent the whole lunch looking at her plate, hiding her eyes. In any case, he should not exhibit her, displaying her as a provocation. I wouldn't do that, nor would you."

It was then that I saw them coming down the road, arms linked, the man loaded with the suitcase, dressed as if to take the train to the capital; they talked a little, standing out in the sun, and then turned toward the store. I leaned over to open the drawer of mail and closed it again without putting my hand in. I looked at them as if I had never seen them, thinking that I could see through them if I faced them for the first time. It was the parting, but he was happy, intimidated, uncomfortable, looking at me and the orderly with a quick smile.

They sat down next to the window grate, at the orderly's table, the table of the English people on New Year's Eve. They ordered coffee and cognac, she, the girl, ordering without ceasing to look him in the eyes. They whispered phrases but were not talking; I continued behind the counter and the orderly in front, his back to me, pointing at the door the expression of understanding and mockery which he would have liked to direct toward the table. The orderly and I talked about the hail, about a mystery which could be suspected in the life of the owner of El Pedregal, about aging and mortality; we talked about prices, about transportation, about the appearance of cadavers, about illusory recoveries, about the comfort which money brings, about uncertainty considered as inherent in the human condition, about the calculations the Barrosos made one afternoon while sitting in a wheat field.

They did nothing but murmur phrases, and that only at first, but they did not converse; each one named a thing, a moment, constructed a sequence of three or four words. In turn, respecting the sequence, they went back and forth, saying something, not trying, discovering in the face of the other, dazzled and unblinking, with a brief whisper, playing to see who remembered more or who remembered the most important thing, without concern about the idea of winning. I did not stop watching them, but neither I nor the orderly could hear them. And when we were discussing the rheumatism of the owner of El Pedregal and his excessive love for horses, they stopped talking, still looking at one another. The orderly did not take note of the silence or believed that it was nothing more than a pause between the phrases with which they tried their luck.

Leaning with his waist against the counter, turning his head a little from the door toward me, he said, "Leiva was a kind of overseer at El Pedregal. I say a kind of one. I imagine that for the foreigner he was no more than a kind of servant. The rest is all a lie; but when the filly broke her leg, he killed her with a shot, and that day they didn't eat on the farm because the old man didn't feel like it. Not even in the bunkhouses."

They were silent, looking at one another, she with her mouth open; the guy was no longer caressing her hand: he had put his hand on his shoulder and held it there, still, rigid, showing it to me. I kept on talking so that the orderly would not turn around to look at them; I spoke about the foreigner's gigantic body, bent over, supported by a cane; I spoke about stubbornness, about the man and the filly, about the foreign voice pointed, hard and persuasive, at the nervous head of the animal, at its startled eye.

And they were mute, looking at one another, through time which cannot be measured or detached, that time we feel running in our blood. They were motionless and permanent. Sometimes she raised her lip without knowing it; perhaps it was a smile, or a new form of memory that was going to give her the victory, or the total, instantaneous confession of who she was.

Some people came in to buy things and bring me stories; a truck driver pulled up alongside the store to ask for water and directions; the last bus for Los Pinos passed by, shaking, unwilling, when the sun began to stretch its long shadow over the mountains. I guessed what time it was and looked at the alarm clock hanging from a shelf. They were quiet at the table: the girl with her arms crossed on her chest, pushing back on the chair to get a little distance and see better; he, with his back toward me, broad and feeble, his hand on his shoulder, his hat hiding the back of his neck. "Without any other purpose than that of looking, tireless, indecisive," I thought while walking back and forth near them, without deciding whether to tell them that the bus for the city was probably about to arrive. Now I could see the man's face, thinner, sad, immoral. The orderly looked at me with a smile full of patience.

"The bus," I told them. "It's going to arrive at any moment."

They moved their heads in agreement; I returned to my place at the counter and spoke to the orderly about how useless it is to try to escape fate. The orderly recalled several examples.

The bus stopped across from the store, and the driver came in to have a beer; he looked at the suitcase next to the girl.

"I don't know," said the orderly, smiling in an unconsciously de-
grading way. "We can ask." He seemed infuriated when he clapped
his hands: "Last bus!"

They did not move; the orderly shrugged his shoulders and again
leaned forward against the counter; I smiled at the driver, face to face.
The bus had already left and the night had begun when I thought that
it was not enough for them to be oblivious to everything, because all
of this kept on existing and waiting for the moment when they
would stop looking at one another in silence, when the man's hand
would become detached from the gray material of his suit in order to
touch the girl. There would always be houses and roads, cars and gas
pumps, and other people who exist and breathe, have forebodings,
imagine, prepare meals, contemplate themselves in a tedious and re-
flexive way, pretend and plan.

Standing against the violet light by the door—he was carrying the
suitcase and smiled at me, blinking, giving me permission to live—
the girl raised a hand and put it on the man's cheek.

"Are you going to go on foot?" she asked him. He kept on looking
at me.

"On foot, yes. Why not? Sometimes I walk much farther than
that. We don't have to hurry to reach the train."

Helpful, as if for a photograph, he was rehearsing—for me, for the
others, for everything I represented, looking out from behind the
deliberate clumsiness of the orderly—a smile of which I would
not have believed him capable and which, nevertheless, she contemplated without surprise; a smile which proclaimed his desire to
look after the girl, to guard her from passing worries, to smooth over
the admitted impossibility of maintaining her separate from what
we—the orderly and I, the store, the height of the mountain range—
symbolized.

They moved their hands in a gesture of parting and went out to
the road. They had to walk two blocks along the Royal's tennis
courts and the back of the dairy; then they would turn to the right to
walk between thick walls of reddish earth, along a zigzagging path,
sloping downward, until coming out next to the light and the flag at
the police station. They would walk arm in arm, much slower than
the night, listening absentmindedly to the noise of fuss and disci-
pline which would come at them from the left, from the brightly
colored buildings of the airport. Perhaps they would remember the
other night's walk, when the girl arrived and they climbed up the
mountainside to the little house; perhaps they carried with them,
secret and active, but not yet available as a memory, that earlier trip,
the obvious meanings of which could be added or taken away.

The letters started coming again, harmoniously now; one of those written in the wide blue handwriting together with one of the type-written ones. I did not feel pity for the man but for what he evoked when he came to drink his beer and ask wordlessly for his letters. Nothing in his movements, his slow voice, or his patience betrayed a change, the trace of the undeniable facts, the visits and the good-byes. This profound ignorance or discretion, or this symptom of the lack of faith which I had guessed in him, can be remembered with assurance and believed. Because, besides, it is true that I was looking for modifications, cracks, or additions, and it is true that I came to invent them.

That is how things were for us while the summer became more intense in January and February and the hordes of tourists filled the hotels and the guesthouses in the mountains. There we were, he and I—although he may not have known it or thought he knew some-thing else—playing the game of pity and protection throughout that driest of summers. To think of him, to accept him, meant to increase my compassion and his misfortune. I got used to not seeing or hear-ing him, to giving him his beer and his letters as if I were delivering them to any one of those who came into the store in the dissimilar uniforms of summer.

"Don't think I don't realize it," the orderly would say. "You don't want to talk about the guy. Why? Did he bewitch you too? It's un-believable what's going on in the old hotel. He does not say hello to anybody, but nobody wants to speak ill of him. They do of the girl, yes. And not even with Gunz; it is impossible to talk to Gunz about the death of the guy. It's as if he didn't know, as if he hadn't seen a hundred others better than this one die."

Every day at noon the man picked up his letters, drank a bottle of beer, and went out onto the road, giving the hint of a greeting, un-hurriedly entering the intolerable heat, attracting me for a moment with the constant ruin of his shoulders, with what there was of sur-feit, heroism, and goodness in his body seen in motion from behind.

Carnival had just ended when the woman got off the bus, her back to me, pausing to help the child. She did not stop by the tree or look for the man's tall, stooped figure; it did not matter to her whether he was there waiting for her or not. She did not need him because he was no longer a man but an abstraction, something more elusive and yet more vulnerable. And perhaps she was happy not to have to face him right away; perhaps she had organized things so as to assure her-self this initial solitude, these minutes of pause in which to mull everything over and acclimatize herself. The boy was about five and did not resemble her or him; he looked around indifferently, without fear or smiles, his recently cropped blond head held up very straight.

It was not possible to know what she was thinking behind her dark glasses; but there was the child, his legs hanging from the chair, and there she was, offering him a soft drink, straightening the knot of the plaid tie, flattening the hair on his forehead with a drop of saliva. She chose not to recognize me because she was afraid of any unforeseen risk, of betrayals and false steps; she greeted me as she left, moving her mouth only as much as necessary, as if her lips, her glasses, her pallor, the wetness under her nose, her whole large and calm body were nothing but a representative of herself, of the purpose into which she had converted herself, and as if she considered it necessary to maintain this purpose free of contact, of wear and tear, without losing what she had been gathering and fortifying for a surprise attack on the old hotel. And perhaps it was not even that; perhaps she did not see me or remember me and, in an uninhabited world, in a world where there was only one thing left to win or lose, she persisted, without real plans, with the simplicity of an animal, in the barely exalted preservation of a period of time spanning from when she met the center of the international basketball team in the dance hall, during the distribution of medals and drinks, until that afternoon in my store, until moments before slipping into a hotel room, pushing the dauntless child forward with her knees to appeal, in succession, in turn, to pity, to memory, to decency, to whatever is sacred.

The three of us were in the empty store, waiting for the horn of the Los Pinos bus to sound. I looked at her round shoulders, at the defensive, almost ironic slowness of the movements she made while watching after the child or emptying her own glass of orange drink. I compared what she could offer with what the girl could, unsure about strengths and weaknesses, without taking sides with either of them. Only it was easier for me to identify with the woman in the sunglasses, to imagine her entering the hotel room, to foresee the movement of holding on and prompting by means of which she would try to fill the child with self-confidence and impel him immediately toward the long, lazy body in the bed, toward the wary, trapped face which was rising out of the nakedness of the nap, recovering its worn-out expression of suspicious integrity.

Between the two, I would have bet against all reason for the woman and the child, for the years, the habit, the impregnation. A good bet to make with the orderly. Because the following day, in a similar landscape, I saw the little suitcase wavering across from the door of the bus, the same gray suit, the little hat squeezed by the white gloved hand.

She entered with her head too tall, though with that slight nod which served to excuse her, which seemed to hint, misleadingly, at a capacity to separate herself, without a real struggle, from everything she saw and thought. She greeted me as if challenging me and stood right in front of the counter, the bag between her shoes, three fingers of one hand half-buried in her jacket pocket.

"Do you remember me?" she said, but it was not a question. "When is something going to the old hotel?"

"You have a half-hour wait. If you prefer, we can try to get a car."

"Like the other time," she commented without smiling.

But I was not going to take her in any case. Perhaps I thought of the impossibility of repeating the first trip and surprise or of the pathos of trying to. She said that she preferred to wait and sat down at the table she was already familiar with; she ate the same lunch as the orderly: cheese, bread and salami, sardines, everything that I could give her. With one arm supported on the grate, she watched me come and go, rehearsing with me the tolerant, open expression she had imagined during the trip.

"Because when I get there they will have already had lunch," she explained, letting herself believe that meal service at the wrong time was the gravest upset she was going to cause at the hotel.

The few customers entered the shade of the store, came up to me and the counter with their heads held motionless, their eyes fixed on my face; they asked for something in a low voice, not concerned about whether they were waited on or not, as if they had only come to interrupt my vigil, and they turned around right away to look at her, spying on the platters that were set before the girl. Afterward they sought out my eyes with an expression of ostentatious surprise, with mockery and malice; and all of them, men and women, especially the inflexible, tired women who came down the mountainside during the siesta time after lunch, wanted to find some sort of complicity in me, my concurrence in a vague condemnation. It was as if they all knew the story, as if they had bet on the same woman as I had and were afraid of seeing her lose. The girl kept on eating, without hiding her face or showing it off. Afterward she lit a cigarette and asked me to sit down and have a cup of coffee with her.

So I could play at prophecies and portents in peace, could worry in earnest about her faults, calculate her age, her goodness. "I would be more comfortable if I hated her," I thought. She smiled at me while lighting another cigarette; she kept on smiling behind the smoke and suddenly, or as if I had just found out, everything changed. I was the weaker of the two, the mistaken one; I was discovering the constant misfortune of my fifteen years in the town, the regret of having paid the price with my solitude, the store, this mode of not being anything. I was tiny, meaningless, dead. She came and went; she had just arrived in order to suffer and fail, to go away to another form of suffering and failure which she did not care to foresee. And she must have realized that I would breathe better if I could hate her, because she wanted to help me and kept on smiling at me between the useless phrases, behind her rigid fingers handling the cigarette, measuring the sustained, cynical, touching smile, the hostile sparkle in her eyes against my need for them.

And perhaps, as it occurred to me later, she was not doing that—the smile, the apathy, the insolence—only in order to facilitate my hate, my comfort, my return to resignation; perhaps she also sought to paralyze my feelings of pity in the immediate future, in the hour of defeat I had prophesied or in the other one, the definitive, distant hour, beyond pride, which she was inscribing as an act of destiny in her life.

"To live here as if time did not pass, as if it passed without touching me, as if it touched me without changing me," I was lying to myself when the bus came.

She smoothed out a ten-peso bill on the sheet of newspaper that served as a tablecloth, put on her gloves again, and walked to the counter with the light bag.

"She has not come to stay," I thought while I counted her change. "She has not brought enough clothing for even the one night she is not going to have. She knows she made the trip to hear a no, to be reasonable and accept it, to remain for the rest of the man's life like a myth of dubious consolation." She hardly murmured a greeting, her smile directed at the floor.

I kept on seeing her and I still remember her like this: proud and pleading, leaning toward the arm that carried the bag, not patient but rather lacking the ability to understand patience, her eyes lowered, generating with her smile a sufficient will to keep on living, to tell anyone, with a wink, with a movement of the head, that this misfortune did not matter, that misfortunes only serve to signal dates, to separate and render intelligible the beginnings and endings of the numerous lives we traverse and live through. All this facing me, across the counter, this set of gratuitous inventions placed, as in a bell, in the semidarkness and the warm, damp, confused smells of the store. The girl had walked behind the bus driver, copying the tilt of the shoulders of the former basketball player.

Then, that same afternoon or weeks afterward (because exactness no longer matters, because from that moment on I no longer saw anything in them but their different styles of failure), the orderly and Reina the maid began telling me the story of the epilogue in the hotel and the little house. "An epilogue," I thought, defending myself, "an end to the disputable story, to the extent that these two are capable of imagining it."

They got together in the store, he and the maid, every afternoon after lunch. They could be seen anywhere, and it would not have mattered to anyone in the town or in the world to see them together; no one would have thought that they were not made to be together. But it occurs to me that the orderly or she herself, Reina—fat, with her mouth half-open, with the unconvincing, cold eyes of women who have waited too long—one of them supposed that they added something if they met during the siesta at the store, if they pretended, before me, before the shelves, before the whitewashed walls with their hardened bubbles of lime, not to know one another, if they greeted one another with brief nods and conjured up miserable pretexts to sit down together at a table and whisper.

They must have felt very poor, without real obstacles, without believable persecutions; they always ended up turning their round smiling faces toward me, careful not to brush against one another; they suspected that I had bet on the plump woman with the dark glasses and dedicated themselves to defending her, to the careful enumeration, for which they were jointly responsible, of the virtues she possessed or represented, of the eternal values that the older of the two women had been vindicating, for forty-eight hours, at the hotel and the little house.

"He should be killed," the maid said. "Him. I don't know what I would do to that little whore, begging pardon. Death is too little if you think that there is a child."

"A child in the middle," the orderly confirmed, but he smiled at me, blissful, vengeful, sure that it was impossible for me to dissent. "You took her to the hotel that night at the end of the year. Of course you couldn't have imagined it all."

"How was he to know!" she shrieked, scandalized, looking me in the eyes to absolve me.

I heard them tell and reconstruct the epilogue; I thought of the high, broken piece of earth where we were living, of the histories of those who had inhabited it before us; I thought of the three of them and the child, who had come to this town to shut themselves in and hate, discuss, and sort out common pasts that had nothing to do with the ground they were standing on. I thought of these and other things, tended the counter, washed the glasses, weighed merchandise, gave and received money; it was always in the afternoon, with the orderly and Reina in the corner, hearing them murmur to one another, knowing they were squeezing one another's hands.

When the girl got to the hotel, the man, the woman, and the child were still in the dining room, quiet, spinning their coffee cups around. She, the woman, raised her head and saw her. The other had stopped two tables away, with the bag she had refused to leave at the desk, proclaiming with her grave, barely arrogant smile, with the calm of her flat eyes, that she did not want to hurt or be hurt, that it did not matter to her whether she won or lost, and that all of that—the meeting of the triumvirate in the mountains, the predictable disputes, the offers of sacrifice—was, as she had just discovered, grotesque, vain, meaningless, just as any accord they came to would have to be unfair. Nevertheless, despite the slight coolness with which she surveyed the empty tables, the spotted glasses, and the disorder of napkins, she pretended—and this was repugnant and inexplicable to Reina—not to have noticed the emaciated group that lingered over the cups of lukewarm coffee.

"She was marking time; even she was ashamed when she saw the child."

The woman saw her stop, then come forward involuntarily; she recognized her right away. She had never seen a picture of her, had never managed to extract from the man adjectives sufficient to construct an image of what she should fear and hate. But, in any case, she had shuffled faces, ages, statures; and the lasting combinations that she succeeded in conjuring up, the changing targets for her rancor—which were, simultaneously, sources of self-pity, of a renewed, inverted pride in her engagement and honeymoon—could not be related to the girl who was drawing her oblique, frightened smile nearer the table. The man stood up, his shoulders sadder and weaker, the tips of his ten fingers on the tablecloth, a slow cigarette, which he allowed himself after meals and had not managed to give up, hanging from his lips. He murmured a name, nothing more; he did not pronounce words of greeting or introduction. He did not sit down again because the girl did not; she remained standing, tall, far above the other's dark glasses and dark mouth, above the child's blinking curiosity, no longer needing her smile, thoughtful, freed of any promises, facing the edge of the checkered tablecloth as an hour before she had been facing me and the counter, with a corner of her bag supported on a chair, to enable her to resist the sudden invasion of weariness.

The woman forgot the anticipated faces she had constructed; she remembered having imagined the girl exactly as she was, recognized her age, her momentary beauty, the power and falsity of her honest, innocent expression. Once again she was hating her, without trying to, guided by the force of long habit, helped by the sudden certainty of having hated her all her life.

The woman let what was left of her cigarette fall in her coffee and lowered her head; she looked at the rings on her fingers and caressed the child, smiling at him, moving her lips in sounds that did not try to form words, as if she were alone with him. Then the man, tall, doubled over, decided to lift his fingers from the tablecloth, take the cigarette out of his mouth, and offer the girl a chair. But she, molding her face into a smile that had nothing to do with arrogance, disdain, or love, without looking at the man's eyes, took her bag off the chair and walked back between the tables the way she had come.

"I didn't tell her to come here," the man explained, without feeling. "Not to the hotel."

"Thank you," said the woman; she stroked the child's hair, caught his cheek in her knuckles. "It's all the same, here or somewhere else, isn't it? Besides, hadn't we decided already? Sometimes we forget who the money belongs to. You should have asked her to eat with us." She looked at him, showing that she could smile. With his mouth open, drowsy, the child hiccuped, shaking; the woman wiped the sweat off his forehead and from under his nose.

The girl had crossed the semidarkness of the bar, opposite the board full of keys by the desk, slowly, with her back decisively to the dining room. She stopped on the terrace to change her bag from one hand to the other and began going down the steps. She was not capable of crying at that time; she gave no sign of defeat or of triumph while she went down, step by step, agile and unhurried. The Junquillo bus stopped across from the hotel, and the driver honked his horn; a man got off to stretch his legs and was walking back and forth, small, withdrawn, with a reddish poncho hanging over one shoulder. Perhaps she looked at the dark children in rags who were running around on the soccer fields.

"And he stood there for a moment without knowing what to do; it must be said he didn't go rushing out after her like a madman," the maid and the orderly recounted. "He stayed looking at the woman and at his little son who looked sick there in the empty dining room. Until the other woman was stronger than shame and respect and he said something or other and left after her, slow as always, tired. Perhaps he begged forgiveness. He caught up with her across from the bus; he grabbed her arm and she didn't even look around to see who it was."

They stood there talking in the sun, while the laborer from the hotel ran to the bus, weighed down with packages. And when the brakes of a car gave way and it began to roll down toward my store, she burst out laughing and let him carry her bag. Holding hands, they slowly climbed the path to the mountainside, skirting the edge of the soccer field beginning to be surrounded by people, turning up above, at the corner by the dentist's, and zigzagging until coming to the Ferreyras' little house. The man stopped on the porch; he looked from there at the dry riverbed, the rocks, the hotel's garbage dump but did not go in; they saw him embrace her and go down the porch steps. She closed the door and opened it again when the man was far away; she could see him until he was lost from sight behind the offices of the quarry; she saw him again, small, blurry, by the side of the soccer field, in the road.

I imagined the man coming downhill at a swift pace toward the hotel, after the embrace: conscious of his height, of his weariness, of the fact that the existence of the past depends on the amount of the present that we lend it, that it is possible to give it little or none. He came down the mountainside, after the embrace, young, healthy, compelled to run all the risks, almost to provoke them.

"They weren't there. When he returned, the lady had withdrawn with the boy, and the boy was kicking things around on the staircase. The door to the room was locked from within, so the man had to knock and wait, smiling at everyone who passed by in the hallway in order to pretend, until she woke up or felt like letting him in," they recounted. "And Dr. Gunz insisted on saying that he hadn't seen anything, although he was in the dining room when she arrived with her bag, but he had no alternative to saying, word for word, that the guy should have gone to the sanitarium from the start. Perhaps in that case we could have some hope."

And he knocked, tall and sinuous against the door, in the narrow brightness of the hallway filled with bustling maids, ashamed to face the old ladies on their way back from walks in the park after lunch; while he waited, he was evoking old names of a faded obscenity, names he had made up long before for a woman who no longer existed. Until she came and turned the key, half-naked, exaggerating her embarrassment and sleepiness, without glasses on now, and moved away to throw herself on the bed once more. He could see the form of her thighs, the bare feet she dragged along, the open mouth of the sleeping child. Before moving forward he thought, rediscov-

ered, that knowing the past is worth no more than knowing someone else's dream.

"Yes, it's better to end this right now," he said when he sat down,
without any feeling of suffering except that of confirming that everything is so easy. "She was right: it's absurd, unhealthy."

Then he crossed his arms and listened with surprise to the
woman's wailing, growing sad, as if he repented vaguely not of an act
but of an evil thought, feeling that the crying referred to him un-
fairly. He was stooped over, smiling, letting himself fill up with
kindness until it became intolerable for him. He patted the woman's
hip cheerfully.

"I am going to die," he explained.

The rest of the afternoon is lost; he probably tried to sleep with
the woman, thinking that it would be possible to transmit to her the
euphoria obtained through lust. When night fell, the man came
down from the room and began joking with the desk clerk and the
bartender.

"He came down dressed the same as always, with that gray suit
which is not for summer or for winter, a collar and tie on, his shoes
shined. He does not have another suit, but it seemed as if he had just
bought everything he had on. And it was as if nothing had happened
at lunch, as if the girl had not arrived and nobody knew what was
happening. Because, as had never happened before, he came down
happy and talkative, cracked jokes with the desk clerk, and forced
the bartender to have a drink with him. It's unbelievable. And he
greeted each person who arrived for dinner with a big smile. So
much so that someone asked Gunz if he had declared him cured."

They had set the table on the terrace for dinner and had just sat
down when the girl came up the steps and approached them, lazy,
friendly. She shook hands with the woman and ate with them. Everyone heard them laugh and ask for wine. The round woman had lost
interest in the child, and it was the other one, the girl, who regularly
moved her hand to brush the hair on his forehead.

But the couple of hours had passed from the time the man came
down from the room until the waiter came to tell him that the table
was ready on the terrace, and he stood up by the bar to offer his arm
to the woman in the sunglasses. The couple of hours and what he
had done in them to reconquer the time in which he had lived in the
hotel, to fill it up, in everybody's memory, with the expressions of
interest and the simple courtesies which would make it bearable,
commonplace, capable of being mixed up with the times when the
others had lived. Everything the man produced and dissipated in two

hours, with their consent, so that they would distribute evenly throughout the previous months: the smiles, the invitations, and the loud greetings; the uneasy questions, of an excusable boldness, about temperatures and diets; the pats on the backs of the men; the respectful and longing glances at the women. He managed to include, also, a short period of clowning around, pirouettes for the benefit of those who joined him at the bar, a sudden gravity, the hand raised to beg for complicity and silence, the look of alarm and respect at Dr. Gunz, who had just come into the lobby and was asking for the afternoon papers as he unbuttoned his vest, the rapid and stealthy steps toward the scale, the tall body totally straight, rejuvenated, steady on the platform. "One hundred and sixty-five," he announced with relief when he settled back down at the bar. Surely he was lying. "I can have another."

Everyone laughed and he showed his gratitude; he held his smile while they returned him some of the claps on the back that he had been spreading around, while he thought with wonder about the ease with which men are terrified by death—hating it, believing in tricks to escape it, to live without it. It didn't matter whether one despaired or played the clown, spoke of politics, or prayed to oneself, taking as text the foreign words on the labels of the bottles on the shelf. And since he was hurriedly and stubbornly paying off all the debts that had been piling up since the day of his arrival, he asked permission from the marble busts that leaned over the tourist posters under the glass countertop and approached the wicker table, a full glass in his hand, where Dr. Gunz was reading the soccer news and the orderly was noting in a little notebook the shots he had to give in his rounds that night.

"I wish you had seen him. It was hard for me to convince myself that it was the same man."

There he was, holding the glass in his clumsy fingers, showing off the splendor of his silk tie and shirt—"as if this were the happiest night of his life, as if he were celebrating"—smiling with alert mildness at Gunz's blond mustache, at the golden sparkle of his glasses, at the rapid, nasal words the doctor was saying to him.

"And I came and went, carrying the tablecloths and the plates into the dining room, because the other girl happens to be sick or says she is. And I came down from the office carrying all that stuff and passed between the bar and the table where they were, before the woman (who a little earlier had asked me for mineral water and aspirin) came down with the child. And she saw him, from the back, with his hair carefully combed, rocking back and forth in the rock-

ing chair, laughing from time to time, drinking from the glass which
was always in his hand. And it was as if they were chatting about
anything at all, about the rain or the hole in the tennis court."

While on the same wave of irrepressible pleasure and friendship
which he had been sustaining for everyone, he consulted with the
doctor about reasonable expectations, about months of life. And at
this moment he had to make more visible, more feely offered—not
for Gunz or for the orderly or for the maid's busy trip back and
forth—the irony without future contained in his swift campaign to
gain back lost time, in the attempt to change the showy, disagree-
able memory he had imposed on the people of the hotel and the
town. In the smile with which he listened to Gunz, there was an almost aggressive display of the essential incredulity which I had
guessed at first sight of him, a dreamy inability to have faith which
he must have discovered when he felt the first shooting pain in his
back and which he had decided to accept fully in the course of the
day the maid and the orderly were witnessing.

"But who catches Gunz unawares? He spoke of total treatment,
as always; he told him that from the beginning he had advised him
to enter the sanitarium for a complete treatment. And the guy, who
must have been drunk by then, but did not lose track of his self-
possession, laughed, saying that he couldn't stand life in a sanitarium. And when the woman appeared on the staircase, the child in
her arms, he began talking about a game against the American team,
which someone said had been lost because of him, and of how he
could hardly keep from crying when they pressed the microphone
toward him at the end of the game. He said goodbye and went back
to the bar; he let the woman go by with the child behind him and go
out to the terrace. I went up to ask the bartender if there had been
any calls for me, and he was telling the same story of the basketball
game with the Americans, now play by play, point by point."

"When I went up to Room 40 to take the aspirin and the mineral
water, she received me with great affection. The little boy was standing on a chair near the window looking outside and calling to a cat.
She helped me put the tray on the table and told me, I remember,
that it was a great idea to use rubber-soled shoes. I told her that they
were very comfortable but made me look very short. She was in a
slip, without her glasses, and has very large, green eyes with dark
circles under them. I felt her looking at me while I opened the bottle,
leaning against the wall, her arms crossed, almost clutching her
shoulders. As if we were friends, as if I had gone up to Room 40 to
tell her something that bothered me and she were waiting. And
when I was leaving she called me with a movement of her arm and

said to me in all seriousness, 'If you saw me, like this, like I am now, without knowing anything about me . . . would I seem like a bad woman to you?' 'Please, ma'am,' I said to her. 'Anyhow, you're not the bad woman.'"

Why had he chosen, out of all of the things that did not matter to him, the story of the basketball game? I saw him sitting up straight on the bar stool, scattering the insignificant tale of blame, defeat, and youth on either side. I saw him choosing it, as the best one to carry off, as the most complete and comprehensible symbol: the memory of that night at Luna Park; the inaccurate memory, distorted so many times, of locker room jokes; of tickets sold by scalpers for a hundred pesos; of struggle, sweat, courage, tricks; of the solitude in disillusionment, of being blinded by the lights, in the middle of the noise of the crowd leaving now, no longer shouting.

Perhaps he had not been choosing a memory but a shameful, public, tolerable fault, an injury for which he recognized himself responsible, which hurt nobody now and which he could live over, ascribing to it, exaggerating it to the point of turning it into a catastrophe, making it capable of covering up all other remorse.

"They ate on the terrace, like the best of friends, as if the four of them formed a happy family, something you rarely see. And when the meal was over the guy accompanied the girl to the chalet, and the woman went down the steps, carrying the child, to go with them to the gates of the hotel. After putting the child to bed, she came back to the dining room and asked for a drink. She was waiting until they left Gunz by himself; then she called him over and they talked for about half an hour, the amount of time that it took the guy to go up and back."

She was neither happy nor sad; she seemed younger and at the same time more mature when the man spotted them from the dining room door and approached, standing straight, emaciated, with a mocking, alert expression on his face. Gunz talked for a few more minutes, slow, thoughtful, while cleaning his glasses. The woman's hand rubbed hard against the man's, careful, unnecessary. Beneath the lie, the compassionate reaction, she felt surprise and curiosity. She examined the man as if Gunz had just introduced him to her after making her hear a short biography which went beyond the present: a prophetic, believable story reaching forward to cover several months after that minute, that coincidence. She had never slept with him; she did not know his habits, his dislikes, the meaning of his sorrow.

Gunz left and they drank a little more, quiet, separated forevermore, in agreement. And when they went upstairs to go to bed, she

felt compelled to walk leaning on the man's proven strength, imagining and correcting the impression that their two bodies could
make, step by step, on the night clerk and on those who remained
yawning at the bar, discovering—with a shy enthusiasm she would
never accept—that nothing remains or is repeated.

"But if what happened that night," the orderly insisted, "was already pretty strange—the two women acting like lifelong friends,
the kiss they exchanged on parting—what happened the next day is
unbelievable. Because after lunch it was she who walked by herself
up to the chalet, with a package that must have been food. The guy
stayed behind with the boy and took him for a walk to the most
beautiful place he had found in all that time: the garbage dump. He
lay down in the sun with his shirt on, his hat over his face, pulling
out dry weeds without looking and chewing on them while the boy
climbed around on the rocks. He could have slipped and broken his
neck. And the guy, see, lying in the sun with his coat for a pillow, the
hat over his eyes, almost at the edge of the pile of papers, broken
bottles, dirty cotton balls, like a pig in its sty, without worrying
about anything at all, about the boy, about what the women up
above might have been saying. And when it began to get cold, the
boy, out of hunger or boredom, came and shook him until the guy
got up and put him on his shoulders to carry him back to the hotel.
She arrived about five; she seemed thinner, older, and stayed at the
bar having a drink, one hand over her face, not moving, not seeing.
Then she went up and had the big talk."

"Not a talk," Reina corrected sweetly. "I was making up the room
across the hall and had no alternative but to listen to them. But you
couldn't hear too well. She said that the only thing she wanted was
to see him happy. He didn't shout either; sometimes he laughed, but
it was a false, angry laugh. 'Gunz told you that I am going to die.
That's the reason for the sacrifice, the renunciation.' At this point
she started to cry and the boy too. 'Yes,' he said, only to torture her,
'I am dead. Gunz told you so. All of this, a six-foot tall corpse, is
what you are giving her as a present. She would do the same, you
would accept the same.'"

"It's not that I'm defending him," the orderly said, "but you have
to realize that he was desperate. It cannot be denied that there was
some kind of deal between them, and although this is what he had
been wanting, when the thing happened he saw the truth. Of course
he already knew it, the truth. But it's always like that. You saw her
come with the child and take the bus, almost sure this time she was
leaving forever. They are living in the chalet; they are brought food
from the hotel and never go out. They've only been seen once, at

night, smoking on the porch. And Gunz told me that the thing is going to go quickly now, that it's no longer even a question of putting him in the sanitarium."

She passed by the store carrying the child, it's true, without coming in, choosing to wait for the bus in the shade of the tree. From the counter, while washing a glass, I looked at her as if spying on her. I would have offered her anything, whatever she wanted to take from me. I would have told her that we agreed, that I believed as she did that what she was leaving to the other woman was not the man's corpse but the privilege of helping him die, the sum total and key to his life.

The other two stayed shut up in the little house until the beginning of winter, until a few days after the first snowfall of the year. No more letters arrived, only a package labeled "used clothing."

Andrade, from the real estate office, went to visit them four times and was always seen by the girl: friendly and taciturn, ignoring the other's curiosity, rendering useless the pretexts for delaying there which Andrade had made up on his way there on bicycle. It was the first day of the month; the knocks on the door could only be those of Andrade. She went out right away, as if she had been waiting for him, in a dark sweater and wrinkled pants, with the quick, exact movements of her boyish body; she greeted him, transacted in silence the exchange of money for a receipt, and greeted him again. Andrade climbed on his bicycle and went zigzagging back to his office, or continued his rounds to the other houses on the mountainside he looked after, thinking about what he had seen, about what it was admissible to deduce, about what he could lie and tell about.

On the day of the departure of the woman and child, the man paid his bill at the hotel and left. So for the guests he was no longer one of them; the courtesies, the appearances he had lavished on his last night began to be forgotten from the moment when he went down the steps, putting away his receipt, the raincoat over his shoulder, dealing out silent greetings with a final enthusiasm, moving his smile from one side to the other. Once more, Gunz and Castro's patients noted, with more exasperation than before, each of the things which separated them from the man; and above all, they came to feel again the intolerable insistence of the man not to accept the sickness which should have joined him to them.

They could not put a name on the vague and unforgivable offense he had personified while he lived among them. They focused their fury on the Ferreyras' little house, visible when they rested on the terrace or when they walked through the park along the banks of the stream. And twice a day (until the nights grew longer and they could only know of the second trip by its prologue), they could celebrate the fact that their hatred subsisted when it was renewed by the trips on foot of the hotel employee who was delegated to carry the food, a newspaper under his arm, up to the little red-and-white house, which they pretended to suppose was closed by shame. They kept track of the requests for bottles which the laborer communicated to the manager and spent their time imagining scenes in the life of the man and girl shut-in up above, provocatively, insultingly free from the world.

The orderly had been talking about the public scandal and affront; it was almost dark when I lit the lamps and asked the Levy boy to tend the store while I went across the road to have a drink and chat about deaths, treatments, and rates with the manager of the Royal. I went out into the blue-and-gray cold, into the wind which seemed not to come down from the mountains but to be formed in the treetops along the road and to attack me from there, time and again, almost at every step, angry and jubilant. I was walking with my head down, hearing the engine of a car taking the shortcut above the airplane factory, predicting that the manager of the Royal would announce to me, with a false sense of apprehension, with a childish hope, that it would be a snowy winter, with blocked roads, when I saw the blinking circles of the light on the dirt road. I stopped. The yellow light of the flashlight shone in my face, and I listened to the laugh; it was a dry, pointed sound, practiced as a challenge. The man pointed the light at the ground once more, looked at the clouds, turned it off.

"I brought it for the return trip," he said. "I discovered it in the garage. We meet by chance—you were on your way out. But I was coming to look for you. I have something to say, need to talk with you and do business."

He was motionless, extremely tall, with his back to the last band of light in the mountains, dark and disheveled. The wind shook his coat around and made him crack with a sound which could be mistaken for that of a very spread-out cough, which the man concealed by raising his hand and his flashlight.

"I hadn't recognized you," I said, not knowing if I should offer him my hand, quickly thinking over his story. "Let's go to the store, all right? At least there's no wind there."

He followed me in silence, treading as if he were trying to crush something. "It's the first time he's talking," I thought as we entered the store. "Everything before was monosyllables, grunts, gestures, just one word. He is drunk, but not on alcohol. He needs to keep talking, as if he were plunging headlong and wanted it to be over as soon as possible."

I was rubbing my hands, taking off my outer layers of clothing, although the cold and some of the wind were inside the store also. I did not want to turn around to look at him. I clapped the Levy boy—absorbed, mouth open, cap drawn down to his eyes, behind the counter—on the back. We were left alone and I filled two glasses with vermouth. He took his hand off the window grate and came toward me, smiling, his arms held away from his body, rocking the long, nickel-plated flashlight back and forth. He leaned over to control his coughing and smiled again, blushing, tearful.

"Excuse me," he murmured. "If you don't mind, I'd prefer rum."

I served him what he requested and said "To your health!" before drinking, without having looked at him yet. I began examining him by looking at his overcoat: old, black, too loose, with very large buttons and a velvet collar which was too new.

"You were on your way out," he said. "I don't want you . . . because of me . . . It will just take a minute." He stopped and looked around, serious, bewildered, inquisitive. He turned his head again, more calmly, raised his glass and emptied it. He looked at me without it mattering whether he saw me, his lip raised and still. He touched the counter with his fingertips, to hold himself straight, in his black, smelly, out-of-date overcoat; the bones of his hairy wrists were exposed, and he bent his head down to look at them, full in turn of pity and affection.

Apart from this, he was no more than cheekbones, the hardness of a smile, the active and childish sparkle of eyes. It was hard for me to believe that a face could be made of so little: I added a wide, yellow forehead, rings under his eyes, blue lines along the edges of his nose, very dark, linked eyebrows.

"Give me another drink," he said. "It's very simple, they cut off our provisions. They could only put up with it for a few months; but I took too long, was not able to kick the bucket on schedule within the limits of decency, as they had hoped. Here I am, still, coughing and on my feet. I am like that: I make plans, believe in them, even swear by them, and then don't keep my word. I don't want to bore you, excuse me. So, today to be precise, at the hotel, they ran out of patience. The employee came at noon with the food and told us he was not coming back. He felt very ashamed, was scraping the floor with his foot, maybe even felt pity for us. We paid him and tipped him well. And she slipped out on the porch so that I would not see her cry. Things are bad, of course; she had made herself responsible for my treatment, for my happiness. She inherited some money from her mother and had the whim to spend it on this, so that I would get better. Anyway, we agree that we must keep on eating until I die. So I came to see you, to ask you if you could have food brought to us, once or twice a day, for a short time. Not because I plan to die, but maybe we will leave soon."

I said I would, lying (because I did not know how I would get them their two meals a day), asking myself why they turned to me and not to some other hotel or guesthouse. He was next to the counter, in profile, clumsy, playing with the light of his flashlight because he could not think of a way to say goodbye. I served another round; I imagined that the girl up above would take advantage of his absence to cry a little more.

An old woman who lived in the mountains had recounted that she had approached the little house one Sunday to ask for matches, that one window was open, and that the man, alone, standing, nude, was looking at himself in the wardrobe mirror; he moved his arms, putting on a curious, slightly surprised smile. And it was not, I reconstructed, it had not been that they had just finished rolling around on the bed and that the man had found himself caught by the mirror in passing. He had undressed slowly in front of the wardrobe to recognize his skeletal self, with patches of hair which were conventional, and not intentionally sarcastic, additions, with the insistent memory of what his body had been, unsure whether his thighbones could hold him up, unsure of the penis hanging down between the bones. He was not just thin there in the mirror but getting thinner, as he could see as often as he got up the nerve to look and measure.

He shook one hand in the pocket of his overcoat, but I spoke before he got it out.

"It's nothing. My treat. It's all set: meals for two people, twice a day."

The light of his flashlight struck the wall and he smiled, with a cautious pride, as if he had just succeeded.

"Thank you. Whatever you send us will be fine. No more letters will come. The fact is, I asked her not to write."

He moved to face me, showing his full face, holding the broad, negative smile. He was aged and dead, destroyed, becoming empty, but, nevertheless, younger than at any time before, reproducing the head he had straightened on the pillow in adolescence, when recovering from the first congestion. He turned his smile into a noise and held out his hand to me. I saw him go out the door, daring, warlike, putting on the billowing overcoat which had once fit tightly around his chest, struggling with the wind: I saw him drag along the light of the flashlight while climbing upward.

I did not see them again for two or three weeks; they brought them food from the Royal, and now it was he who received the emissary—the Levy boy—and paid him every day.

The girl reappeared in the orderly's gossip, coming down the mountain one evening to look for Gunz at the hotel and install herself on the terrace waiting for him, smiling and silent with the waiters, with the guests who could recognize her. In the orderly's version, Gunz shrugged his shoulders and said no; afterward he whispered with his head bent toward her and the table; over the doctor's body the girl looked into the distance as if she were alone. Finally, she thanked him and offered to pay for the cups of coffee; Gunz walked with her as far as the gates of the hotel and stood there for a while with his hands in his pants pockets, watching her move away and climb, her tightly filled vest advancing in the twilight.

In the maid's story—she was no longer going to marry the orderly and came to the store by herself at hours when she would not run into him—the girl came down one night to pull Gunz out of bed and display to those who chatted drowsily in the bar a face in which there was more fright than grief. Gunz, unenthusiastically, finally agreed to go up to the chalet holding onto one of the girl's arms.

I saw them again, by surprise, without the maid or the orderly having been able to inform me that they were leaving. They chose the morning, between six and seven, to arrive at the store together, alone in the cold, each one with a bag.

"Once again," said the man, standing up straight.

They sat down by the window and ordered coffee. Sleepily, she followed me for a while with a smile which sought to explain and give her peace. I looked at their sleepless eyes, their hardened, sated, willful faces. It was easy for me to imagine the night they had just been through; it tempted me, in the morning excitement, to go on filling in the details of the hours of wakefulness and of definitive, affected embraces.

Wrapped in her wool coat, with a blue ski cap, the girl blinked, looking outside; she had a round, childish, inquiring face. With a huge watch jumping around on his wrist, the man opened his enormous hand to hold onto his jaw, alone and bewildered, facing his empty cup. Mist clouded the morning behind the windows and the grates; the sun shone intermittently; the cold was becoming palpable in the middle of the dirt floor of the store.

"We are going to the sanitarium," the man said when I approached to give them their check because he had waved a bill in the air; the girl wrinkled her nose and mouth to say something, but kept on looking at the morning through the grate. "Yesterday I told the boy; in any case, I wanted to tell you that it's over. And to thank you."

I leaned on the table and performed a good farce, asking him to forgive the quality of the food, as if I had cooked it. Someone, Mirabelli probably because of the hour, went past, driving a cow with a bell on. She had her neck resting on the man's arm, listening to the birds, the first car motors, the end of the night.

"Dr. Gunz says it's a sure thing," the man said from the hollow of his hand, with a lazy and vigilant smile, with a voice which would not awaken the girl if she slept. "Three months in the sanitarium, with a very strict regimen."

"Gunz is a very good doctor. And he has a lot of experience."

"A lot of experience," he repeated slowly, enjoying himself; he looked toward the middle of the room, right at the spot where I could feel the cold collecting; now his face fit in his hand, his fingertips touched the long, uneven locks of hair on his forehead. "And then, to start again. Don't you see? It's only for three months; and even if it were six."

It seemed to me that he had not raised his voice, but she stopped looking at the watery cloud on the window and pointed her eyes, as the man did, at the center of the floor of the shop. The first real customer entered with a hoarse, indirect greeting, his sandals making a sad scraping sound; he was wearing a beret and had a long mustache and a black handkerchief of mourning. The girl's hand ran over the man's chest, went up until it clasped onto the giant fingers supporting his head.

Chilled to the bone, clearing his throat, the man with the black handkerchief smoothed out a bill on the counter and ordered gin. While I was filling his shot glass, I saw the recently painted sanitarium van approach, rocking slowly back and forth. The girl and the man guessed it was there and got up with effort, numb; they did not greet me on leaving. He carried the two bags; she started joking with the driver who had gotten out of the van and clutched his captioned, visored cap to his stomach.

Three months, Gunz had lied; six months the man had admitted. I imagined them motionless in white iron beds, up there, placed temporarily in a room in the sanitarium, noses and chins pointing resolutely at the whitewashed ceiling, still pretending not to understand, on their word to wait without protests, without idle comments, for the hour when the others would recognize their mistake and decide, with little excuses, with phrases which denied time, with friendly little pats on the back, to send them back to the world, to helplessness, to controversy, to postponement. I imagined the furtive lust, the man's attempted allures, the girl's refusals, promises, and pitiless rages, her persistent, masculine postures.

Very few days of the six or three months had passed when, with the help of the youngest of the Levy boys, I started cleaning the store and taking inventory. Then I saw once more, at the bottom of the drawer of mail, under the black notebook for the certified letters, the two envelopes in the wide, blue hand which I had not felt like giving to the man when they arrived during the summer. I did not think about it much; I put them in my pocket and that night read the letters, by myself, after closing the blinds. One, the first one, was of no importance; it spoke of love, of separation, of the guessed-at or imposed meaning of past phrases or acts. It spoke of intuitions and discoveries, of surprises, of long waiting. The second one was different; the paragraph that matters said: "And what can I do? Less now than ever before, considering that when all is said and done she is your blood and wants generously to spend her money to restore you to health. I would not venture to say that she is an intruder because properly speaking I am the one who has come between you two. And I cannot believe that you really mean it when you say that your daughter is the intruder, knowing that I have given you so little and have been more of a nuisance than anything else."

I felt shame and rage; my skin crawled with shame for several minutes, and within it I felt the rage growing, the humiliation, the writhing of a small tormented pride. I thought of doing various things, of going up to the hotel and telling everyone, mocking everyone up there as if I had always known and it had been enough for me to look at the girl's cheeks or eyes at the New Year's Eve party—and not even so much as that: her gloves, her bag, her patience, her quietness—in order not to share the mistake the rest had made, in order not to help with my unconscious desire to bring about the defeat and the exhaustion of a woman who did not deserve that; I thought of going up to the hotel and walking among them, not saying a word about the story, holding the letter in my hand or in a pocket. I thought of visiting the sanitarium, taking them a box of fruit, sitting down by the bed to watch the man's beard grow with a friendly smile, to breathe secretly, with a feeling of relief, each time she caressed him timidly in my presence.

But all my excitement was absurd, more worthy of the orderly than of me. Because, supposing that I had guessed right when I interpreted the letter, it did not matter, with respect to the essential thing, the link between the girl and the man. She was a woman, in any case; another one.

All I did was to burn the letters and try to forget; and I could, finally, recover from the defeat successfully, alone before myself, scorning the chance that the orderly, Gunz, the sergeant, and Andrade heard me, uncovering and covering up the man's face, shrugging my shoulders, moving away from the body on the bed to go toward the porch of the Ferreyras' house, toward the biting cold night, and saying in a low voice, with spirited pity, with exhausted contempt, that the man had nothing left but death and had not wanted to share it.

"What?" the orderly asked me, respectful, unsure, containing his excitement.

I went out and leaned against the porch railing, trembling with cold, looking at the lights of the hotel. It sufficed for me to place my recent discovery before the beginning of the story for everything to become simple and foreseeable. I felt myself full of power, as if the man and the girl, and also the older woman and the child, had been born of my will and lived what I had determined for them. I was smiling while I thought this once more, while I agreed to forgive the basketball champion's final greed. The air smelled of cold, of drought, of nothing green or growing.

I went into the room, and, full of kindness, crossed the whispering of the four men. I slowly examined the little house, looked at and lightly touched the prints, antimacassars, curtains, pillows, pillowcases, dry flowers, everything the four dead women had made and had left behind there, the knickknacks their hands had created, amid silly, mechanical chatter, forebodings and rebellions, words of advice, recipes. I counted the death throes under the roof striped by new, black, useless beams, capriciously using my fingers. I thought, absentmindedly and without respect, about the virginity of the three sisters and about that of their friend, a very young woman, blond, stout. In the room at the back I found the pile of unopened newspapers, the ones they had made the hotel employee bring, and in the kitchen a row of wine bottles, nine of them, never opened.

I returned, step by step, to the room where the body and the others were.

"He lacked patience, ma'am," Gunz was explaining to a thin woman, whose head, covered by a shawl, marked assent.

"That's right," said Andrade, sad and flattering.

The orderly was talking about procedures and removals with the sergeant; he smiled when he saw me come in and wanted to ask

something, but I turned toward the shoes and the visible pants of the
dead man, toward the incomprehensible form under the sheet.

"Not much blood, ma'am," the orderly reported, with a question-
ing tone directed at Gunz.

"What he had left," the doctor joked, yawning.

I looked toward the bed with all my strength, believing it possible
to find out why they had asked for the papers in order not to read
them, why they had bought the bottles in order not to open them,
believing that I needed to know.

"How would it be if I left the certificate to you?" asked Gunz.

"However you want, doctor," the sergeant sang out. "But if you
would wait a moment . . ."

And there it was, on the ground: the dark, short, sufficient revolver, which he had brought hidden amid the whiteness of under-
shirts and handkerchiefs, which he carried in a pocket or on his belt,
hiding it with cunning and impudence, knowing that he was hiding
it from himself, calm and strong because it was an object that could
be hidden from one woman and the other, from the part of him that
lacked a foundation.

The sergeant and Gunz had gone out on the porch to wait for the
police chief; only the slow sound of their words reached me, the image of the ribbons of steam from their mouths. Behind me, rising up
out of her perplexity, curiosity, fear, the thin woman began to ask
questions.

"Didn't you see him?" said the orderly happily. "He looks the
same as always. Thinner, perhaps; calmer." He stopped and I know
that he was looking at me in anguish; he repeated his story softly, so
that I would not hear it again.

"He was a hopeless case although, of course, they never told him
so. You know how it is. They had been at the sanitarium for three
weeks, and we kept him quiet with shots. A very strict regimen.
Neither worse nor better. Always happy, always a gentleman. The
girl was with him—I don't know, ma'am, taking care of him—And
this morning, when she woke up and the patient was not in the
room, we went out looking for him all over the sanitarium; afterward we found out that he had gone down in the bus. The driver was
used to it, people who can hardly walk and suddenly have the idea of
going out. It's not possible, ma'am; that's how the sanitarium is—
freedom. But he did not come back, the driver got tired of waiting for
him, and there we were, not knowing what to think, until Andrade,
here, called us."

"That's right, ma'am," Andrade confirmed. Now I was looking at
them, amused, rocking back and forth to get warm. "They told me

that they had seen him come in at noon, although he had returned the keys to me, and I refused to believe it. I hadn't even come to clean up. But there was a window lit up after sunset, and I came and knocked. Imagine, when I opened the door and came in. Perhaps he had kept a key to the kitchen door."

"And he was still young, the poor thing," the woman said; she tried to burst into tears.

The orderly, Andrade, and I shrugged our shoulders and listened just then to the sound of a car engine coming to a halt. The sergeant and Gunz walked across the porch, beating with every step, as if on purpose, on the luminous, cold silence, the hardness of the impartial night.

"The police chief," the orderly announced solemnly, and the old woman said yes again, nodding.

I sat down on the couch, shaken and at peace; I preferred not to move when the girl entered and went straight to the bed, with incredible slowness copying my gesture of uncovering and covering up.

The sergeant and Gunz stood in the doorway; the old woman and the orderly flattened themselves against the wall; Andrade moved back with the beret in his hand. Almost without breathing, I looked at the girl leaning her head over the untimely ensemble, angrily horizontal, of shoes, pants, and sheets. She was motionless, without tears, her brows locked, slow to understand what I had discovered months before, the first time the man came into the store—she had nothing more than that and did not want to share it—dignified, eternal, invincible, already preparing herself, without foreboding, for any future violent night.

# A Dream Come True

The one who came up with the idea for the joke was Blanes. He would come to my office—back when I had an office, or to the cafe when things were bad and I was without one—and would stand on the rug, a fist resting on the desk, a brightly colored tie held to his shirt by a gold tie pin. His head—square, closely shaven, with dark eyes that could stare unblinking at something for more than a minute, eyes that would relax all at once as if Blanes were about to fall asleep or were remembering some pure moment of feeling, a moment that, of course, he had never experienced—a head without even a single unnecessary spot, facing a wall covered with pictures and posters, would let me talk and then comment, the mouth becoming round: "For you, naturally enough, got ruined giving *Hamlet*." Or then again: "Yes, we all know. You have always sacrificed yourself for art, and if it weren't for your mad love for *Hamlet* . . ."

And I spent all those years dealing with so many nasty people, authors and actors and actresses and theater owners and newspaper critics and the families, friends, and lovers of all of them, all the while losing and winning money that both God and I knew I would lose again the next season, with that water torture on my bald head, that fist in the ribs, that bittersweet drink, Blanes's joke that never quite made sense: "Yes, of course. The mad acts to which your endless love for *Hamlet* have carried you . . ."

If I had asked him the meaning of all of that the first time, if I had confessed to him that I knew as much about *Hamlet* as a first reading allows you to guess how much money a play will bring in, the joke would have been up. But I was afraid of the crowd of jokes yet unborn that this question would inspire, so I only frowned and told him to get lost. And that's how I was able to live for twenty years without knowing what *Hamlet* was, without ever having read it, but knowing, by the pointed intention I could see in Blanes's face and in the movements of his head, that *Hamlet* was art, pure art, great art, and knowing too, because I absorbed the idea without realizing it, that he was also an actor or actress, in this case inevitably an actress with bizarre hips dressed in tight black clothes, a skull, a cemetery, a duel, revenge, a girl who drowns herself. And also, W. Shakespeare.

That is why, when now, only now, wearing a blond wig parted down the middle that I prefer not to take off even when I go to sleep, a denture that never fit very well and makes me hiss and speak in an affected way, I found myself in the library of this home for impoverished theater people called by some name that puts a better appearance on things and came upon a tiny book in dark blue binding with embossed gold letters that said *Hamlet*, I sat down in an armchair without opening the book, resolving never to open the book, never to read even a single line of it, thinking of Blanes, of how this way I could get back at him for his joke, thinking of the night Blanes went to meet me in a hotel in some provincial capital and how, after letting me talk, smoking, looking at the ceiling and at the people who were coming into the room, he let his lips jut out to tell me, in front of the poor crazy woman: "And to think that a guy like you ruined yourself for *Hamlet*."

I had made an appointment with him in the hotel to arrange for him to play a character in a short bit of nonsense called, I think, *A Dream Come True*. In the cast of that silly piece, there was a nameless gallant who could only be played by Blanes because when the woman came to see me, only the two of us, he and I, were left; the rest of the company had managed to escape to Buenos Aires.

The woman had been at the hotel at noon, and since I was asleep she had returned at the time of day that, for her and for everyone else in that hot region, was the end of the siesta; at that hour I was in the coolest corner of the dining room, eating a breaded cutlet and drinking white wine, the only good thing to be had there. I won't say that at first glance—when she paused in the circle of heat by the curtained door, her eyes widening in the darkness of the dining room, and the waiter pointed her to my table and all at once she began walking straight toward me, her skirt billowing—I guessed what was going on inside the woman or that thing resembling a spongy, whitish ribbon of madness that she had been unraveling, pulling at with little tugs, as if it were a bandage stuck onto a wound, from her former, solitary years, only to come wrap me in it, as if I were a mummy, wrapping me and some of the days spent in that dull place, full of fat, badly dressed people. But yes, something about the woman's smile made me nervous, and I found it impossible to look for very long at her small, irregular teeth, all exposed to view like those of a sleeping child breathing with mouth open. Her hair, almost gray, was combed in twisted braids; her dress followed some older fashion. It was not the suit a lady would have worn at the time it was designed, but (that's right) what a teenage girl would have worn. Her skirt extended to her shoes, the kind called ankle boots; the skirt was long and dark, and when she walked it opened and then contracted, only to tremble again when she took her next step. Her blouse was of lace; it was tight, and a large cameo hung between her pointed, girlish breasts. The blouse and skirt were joined and divided by a rose at her waist, maybe an artificial one (now that I think about it), a flower with a large corolla and low top, the stiff stem threatening her stomach.

The woman must have been about fifty, and what you couldn't forget about her, what I feel even now, remembering her walking toward me in the hotel dining room, was that girlish air from some other century, as if she had fallen asleep and only awakened now, her hair in disarray, hardly aged but seemingly at any moment about to reach her own age all of a sudden and then shatter in silence, collapse as if gnawed away by the secret work of time. And it was bad to look at her smile because you would think that, in spite of the ignorance the woman displayed about the danger of aging and sudden death, all so imminent, that smile knew, or at least the little exposed teeth had a foreboding, of the horrible defeat that awaited them.

All of that was now standing in the shadows of the dining room, and I clumsily put the silverware down by my plate and stood up. "You are Mr. Langman, the theater patron?" I nodded, smiling, and invited her to sit down. She didn't want to have anything to drink; across the table I studied her mouth, its form intact. There was no lipstick at the middle of the mouth, in the spot where her voice, sounding slightly Spanish, had hummed a little, sliding between the uneven surfaces of her teeth. I couldn't read anything in her eyes: small, quiet, intent on looking bigger than they were. I had to wait for her to speak. I thought that any form of woman and existence her words might evoke would fit her odd appearance well, so her appearance would not seem so odd.

"I wanted to see you about staging a play," she said. "I mean, I have a dramatic work."

It seemed as if she was going to go on, but she stopped and waited for my answer; she surrendered to me with an irresistible silence, smiling. She waited calmly, her hands clasped on her lap. I pushed aside the half-eaten cutlet and ordered a cup of coffee. I offered her a cigarette and she shook her head, broadening her smile a bit, which was supposed to mean that she didn't smoke. I lit mine and began speaking to her, trying to escape from her without violence, quickly and definitively, though in a cautious way I assumed for some unknown reason.

"Ma'am, it's really a pity . . . You've never had anything put on, right? Of course. And what's the name of your play?"

"No, it doesn't have a name," she answered. "It's so hard to explain . . . It's not what you think. Of course, I could give it a title. It could be called *The Dream, The Dream Come True. A Dream Come True*."

I understood now, beyond a doubt, that she was crazy, and I felt more at ease.

"Fine. *A Dream Come True*, it's not a bad title. The title is very important. I have always had an interest, let's say a personal interest, but in a sense a disinterested one, in helping those who are just getting started. To provide new blood for the national theater. Though it goes without saying that nobody thanks you for the effort, ma'am. There are lots of people who owe their first step to me and who now earn huge sums along Corrientes and win the annual prizes. They no longer remember the times when they came to me, almost begging . . ."

Even the waiter would have understood, there in the corner by the refrigerator where he waved a napkin to chase flies and the heat, that that strange bird couldn't care less about what I was saying. I looked at her out of the corner of my eye, from just above the hot demitasse of coffee, and said to her, "Anyway, ma'am. I'm sure you know that our season here has been a failure. We have had to cut it short, and I have only stayed on because of some personal affairs. But early next week I will be going to Buenos Aires too. I have failed again, but there's nothing to do about it now. The atmosphere here isn't ready, and even after resigning myself to a season of musical comedies and things like that . . . you can see how I've done. So . . . Now, we can do one thing, ma'am. If you could give me a copy of your play, I will see whether in Buenos Aires . . . Is it three acts long?"

She had to answer, but only because I, turning the game around on her, stopped and leaned toward her, pressing the end of the cigarette in the ashtray. She blinked, "What?"

"Your play, ma'am. *A Dream Come True*. Is it three acts long?"

"No, there are no acts."

"Or scenes. It is now common enough to . . ."

"I don't have a copy. It's not something I have written down," she continued. It was the moment to escape.

"I will leave you my address in Buenos Aires, and as soon as you have written it . . ."

I saw her hunching up, her body curling, but she raised her head, her smile in place. I waited, certain that she would get up, but a moment later she gestured, her hand in front of her face, and kept on talking.

"No, it's completely different from what you think. It's a moment, a scene you might say, and nothing happens, as if we were playing this scene here in the dining room and I should leave and nothing else were to happen. No," she answered, "it's not a matter of plot, there are some people in a street and houses and two cars that go by. There I am and a man and some woman who comes out of the shop in front and gives the man a glass of beer. There isn't anybody else, just the three of us. The man crosses the street to the place where the woman is coming out of the door, then he sits down at the table, near me, where he was at the beginning."

She paused for a moment; now her smile wasn't directed at me or at the cupboard full of tablecloths half-open by the dining room wall. She concluded, "Do you understand?"

I managed to escape because I remembered the term "intimate theater" and told her about that and about the impossibility of producing pure art in such places and that nobody would go to the theater to see it and that in the whole of the province I was probably the only one capable of understanding the quality of that play and the meaning of the movements and the symbolism of the cars and the woman who offers a mug of beer to the man who crosses the street and comes back near her, near you, ma'am.

She looked at me and there was something about her face that resembled Blanes's face when he asked me for money and talked to me about *Hamlet:* some pity, some ridicule and antipathy.

"It's not like that at all, Mr. Langman," she said. "It's something I want to see, nobody else, no audience. The actors and I, that's all. I want to see it once, but for that once to be exactly the way I'm going to tell you, and you have to do what I say and no more. All right? Now, please, tell me how much it's going to cost and I'll pay you."

It wouldn't work any more as intimate theater or anything like that; there I was, face to face with the madwoman, who opened her purse and took out two fifty-peso bills. "With this you can hire the actors and cover the first expenses and later you tell me how much you need." I, who needed cash desperately, could not get out of that damned hole until someone in Buenos Aires answered my letters and sent me a few pesos. So I offered the woman my warmest smile and nodded several times while putting the folded money away in the pocket of my vest.

"Fine, ma'am. I think I understand the sort of thing you . . ."

While I spoke I didn't want to look at her because I was thinking about Blanes and I didn't like coming upon Blanes's expression of humility on the woman's face. "I will spend the afternoon working on this matter, and if we can see one another . . . Tonight? Fine, right here; we'll have the first actor by then and you'll be able to explain that scene clearly and we'll come to an agreement so that *Dream, A Dream Come True. . ."*

Perhaps it was just that she was crazy, but also it may have been that she understood, as I did, that I could not just steal the hundred pesos from her, so that was why she did not ask me for a receipt. It did not even occur to her. She left after shaking my hand, her skirt turning slightly with every step, standing very straight in the twilight of the dining room, then going out into the heat of the street. It was as if she was returning to the temperature of a slumber of many years; she had retained that impure youth that seems always on the verge of rotting away.

I was able to find Blanes in his messy, dark room, with walls of badly mortared bricks, behind the plants, the green mats, behind the damp heat of the sunset. The hundred pesos stayed in my vest pocket, and I couldn't spend a cent until I found Blanes, until I persuaded him to help me give the madwoman what she wanted in exchange for her money. I woke him up and waited patiently for him to bathe, shave, lie down again, get up to drink a glass of milk—which meant that he had been drunk the night before—and then go back to bed once more to light a cigarette. He refused to listen to me before and even then, when I drew up the remains of a boudoir armchair I was sitting on and leaned over with a serious air to make him the proposal, he stopped me, saying, "But look for a moment at the roof!"

It was a tile roof, with two or three greenish beams and some bamboo fishing rods that came from God knows where, long and dried out. I looked at the roof for a moment, and he did nothing but laugh and shake his head.

"OK. What's up?" he said then.

I explained what the deal was, and Blanes interrupted me every few moments, laughing, telling me that it was all a lie I was telling, that someone had sent the woman to me as a practical joke. Afterward he asked me what the business was once more, and I had no alternative but to offer him half of what the woman had paid me, after deducting the expenses. I answered that actually I didn't know what it was about or why or what the hell the woman wanted from us but that she had given me fifty pesos, which meant we could

leave for Buenos Aires, or at least I could go, if he wanted to keep on
doing nothing there.

He laughed and then a moment later got serious; of the fifty pesos
I told him I had received as an advance, he wanted twenty right
away. So I had to give him ten, which I repented of right away because that night when he came to the hotel dining room he was already drunk, frowning, his head leaning down over the plate of ice.
He began to say: "You never learn. The patron of Corrientes Street
and of whatever street in the world where a burst of art . . . A man
who went broke a hundred times for *Hamlet* is now altruistically
going to risk everything for an unknown genius in a corset."

But when she came, when the woman came out from behind me
completely dressed in black, veiled, with a tiny umbrella hanging
from her wrist and a watch and chain from her neck, and she greeted
me and stretched her hand out to Blanes, that smile of hers a bit
drawn in the artificial light, he stopped bothering me and said only,
"Wonderful, ma'am, the gods have guided you to Langman. A man
who has sacrificed hundreds of thousands of pesos for a proper pro-
duction of *Hamlet*."

Then it seemed as if she was making fun of us, looking first at
one, then at the other. She turned serious and said she was in a
hurry, that she would explain the whole thing in such a way that
there would not be room for the slightest doubt, and that she would
come back only when everything was ready. Under the smooth clean
light, the woman's face and the glowing spots on her body, clothing,
the nails on the bare hand, the umbrella handle, the watch and chain,
all seemed to become simply themselves freed from the torture of
the daylight. I soon felt relatively comfortable; the whole rest of the
night, I never once thought that she was crazy. I forgot that there
was an air of a confidence game about the whole thing; instead, a
feeling of a frequent, even ordinary, business proposition left me
with a sensation of perfect peace. Although I had no reason to worry
about anything, now that Blanes was there, proper, drinking, talking
to her as if they had already met two or three times, offering her a
glass of whiskey, which she exchanged for a cup of herb tea. So what
she had to tell me, she told him instead; I did not want to break in
because Blanes was the principal actor and the better he understood
the work, the better things would turn out. (She told Blanes the
whole thing in a different voice; even though she didn't look at him,
even though she lowered her eyes while talking about all of that, I
felt that she was telling him now in a personal way, as if she were
confessing some intimate detail of her life, while she had told me

the whole thing as if in an office, for instance, as if she were asking for a passport or something like that.)

What the woman wanted us to perform for her was this: "There are houses and sidewalks on the stage, all confused, as if it were a city, everything piled up to give the impression of a large city. I go out—the woman I am going to represent goes out of a house and sits down on the curb next to a green table. Next to the table there's a man sitting on a kitchen stool. That's your character. He is wearing a sweater and a cap. On the sidewalk across the way, there is a market with boxes of tomatoes in the door. Then a car appears, begins crossing the stage, and the man, you, gets up to cross the street, and I am afraid, thinking that the car will run you over. But you get across before the car comes; you arrive at the sidewalk on the other side at the very moment that a woman appears, dressed as if she were going out, with some beer in her hand. You drink it down in one gulp and start back just at the moment that another car comes, this time from the opposite direction, at full speed; once again you get across just in time and sit down on the kitchen stool. Meanwhile, I am lying on the sidewalk as if I were a little girl. And you lean over a little to pat me on the head."

The thing was easy to do, but I told her that the obstacle, now that I thought about it some more, was that third character, the woman who comes out of her house to take a walk with a glass of beer.

"A pitcher," she told me. "It is an earthenware pitcher with a handle and a top."

Then Blanes nodded his head and said, "Of course, how about a drawing, a sketch?"

She agreed and it seems that what Blanes had said made her very happy, content, with that joyful expression that only a woman can have and that makes me want to close my eyes to avoid seeing it when it happens, as if good manners demanded that. We went back to speaking about the other woman, and Blanes ended up squeezing her hand and saying that he already had everything he needed, that we didn't need to worry anymore. I thought then that the crazy woman's madness was contagious, because when I asked Blanes what actress he was counting on for that role, he told me that it was Rivas, and even though I didn't know anyone by that name, I didn't want to say anything because Blanes was looking at me furiously. So everything was arranged; the two of them arranged it all, and I didn't have to think about the play at all. I left right away to look for the owner of the theater and rented it for two days for the price of one, giving him my word that nobody would go in except the actors.

The next day I found a man who understood electrical installations, and for a day's wage of six pesos, he helped me move the side flats around and paint them a bit. That night, after working about fifteen hours, everything was ready; sweating and in shirtsleeves, I had some sandwiches and beer while listening inattentively to the stories the man was telling me about the town. The man paused and then said, "Today I saw your friend in good company. This afternoon, with that woman who was at the hotel last night with the two of you. Here everybody knows everything. She isn't from here; they say she comes in the summertime. I don't like to intrude, but I saw them go into the hotel. Yes, how funny. It's true that you live in the hotel also. But the hotel they entered this afternoon is different . . . One of those—you know what I mean?"

When Blanes arrived after a while, I told him that all that was missing was the famous actress Rivas. I had settled the business about the cars, but I could only rent one, the one belonging to the man who had been helping me, who was willing to rent it to me for a few pesos and to drive it himself as well. But I had my own solution to that, because since the car was an old wreck with a convertible top, it sufficed to have it go by first with the top down and then later with it up or backward. Blanes didn't answer me at all because he was completely drunk; I could not guess where he had gotten the money from. Later it occurred to me that perhaps he was cyncial enough to take money directly from the unfortunate woman. This idea made me bitter, and I kept on eating the sandwiches in silence while he, drunk and humming slightly, wandered around the stage, assuming poses of a photographer, a spy, a boxer, a rugby player, constantly humming, his hat slouched in back, looking all around, from every side, searching meticulously for the devil knows what. Since I was more and more convinced that he had gotten drunk with money stolen, practically, from that poor, sick lady, I didn't want to speak to him; when I finished eating the little sandwiches, I ordered the man to bring me a half dozen more and a bottle of beer.

By that time Blanes had tired of dancing pirouettes; his indecent drunkenness brought out his sentimental side, and he came over near where I was, sat down on a crate, his hands in his pants pockets and his hat on his knees, staring with troubled eyes in the direction of the stage. For a while we didn't speak, and I could see he was growing old and that his blond hair was fading and thin. He didn't have many years left in his career as a beau, taking ladies to hotels, or for anything else.

"I didn't waste my time either," he said all of a sudden.

"Yes, I can imagine," I answered with indifference.

He smiled, grew serious, straightened his hat, got up again. He kept on talking to me while walking back and forth, as he had seen me do so often in the office, all full of autographed photos, dictating a letter to the girl.

"I was investigating about the woman," he said. "It appears that the family or she herself had money and that later she had to work as a teacher. But nothing, hey, nothing proves she's crazy. Yes, she always was a bit peculiar. But not crazy. I don't know why I've come to tell you this, oh adoptive father of sad Hamlet, with your snout covered with the butter from the sandwich . . . talking to you about this."

"At least," I told him calmly, "I don't go around spying on the lives of others. Or devoting myself to seducing women who are a bit peculiar." I wiped my mouth with a handkerchief and then turned to look at him with a bored expression. "Nor do I get drunk with God knows whose money."

He paused there with his hands on his kidneys, standing there looking at me, in turn, pensive, and went on telling me unpleasant things, but anyone could see that he was thinking about the woman and that he wasn't insulting me with all his heart but instead just trying to do something while thinking, something to keep me from realizing that he was thinking about her. He turned to me, squatted down, picked up the bottle of beer, and drank down what was left, not hurrying, his mouth fixed to the neck of the bottle until it was empty. He paced around the stage a bit more and then sat down again with the bottle between his feet, covering it with his hands.

But I spoke to him and he was talking to me. He said, "I wanted to know what this was all about. But I don't know if you understand that it's not just a matter of putting the money in our pockets. I asked her what it was that we were going to represent, and that's when I found out she was crazy. Do you want to know? It's all a dream she had, do you understand? But the craziest part is that she says that dream has no meaning for her, that she doesn't know the seated man in the blue sweater or the woman with the pitcher, and she didn't even live on a street that looked like that ridiculous pile of junk you put together. And why, then? She says it's because while she was sleeping and dreaming about all of that, she was happy—but happy isn't the word, something else. So she wants to see it all over again. And even though it's crazy it has its reasonable side. And I also like the fact that there isn't the usual rubbish about love in all of this."

When we left to go to bed, he half stopped in the street—the sky was blue and it was very hot—to grab me by the shoulders and the lapels and ask me if I understood, God knows what, something that he must not have understood either, because he never finished explaining it.

The woman arrived at the theater promptly at ten and was wearing the same black suit with the watch and chain as the other night, which didn't seem appropriate to me considering the poor neighborhood where the theater was, and all in order to sit down on the curb while Blanes patted her on the head. But it didn't matter: the theater was empty; there was nobody in the orchestra except for Blanes, drunk as always, smoking, dressed in a blue sweater and wearing a gray cap over one ear. He had come early accompanying a girl—the one who had to look out of the door next to the market and give him the pitcher of beer—a girl who didn't fit the sort of character, the sort I imagined, of course, because only the devil knows how it really was supposed to be, a sad, thin girl, badly dressed and made up, that Blanes had picked up at some corner cafe, taking her out for a walk in the street at night, telling some absurd story to bring her along, no doubt, because she put on airs of a grand actress; when I saw her stretch out her arm with the pitcher of beer, I felt like crying or throwing her out of the place. The other woman, the crazy one, dressed in black, stood for a while looking at the stage as soon as she arrived, her hands clasped before her. She seemed enormously tall to me, much taller and thinner than I had believed until then. Then, without saying a word to anyone, constantly displaying (but no longer overdoing) that invalid's smile that made my nerves stand on end, she crossed the stage and hid behind the side flats where she was supposed to come on. I had followed her with my eyes; I don't know why my gaze held the precise form of a tall body dressed in black, clung to it, hugged it, followed it as far as the edge of the curtain that separated my gaze from the body.

And now I was the one who was in the middle of the stage, and as everything was in order and it was after ten, I raised my elbows to clap to the actors. But that was when, without my understanding completely what was happening, I began knowing things and exactly what we had gotten ourselves into, though I could never say it, just as one knows what a person's soul is like but can't describe it in words. I preferred summoning them with gestures; when I saw Blanes and the woman he had brought along starting to move to occupy their spots, I slipped behind the curtain where the man was sitting at the wheel of his old car, which was starting to shake with a tolerable amount of noise. From there, standing on a crate, trying to hide because I had nothing to do with the craziness that was just starting, I saw how she came out of the door of the hovel, moving her body like a girl. The hair, thin and almost gray, was loose at her back, tied at shoulder level with a light-colored ribbon. She took long steps that were no doubt those of the girl who had just set the table and looked out for a moment at the street, watching the sunset, still, not thinking about anything. I saw how she sat down near Blanes's bench and held her head in one hand, her elbow resting on her knee, her fingertips touching her half-open lips, her face turned toward a distant place off beyond where I was, beyond the wall behind me. I saw how Blanes got up to cross the street, crossing a moment before the car, its hood high, went by giving off lots of exhaust and then was gone. I saw Blanes's arm and that of the woman who lived in the house across the street join together over the pitcher of beer and how the man drank it all down in one gulp and left the pitcher in the hand of the woman, who sank down again, slowly and noiselessly, by her front door. I saw, once again, how the man in the blue sweater crossed the street a moment before a fast car with its hood down went by close to me and then suddenly turned off its motor, and while the bluish exhaust smoke cleared, I noticed the girl on the curb, yawning and then lying down on the flagstones, her head resting on one arm that concealed her hair, one of her legs bent. The man in the sweater and cap leaned over then and patted the girl on the head; he began caressing her, his hand going back and forth, getting entangled in her hair, the palm rubbing her forehead, the fingers squeezing on the light-colored ribbon in her hair, the caresses being repeated over and over.

I got up from the bench, breathing more freely, and tiptoed toward the stage. The owner of the car followed me, smiling nervously, and the thin girl Blanes had brought came out of her hallway to join us. She asked me a question, a brief question, just one word about all of that, and I answered without ever taking my eyes off Blanes and the woman who was lying down. Blanes's hand kept on caressing the woman's forehead and loose hair, not stopping, not realizing that the scene was over and that this last thing, caressing the woman's hair, couldn't go on forever. Bent over, Blanes was patting the woman's head; he stretched out his arm, running his fingers over the length of the gray hair from the forehead to the ends resting on the shoulders and back of the woman lying on the floor. The man in the car kept on smiling, coughed, spit off to one side. The girl who had given Blanes the pitcher of beer started walking toward the spot where the woman was lying and the man was bent over caressing her. Then I turned around and told the owner of the car that he could take it away; that way we would get out of there early. I walked with him, putting my hand in my pocket to give him a few pesos. Something strange was happening off to my right where the others were, and when I tried to think about it, I stumbled against Blanes, who had taken off his cap and had an unpleasant smell and punched me in the ribs, shouting: "You son of a bitch, don't you realize she's dead!"

I was left by myself, doubled over by the blow, and while Blanes went back and forth on the stage, drunk, half-crazy, and the girl with the pitcher of beer and the man with the car bent over the dead woman, I understood what it was all about, what the woman had been searching for, what Blanes had drunkenly been trying to find out the night before on stage and seemed to be searching for even now, walking back and forth with the haste of a madman: I understood it all clearly, as if it were one of those things that one learns once and for all as a child, something that words can never explain.

# Esbjerg by the Sea

At least the afternoon has warmed up a little, and a watery sun occasionally lights up the streets and walls, because just at this hour they must be walking in Puerto Nuevo by the boat or passing the time going from one dock to another, from the newspaper stand by City Hall to the sandwich place—they: Kirsten, heavy, not wearing heels, her hat squashed on her yellow hair; and Montes, short, bored, nervous, spying on her face—learning the names of ships without realizing it, absentmindedly watching the ropes being pulled this way or that.

I imagine him chewing on his mustache as he toys with a fantasy of pushing the woman's body, the body of a country woman grown fat in city idleness, making it fall into the wedge of water between the wet stone and the black metal of the ships, where there is a boiling sound and little space for a person to stay afloat. I know they are there because Kirsten came looking for Montes today at noon in his office and I saw them walk out together in the direction of Retiro— she with her face of rain: the face of a statue in winter, the face of someone who has fallen asleep, eyes open, in the rain. Kirsten is fat, freckled, hardened; perhaps she smells of stables and cream, the penetrating odor I imagine must exist in her country.

But other times they have to go to the docks at midnight or at dawn, and I think that when the whistles of the ships let Montes hear her pressing forward on the cobblestones, the poor devil must feel that he is going hand in hand with misfortune into the darkness. Here in the paper there are notices of the departures of ships for this month, and I could swear I can see Montes standing still, from the time the ship blows its whistle and begins to move until it's so tiny that it's not worth watching any more. His eyes move sometimes— asking, over and over, without ever understanding, without getting any reply—glancing toward the woman's fleshy face, squeezed for long periods at a time, sad and cold as if it rained while she was asleep and she had forgotten to close her eyes, enormous, almost beautiful eyes, eyes the shade of the river on those days when the mud isn't stirred up.

I learned the story, without understanding it very well, the same morning that Montes came to tell me that he had tried to rob me, that he had hidden many Saturday and Sunday bets from me in order to take the profits himself, and that now he couldn't pay off the winners. I was not concerned with why he had done it, but he was infuriated by the need to tell me, and I had to listen to him while thinking about luck, so faithful to her friends, and only to them; I had to know everything so as not to get angry, because after all if that fool hadn't tried to rob me, the three thousand pesos would have had to come out of my pocket. I insulted him until I could no longer think of new ways to do so and used all the means of humiliating him that I could think of, until it was perfectly clear that he was a sucker, a faithless friend, a scoundrel, and a thief. It was also perfectly clear that he agreed with me, that he had no compunctions in admitting all of that to anyone, if I should some time feel like ordering him to do so. And also, ever since that Monday, it was established that every time I insinuated that he was a scoundrel, indirectly, mentioning the fact in passing in the middle of any conversation whatsoever, he would instantly understand the meaning of my words and would show me with a slight smile, barely moving one side of his mustache, that he had understood what I had said and that I was right. We did not make a verbal agreement, but that's how it has worked ever since. I paid the three thousand pesos without telling him, and I left him hanging for several weeks not knowing whether I had decided to help or punish him; a bit later I called him in and told him that yes, I accepted his proposal, and that he could start working in my office for a salary of two hundred pesos a month that he would not collect. And that in a bit more than a year, less than a year and a half, he would have paid what he owed me and would be free to go and look for a rope to hang himself. Of course, he does not work for me; I could not use Montes for anything, now that it was impossible to have him go on taking bets on the horses. I have this auction house so that I can feel more at ease, being able to receive people and use the phone. So he began working for Serrano, who is my partner in some portions of the business and has an office next to mine. Serrano pays him the salary, or rather pays it to me, and has him running all day long from customs to the warehouses, from one end of the city to the other. I didn't want anyone to know that an employee of mine was less reliable than a window at the racetrack; this way nobody knows.

I think he told me the story, or almost all of it, the first day, the Monday, when he came to see me all hunched up like a dog, his face greenish, with a repellent glow of cold sweat on his forehead and on either side of his nose. He must have told me the rest of the business afterward, on the few occasions we talked.

It started at the beginning of winter, with the first dry blasts of cold that made all of us think, without realizing what we were thinking, that fresh clean air is good for business, for outings with friends, for ambitious projects: an air of luxury, maybe that's it. He, Montes, returned home one evening like that and found his wife sitting next to the cast-iron stove, watching the fire burn inside. I don't see the importance of this part; but that is how he told it and how he told it over again. She was sad and didn't want to say why, and continued sad, not wanting to talk, all that night and for a whole week afterward. Kirsten is fat, heavy, and must have very lovely skin. She was sad and didn't want to say what the matter was. "It's nothing," she would say, as all women always say in every country. Later she started filling the house with photographs of Denmark, of the King, the ministers, the landscapes with cows and mountains or whatever. She kept on saying that nothing was wrong, and that fool Montes imagined one thing after another without ever getting it right. Later, letters started arriving from Denmark; he did not understand a word, and she explained that she had written to some distant relatives and that now the replies were coming, although the news was not too good. He said jokingly that she wanted to go back, and Kirsten denied it. And that night or some other one fairly soon thereafter, she touched his shoulder when he was falling asleep and began insisting that she did not want to leave; he started smoking and agreed with everything she said when she spoke, as if she were saying the words by heart, about Denmark, the flag with a cross on it, and the path in the woods that led to the church. All in such a way as to convince him that she was completely happy with the New World and with him, until Montes fell asleep in peace.

For a time letters kept going and coming, and suddenly one night she turned out the light while they were in bed and told him, "If it's all right with you, I'll tell you something, but you'll have to listen to it without saying anything." He agreed and lay there stiffly, motionless at her side, letting the cigarette ashes fall on the crease in the sheet, as attentive as if he had a finger on the trigger, waiting for a man to appear in what his wife was telling him. But she did not speak of any man, and with a soft, hoarse voice, as if she had just finished crying, she told him that they could leave their bicycles in the street, or leave the shops unlocked when they went to church or wherever, because there are no thieves in Denmark; she told him that the trees are taller and older than those anywhere else in the world and that they smelled: each tree had a distinct smell, which stayed unique even when mixed with that of the other trees in the woods. She said that in the morning you woke up to the cries of sea-birds and could hear the sound of the hunters' shotguns and that the spring there grows in hiding beneath the snow until it leaps out and invades everything like a flood, and people make comments on the thaw. That is the period, in Denmark, when there is most activity in the fishing villages.

She also repeated: "Esbjerg er naerved kyssten," and this is what made the strongest impression on Montes, although he could not understand it: he said that this made him want to cry, a desire also present in the woman's voice as she told him all of this, in a low voice, with that music that people use unintentionally when they pray. Over and over again. What he couldn't understand made him feel more tender, filled him with pity for the woman—heavier than he, and stronger—and made him want to protect her as if she were a lost child. It must be, I think, because the phrase he could not understand was the most distant, the most foreign, what came from the most unknown part of her. From that night on, he began feeling a pity that grew and grew, as if she were sick, as if each day her condition were more serious, with no hope of cure.

That was how he came to think that he could do a great thing, a thing that would do him good too, that would help him to live and would console him for the rest of his existence. It occurred to him to get the money to pay for Kirsten's trip to Denmark. He went around asking even before he really planned to do it and discovered that two thousand pesos would be sufficient. But he didn't realize that he had an inner need to get two thousand pesos. It must have been like that, that he didn't know what was happening to him. To get the two thousand pesos and tell her some Saturday night, at the end of a dinner in an expensive restaurant, while they were drinking the last glass of a good wine. To tell her and see in her face, a little flushed by the food and wine, that Kirsten did not believe him, that she thought he was lying, for a while, only then to watch her feelings turn, slowly, into enthusiasm and joy, and then finally into tears and a decision not to accept. "I'll get over it," she would say, and Montes

would insist until he convinced her, and convince her also that he
did not want to break up with her and that he would be waiting for
her here as long as necessary.

Some nights, when he thought in the darkness about the two
thousand pesos, about some way of getting them, about the scene
when they would be sitting at a reserved table at Scopelli's, on a Saturday, with a serious expression, with a bit of happiness in his eyes
as he began telling her, as he began by asking her what day she
wanted to embark—some nights when he dreamed her dream, while
waiting to fall asleep, Kirsten spoke to him once again of Denmark.
Actually it wasn't Denmark; it was just a bit of the country, the tiny
piece of earth where she had been born, where she had learned a language, where she had danced with a man for the first time and had
seen someone she loved die. It was a place she had lost, the way a
person loses something without being able to forget it. She told him
other stories, although she almost always repeated the same ones,
and Montes came to believe that there in their bedroom he could see
the paths where she had walked, the trees, the people, the animals.

Very fat, pushing him off the bed without realizing it, the woman
was lying on her back, talking; and he was always sure that he knew
how her nose was arched over her mouth, how her eyes were squint-
ing a bit amid the little wrinkles, and how Kirsten's chin shook a
little as she spoke in a tremulous voice that came from the depth of
her throat, a bit trying to listen to.

Then Montes thought of getting credit in the banks, of the loan
sharks, and even thought that I might lend him money. One Saturday or Sunday he found himself thinking about Kirsten's trip while
he sat with Jacinto in my office answering the phones and taking
bets for Palermo or La Plata. There are slow days when we barely get
a thousand pesos in bets; but sometimes one of the high rollers appears and the money flows in and sometimes even exceeds five thousand. He was supposed to call me on the phone before each race and
tell me how the betting was going; if there was much danger—sometimes you can feel it—I would try to cover myself by passing some of
the bets to Velez, Martin, or Vasco. It occurred to him that he could
fail to call me, that he could hide three or four of the largest bets
from me, take on a thousand or so himself, and, if he had the nerve,
wager his wife's trip against a bullet in the head. He could do it if he
had the nerve; Jacinto did not have any way of knowing how much
was being bet with each phone call. Montes told me that he thought
about it for a month; it seems reasonable, because a guy like him
must have doubted and suffered a lot before sweating nervously with
each ring of the phones. But I would wager a lot of money that he's

lying about that; I would bet that he did it at any moment, that he decided all of a sudden, had an attack of self-confidence and started stealing from me quietly while sitting next to that fool Jacinto, who didn't suspect anything, whose only comment later was: "I said already that it seemed like too few bets for an afternoon like that one." I'm sure that Montes had an intuition and felt that he was going to win and had not planned any of it.

That was how he began swallowing the bets that turned into three thousand pesos and started walking back and forth, sweaty and desperate, around the office, looking at the ledgers, looking at the gorilla body in a raw silk shirt that was Jacinto, looking out the window at the diagonal avenue that was filling up with cars in the twilight. That was how, when he started to realize that he was losing and that the debts were growing, hundreds of pesos with each phone call, as he sweated the special sweat of cowards—greasy, slightly greenish, ice-cold—that covered his head the Monday noon when he finally felt his legs strong enough to return to the office and speak to me.

He told her before trying to rob me: he said that something very important and very good was going to happen, that she was going to receive an incomparable present, which was not a concrete thing that could be touched. So later he felt obligated to speak to her and tell her of the misfortune; and it was not at Scopelli's, or drinking an imported Chianti, but in the kitchen at their house, sipping on yerba mate while her round face, in profile, reddened by the glow, watched the flames leap within the cast-iron stove. I don't know how much they cried; after that he decided to pay me back by working and she got a job.

The other part of the story began when she, some time later, got used to staying away from home for hours even when she wasn't working; she arrived late when they made an appointment and sometimes got up very late at night, got dressed, and went out without a word. He didn't have the nerve to say anything much or make a frontal attack, because they were living on what she earns and all that comes of his working for Serrano is an occasional drink that I buy him from time to time. So he kept quiet and took his turn bothering her with his bad moods, moods different from those they suffered since the afternoon when Montes tried to rob me, moods that I think will not leave them alone for the rest of their lives. He was suspicious and his head filled up with stupid ideas until one day he followed her and saw her go to the port, dragging her shoes on the cobblestones, alone, and stand there for a long time, stiff, looking out at the water, near but not next to the people who go there to say goodbye to passengers. As in the stories she had told him, there wasn't any man. That time they spoke, and she explained to him. Montes also insists on something else that is unimportant: he insists, as if I doubted his word, that she explained it all to him in a normal tone of voice without any hint of sadness or hatred or confusion. She said that she always went to the port, at whatever hour of the day or night, to watch the boats leaving for Europe. He was afraid for her and wanted to struggle against this, tried to convince her that what she was doing was worse than staying home; but Kirsten kept on speaking to him in a normal tone of voice and told him that going there did her good and that she would have to keep on going to the port, as often as she could, to watch the boats leave, to wave to someone or just look until her eyes got tired.

And he ended up convincing himself that it was his duty to go with her, so that he would pay his debt to her in installments, as he was paying me back; and so now, on this Saturday afternoon, like so many nights and middays, in good weather or sometimes in the rain that mixes with what always bathes her face, they go together beyond Retiro, walk along the dock until the ship departs, mix a bit with people carrying overcoats, suitcases, flowers, and handkerchiefs, and when the ship starts to move, after the whistle call, they stiffen and watch, watching until they cannot see anymore, each one thinking of different, hidden things, but united, without knowing it, in their hopelessness and in the sensation that each one is alone, a sensation that is always frightening when you think about it.

# The House on the Sand

When Diaz Grey, with a feeling of indifference, accepted the idea that he had been left alone, he started playing the game of recognizing himself in the only memory that he had left, shifting, already freed of dates and time. He saw the images of the memory and saw himself as he moved it around and corrected it, trying to keep it from dying away, fixing the damage done by each awakening, sustaining it with unforeseen additions, all the time resting his head on the office window, while he took off his white smock at the end of the day, while he sat smiling and bored at the bar in the hotel. His life, he himself, now consisted of nothing more than that memory, the only one worthy of being evoked and corrected, of having its meaning occasionally falsified.

The doctor suspected that with the passage of years he would end up believing that the memorable first part of the story already held within it everything that, with different variations, happened later; he would end up admitting that the woman's perfume—which throughout the journey had reached him from the back seat of the car—contained in a sort of code all of the later events, what he remembered now, even as he denied it, what would perhaps reach plenitude in old age. He would then discover that Rusty, the shotgun, the violent sun, the legend of the buried ring, the premeditated failed meetings in the decaying cottage, and even the final bonfire were all contained in that unknown brand of perfume, a perfume that even now, on certain nights, he could smell on the surface of sweet drinks.

After the journey together to the coast (at the beginning of the memory), the car left the road and went bouncing along, slow and unsteady, until Quinteros brought it to a halt and turned off the headlights. Diaz Grey refused to pay attention to the landscape; he knew that the house was surrounded by trees, high above the river,

isolated among the dunes. The woman did not leave her seat; the
two men walked some distance away. Quinteros gave him the keys
and the folded bills. Perhaps the glow of the lighter she lifted to her
cigarette passed for a moment over their profiles.

"Don't move or get impatient. To the right along the beach you
can get to the town," Quinteros said. "Above all, don't do anything.
We'll see soon enough what can be done. Don't try to see or call
me. OK?"

Diaz Grey climbed up toward the house, pretending to try to hide
his white coat as he zigzagged among the trees. The car reached the
road and accelerated until the sound of the motor was confused with
that of the sea, until he was left alone listening to the sea, his eyes
closed, tenaciously repeating what he had survived during a month
of autumn, remembering the last few weeks given over almost
exclusively to signing prescriptions for morphine in Quinteros's
brand-new office, in glancing furtively at Quinteros's English girl-
friend—Dolly or Molly—who put them away in her pocket and
placed ten-peso bills on a corner of the table, without giving them to
him directly, without ever speaking to him, without even showing
that she saw him or was paying close attention to the rapid, obedient
movement of Diaz Grey's hand on the prescription note pad.

The sunlit days that followed one after another until Rusty's arrival turned in memory into a single day, of normal length though all
the events somehow fit into it: an autumn day, almost hot, into
which his own childhood and a whole crowd of unfulfilled wishes
could have fit. He didn't need to add a single minute in order to see
himself talking with the fishermen at the left end of the beach, pulling crabs apart for bait, to see himself following the shore toward the
town, to the store where he bought food and got a little drunk, responding to each of the owner's affirmations with a monosyllable.
He was there, the same almost burning day, swimming in the complete solitude of the beach, inventing, among many other things, a
worm-eaten log bouncing on the waves and three gulls screaming
overhead. He was climbing up and slipping down the dunes, chasing
insects through the edges of the bushes, having forebodings of the
place where the ring would be buried.

Meanwhile, Diaz Grey was yawning in a hallway in the cottage,
stretched out on a beach chair, a bottle on one side, an old magazine
on his lap. Rusted, useless, and vertical against the trunk of the vine,
the shotgun was propped in the open shed.

Diaz Grey was there with the bottle, his disillusionment, the
magazine, and the shotgun when Rusty came out from among the
trees and climbed up toward the house, his jacket hanging from his

shoulder, his huge back doubled over. Diaz Grey waited for the other man's shadow to reach his legs; then he raised his head and looked at the unkempt hair, the thin, freckled cheeks. He was filled with a mixture of pity and repulsion that he would have to preserve intact in his memory, something stronger than the will of memory or imagination.

"Dr. Quinteros sent me. I am Rusty," he announced with a smile; with an arm resting on his knee, he was waiting for the astonishing changes his name would work in the landscape, in the morning that was coming to an end, in Diaz Grey himself and his past. He was much burlier than the doctor, even when bent over like that, his back appearing prematurely hunched. They barely talked; Rusty showed the edge of his teeth, tiny as those of a child, and stuttered, turning his eyes toward the river.

Diaz Grey succeeded in holding still, as alone as if the other had never come, as if he hadn't stretched out his arm and opened his hand to let his jacket fall, as if he hadn't squatted down to sit on the porch, his legs hanging out, his torso twisted too far around in the direction of the beach. The doctor remembered Rusty's clinical history, the bombastic description of his pyromania written by Quinteros, in which this half-idiot redhead, manipulating matches and cans of gasoline in the northern provinces, appeared to be trying to identify with the sun and to prevent its immolation in the maternal darkness. Perhaps now, looking at the reflections in the water and the sand, he was evoking the (idealized and imperious) bonfires he had confessed to Quinteros.

"Isn't there anything to eat?" Rusty asked at dusk. Then Diaz Grey remembered that the other was there, hunched over, his round head stretched toward the sand stirred up by the whirlwinds. He made him come into the house and they ate; he tried to make him drunk so as to find out something of no interest to him: if he had come to hide or to keep watch on him. But Rusty barely talked while he ate; he drank all the drinks he was offered and lay down barefoot next to the house.

Then came days of rain, a period of mists that got tangled together and hung, withering suddenly, from the trees, sometimes erasing, sometimes intensifying the colors of the leaves trampled in the sand. He isn't here, thought Diaz Grey, looking at Rusty's hunched, silent body, seeing him walk barefoot, pushing back the dampness with his shoulders, shaking off like a wet dog.

With one arm hanging partly down, with a smile that revealed his having waited long for an impossible miracle, Rusty took possession of the shotgun. He began bending over it at night, by the lantern, to oil and work the screws and springs, suspiciously and awkwardly; in the morning he would go out into the fog with the gun over his shoulder or hanging by his leg.

The doctor searched for the remains of boxes, papers, rags; he gathered some almost dry branches and one night lit a fire in the fireplace. The flames lit up the hands that were bent over the open shotgun; Rusty finally raised his head and looked at the fire, staring at it with no more than the absentminded expression of someone who helps himself dream with the wavering light and the soft surprise of sparks. Afterward he got up to correct the position of the logs, carelessly touching them, then sat down again on the little kitchen chair he had chosen and picked up the shotgun once more. Long before the fire went out, he left to look at the night, at the fog that was turning to drizzle and that could already be heard on the roof. He came back shaking off the cold, and the doctor saw him pass indifferently by the glow of embers that reddened his soaked face, then throw himself on the bed and fall instantly asleep, his face toward the wall, hugging the shotgun. Diaz Grey threw a rag over his muddy feet, clapped his face with his hand, and left him to sleep, turned into a dog, while all the while he himself felt doubly alone for various days and nights, until there was a morning of intermittent sun. Then they went down to the beach—Rusty saw him go out and followed him, stopping occasionally to point the shotgun at the few birds he was capable of imagining, trotting along afterward until almost catching up with him—and followed the shore toward the town. With a beach bag full of food and bottles, they returned beneath an already gloomy sky; the doctor saw Rusty's broad bare feet treading on the various places where the ring would later be buried.

It rained all day, and Diaz Grey got up to light the lantern a minute before hearing the sound of the car on the road. Here is where the moments that form the rest of the memory begin, giving it a variable meaning; and just as the days and nights before Rusty's arrival turned into one sunny day, this part of the memory stretches out and repeats itself in a rainy late afternoon, lived inside the house.

He heard them talking as they approached the cottage, recognizing Quinteros's voice, guessing that the woman who stopped to laugh was the very same one. He looked at Rusty, still and silent, hugging his knees on the little chair; he placed the lantern on the table, where it would stand lighted between those who were about to enter and himself.

"Hello, hello," Quinteros said. He smiled, exaggerating his happiness; he touched the woman's damp shoulder, as if guiding her to greet him. "I think you know one another, right?"

She gave him her hand and in a question mentioned boredom and solitude. Diaz Grey recognized the perfume, discovered that she was named Molly.

"Things are almost arranged," Quinteros said. "Soon you'll be back to your cotton balls and iodine, with an immaculate diploma. I had no choice but to send this beast; I hope he doesn't bother you, that you can stand him. I couldn't fix it any other way. Beware of matches."

Molly went into the corner where Rusty was making his chair squeak, leaning back on it. She touched his head and squatted down to ask him useless questions, then herself supplied the obvious answers. Diaz Grey understood, deeply moved, that she had been able to tell, with a single glance, perhaps by the smell, that Rusty had been turned into a dog. She leaned over, turning down the flame of the lantern to conceal her face from Quinteros.

"I'm doing fine. The best vacation in my whole life. And Rusty doesn't bother me; he doesn't talk, he's in love with the shotgun. I can go on this way forever. If you'd like to eat something . . ."

"Thanks," Quinteros said. "Just a few days more, it's all working out." She stayed on, dwarfed by Rusty's smile, her raincoat sweeping the floor. "But I think I'll have to ruin your vacation. Would it be all right if Molly stayed here for a couple of days? It's good to take her out of circulation."

"No problem as far as I'm concerned," Diaz Grey replied; he quickly withdrew his trembling hands from near the lantern. "But for her, living here . . ."

He moved away from the table, pointing at the windows of the room with both arms, going in and out of the zone of perfume.

"She'll get along," said Quinteros. "Isn't that right, that you'll get along? Two or three days."

She raised her head to look at Quinteros.

"I have Rusty here to sing to me."

"She will explain it all to you, if you like," said Quinteros. He said goodbye almost immediately, and he and the woman went down slowly toward the car, hugging one another, despite the rain that moistened and straightened her hair.

Now Quinteros disappears until the end of the memory; in the motionless single rainy late afternoon, she chooses the corner where she will put her bed, guides Rusty through the task of cleaning out the little room that faces west. When the bedroom is ready, the woman takes off her raincoat, putting on a pair of beach thongs; she changes the position of the lantern on the table, imposing a new style of life; she serves wine in three glasses, deals the cards, and

tries to explain everything with nothing more than a smile, all the
while stroking her damp hair. They play one game and then another;
the doctor begins understanding Molly's face, her restless blue eyes,
the hardness of her broad jaw, the ease with which she can make her
mouth appear happy and then turn inexpressive just as suddenly.
They eat something and have another drink; she says good night and
goes to bed; Rusty drags his bed near the door of the woman's room
and lies down, the shotgun on his chest, one heel brushing against
the floor so that Diaz Grey will know he is not alseep. They play
cards again, until the moment when she, having had too much to
drink, lets fall the cards Rusty has just passed her, her fingers barely
opening, in a manner more final than if she had thrown them vio-
lently on the table, establishing in this way that they would not play
anymore.

Rusty gets up, picks up the cards, and throws them into the fire
one by one. All that's left, thinks the doctor, is to caress Molly or
talk to her, to find and speak some words that would be clean yet
would allude to love. He stretches out one arm and touches her hair,
pulls it away from her ear, lets it go, lifts it up again. Rusty lets the
shadow of the shotgun, held by the barrel now, fall on the table. Diaz
Grey lifts the hair and lets it go, each time imagining the soft blow
that she must be feeling against her ear.

Rusty is speaking over their heads, brandishing the shotgun and
its shadow; he repeats the name of Quinteros, finishes a phrase and
starts it over again, giving it a more transparent or more confused
meaning, according to whether Molly looks at him or lowers her
eyes. The shotgun bangs against Diaz Grey's wrist and pushes it toward the table.

"That's not allowed," shouts Rusty.

Diaz Grey once again pulls her hair from her ear with fingers he
can extend only with difficulty; Molly raises her hands and clasps
them together over her yawn. Then Diaz Grey feels the pain in his
wrist and thinks, without finding consolation in the idea, that it
may be broken. She places one hand on the chest of each man. Rusty
sits down again in his little chair, next to the fire that has gone out,
and Diaz Grey strokes the pain that is coming up his arm, pushes
the wounded hand against Molly's mouth, which draws back, re-
sists, and opens.

Then the moment comes when the doctor decides to kill Rusty
and subjects himself to the humiliation of hiding the fish-cleaning
knife between his shirt and his stomach and walks back and forth in
front of the other man until the cold blade warms up, until Molly
advances, from the door, from various corners of the room, stretches

out her arms and accuses herself, alluding to an imprecise and personal fate.

The doctor, relieved of the knife, is lying on the bed smoking; he listens to the patter of the drizzle on the roof, on the surface of the still afternoon. Rusty walks back and forth in front of Molly's door, the useless shotgun over his shoulder: four paces, turn, four paces.

The sound of the water turns furious on the roof and on the foliage, uses itself up; now they walk in an expectant silence, examining the gray landscape from the doors and windows, imitating the gestures of statues on the porch, an arm outstretched, all senses united on the back of one hand. At least she and Diaz Grey. Rusty has a foreboding of misfortune and walks in circles inside the room; he drags a moan and the butt of the shotgun around the floor. The doctor waits for the speed of his march to increase, to turn frantic, to frighten Molly, to slacken.

When Diaz Grey starts his trips back and forth between the shed and the fireplace, carrying everything that can be burnt, the other man keeps on walking around, panting, repeating a song she does not want to hear but pretends to pay attention to with a movement of her head. Leaning against the doorframe, she seems at once taller and weaker, with her beach pants and a sailor's sweater. Rusty drags his feet and sings; she rocks her head astutely and hopefully, while Diaz Grey lights the matches, while the flame leaps up and crackles in the air. Without looking back,without trying to find out what is happening, Diaz Grey enters Molly's room. She is lying on her bed, repeating Rusty's song in a low voice; he sees her fingers on her belt buckle; she becomes silent when she guesses that silence turns into lust. The rain resounds once more and the clouds tear themselves apart, bearing the sad light of an eternal afternoon of bad weather. Cheek to cheek in the window, they see Rusty crossing the beach diagonally until reaching the strand, the hardened stripe of foam separating sand and water.

"Molly," says Diaz Grey. He knows that it is necessary to avoid words for both of them to be able to deceive themselves, to believe in the importance of what they are doing and draw to them the stubborn feeling that there is something lasting in it. But Diaz Grey cannot help calling her by name.

"Molly," he repeats, bending toward the last smell of her. "Molly."

Now Rusty is standing rigid beside the cold fireplace, with the shotgun resting on his toes. She sits down at the table and drinks; Diaz Grey keeps a watch on Rusty without taking his eyes off Molly's wine-stained teeth, displayed in an insistent grimace that never tries to pass for a smile. She puts down the glass, shivers, speaks in a for-

eign language to nobody in particular. Rusty is still guarding the
cold fireplace when she asks for a pencil and writes some verses,
forces Diaz Grey to look at them and hold onto them forever, come
what may. The part of the woman's face that he dares to look at
shows such desperation that Diaz Grey moves his lips as if he were
reading the verses, then carefully puts away the piece of paper while
she floats between passion and weeping.

"I wrote it, it's mine," she lies. "It's mine and it's yours. I want to
explain what it says to you, and I want you to learn it by heart."

Patient and touched, she forces him to repeat the poem, corrects
him, encourages him.

> *Here is that sleeping place,*
> *Long resting place,*
> *No stretching place,*
> *That never-get-up-no-more*
> > *Place*
> > *Is here.*

They go out looking for Rusty. Their arms linked, they follow the
trail they saw him take earlier, in another moment of the unpleasant
afternoon; with difficulty they climb down, step by step; they walk
on a diagonal to the strand and then follow the hard wet sand to the
town, to the store. Diaz Grey asks for a glass of wine and leans on
the counter; she disappears into the store, shouts and mumbles in
the phone booth. When she comes back, she is wearing a new smile,
a smile that would frighten the doctor if by chance he discovered it
directed toward another man.

They go back along the path under a light drizzle that hits their
faces once more. She stops.

"We didn't find Rusty," she says without looking at him. She lifts
her mouth so that Diaz Grey can kiss her and leaves a ring in his
hand when they draw apart. "With this we can live for months, anywhere at all. Let's go get my things."

While they hurry along the shore, Diaz Grey searches in vain for
the phrase and the sort of look that he would like to leave Rusty
with. Now, by the coast, a rotten log is floating, lifted by the waves
and then dropped; three gulls pass, raising a ruckus in the sky.

She sees the car before Diaz Grey does and starts running, slipping in the sand. The doctor sees her climb up a sand dune, her arms
wide, then lose her balance and disappear; he is left alone before a
deserted patch of beach, his eyes hurt by the wind. He turns around
to shield them and ends up sitting down. Then—sometimes at the

end of the afternoon, sometimes in the middle of it—he digs a hole in the sand, throws the ring in it, and covers it: he does it eight times, in the spots where Rusty's footprints are, in the very spots he had pointed out with a single glance. Eight times he buries the ring in the rain, then draws away; he walks toward the water, tries to confuse his eyes by looking at the dunes, the stunted trees, the roof of the house, the car parked on the slope. But he always returns, in a straight line, without hesitation, to the exact spot of the burial; he sinks his fingers in the sand and touches the ring. Lying down facing the sky, he rests, lets the rain wash over him, unconcerned. Then, slowly, he starts up the path toward the house.

Rusty is stretched out next to the cold fireplace, chewing slowly; he has a glass of wine in his hand. Molly and Quinteros are whispering quickly, their faces together, until Diaz Grey draws near, until it's impossible for them to not hear his steps.

"Hi," Quinteros says, smiling at him, and holding out one arm; he still has his hat on, aslant.

Diaz Grey pulls up a chair and sits near Rusty; he strokes Rusty's head and pats it, harder and harder, waiting for him to get furious and punch him in the jaw. But the other man keeps on chewing, barely turning around to watch; then Diaz Grey lets his hand fall on his reddish hair and turns to look at her and Quinteros.

"Everything is arranged," says Quinteros. "The benefit of the doubt, to repeat the judge's words. If you were worried, I hope that now . . . Although, of course, you can both stay here as long as you like."

He comes near and leans over to give him some more folded bills. When Molly has finished making herself up and buttoning her raincoat around her neck, Diaz Grey stands up and, under the light, by the woman's face, opens his hand, the ring in his palm. Without a word—and now it is necessary to accept that the scene is taking place at the end of the afternoon—she takes his fingers and bends them over, one after another, until the ring is concealed.

"As long as you want," Quinteros says by the door. Diaz Grey and Rusty hear the sound of the motor farther and farther away, silence, the murmur of the sea.

This is the end, in the memory, of the long rainy afternoon that began when Molly arrived at the beach house; now time can be used to measure once again.

As dramatically as if he wanted to convince Diaz Grey that he had understood everything first, Rusty sits up and turns toward the door, toward the rain that is starting to abate, his face humanized by surprise and anguish. He touches the doctor for the first time, grabs him

by the arm, seeming to gain strength from that contact; then he gets
up and goes running out of the house.

Diaz Grey opens his hand, comes up to the light to look at the
ring and blow away the grains of sand that have stuck to it; he leaves
it on the table, drinks a glass of wine slowly as if it were a good wine,
as if there were still something to think about. There's still time, he
thinks to himself; he is sure that Rusty doesn't need his help. When
he decides to go out he discovers, then, with a feeling of indifference,
and examines the last moment that can be made part of the foggy
afternoon: a band of reddish light stretches high over the river. He
lights a cigarette and walks toward the side of the house where the
shed is; he thinks lazily that he ended up keeping the ring, that he
left the piece of paper with the verses on the table, that perhaps deliberate cynicism is sufficient to wipe away what's left of passion
and its absurdity.

When Diaz Grey, in his house facing the main square of the provincial city, gives himself up to the game of knowing himself by
means of this memory, his only memory, he is forced to confuse the
sensation of his blank past with that of his weak shoulders, with
that of his head topped by thin blond hair, leaning toward the glass
of the window, with the sense of solitude recognized all at once, now
that it is beyond help. He is also forced to acknowledge that his me-
ticulous life, his very body deprived of desire, his bland beliefs are
symbols of the essential vulgarity of the memory he has dedicated
himself to preserving for so many years.

In his favorite ending to that memory, Diaz Grey lets himself fall
to one side of the house, upon the wet sand. Rusty in his frenzy piles
branches, papers, boards, pieces of furniture next to the wooden door
of the cottage, making Diaz Grey burst out laughing, cough, and roll
over; when he inhales the smell of kerosene, he forces the other man
to stand still with an imperious whistle and walks up to him, sliding
on the dampness and the leaves, then takes a box of matches from
his pocket and shakes it by the other's ear as he stumbles forward.

# The Photograph Album

While standing at the door to the newspaper office, I saw her leaning on the wall under the sign with the name of my grandfather, Agustin Malabia, the founder. She had come to bring an article about the harvest or about the cleanliness of the streets of Santa Maria, one of those irresistible pieces of silliness my father calls editorials, which when printed fill a mass of type, broken only by a few numbers, noticeably weighing down the third page, always on the upper right.

It was Sunday afternoon, damp and hot at the beginning of winter. She was coming from the port or from the city, carrying a light flight bag, wrapped in a fur coat that must have stifled her, walking step after step along the shiny walls, against the watery yellowish sky, a bit stiff, grief-stricken, as if she were being carried to me by the afternoon, the river, the waltz snorted by the band in the bandstand, the girls going around the bare trees in pairs.

Now she was walking alongside the Berna Hotel, younger, smaller in her open coat, her feet possessing an odd lightness not imparted to her legs, not lessening the stiffness she shared with the statues in the town.

Vazquez, the distributor, came down the hall and stood next to me, seeing me watching her, cleaning his fingernails with a letter opener, also granted momentary prestige by the two words of my grandfather's name. I lit my pipe, awaiting the moment to start crossing the street at a diagonal, perhaps brushing against the woman, finding out her age for certain, and then slamming the door of my car, the new one, the one my father had let me take. But she stopped at the corner, her head and wool cap hiding the faded pitcher raised by a mustachioed wop on the brewery sign. She stopped, her knees together, without meaning to, simply because the impulse that had dragged her up the street had died away.

"She must be a little crazy," said Vazquez. "She's been at the
hotel, at the Plaza, for a week. She came by herself, they say, with a
whole load of trunks. But she spends every morning and afternoon
with that flight bag, going back and forth to the dock, at hours when
no ferries or boats arrive or depart."

"She's ugly, must be getting on in years," I said, yawning.

"Depends how you look at her, Jorgito," he affirmed softly. "There
wouldn't be any lack of takers." He patted my shoulder in parting
and crossed at an angle, almost as I had planned to do, small and
gray, with the gait inherited from his friend Junta, as if balancing a
girth and heaviness not his own on the muddy pavement. He passed
very near the woman at the corner of the Berna, without moving his
neck to look at her, and went into his store.

I knew that it wasn't for my sake—perhaps it wasn't for anybody's, not even for her own—that the woman had stopped on the
sidewalk, motionless and ocher in the middle of the Sunday afternoon, passively joining the heat, the dampness, the pointless nostal-
gia. But I stayed there without stirring, staring at her, until my pipe
sputtered and went out; at that very moment she lifted one foot and
went down, continued advancing toward the hotel, beside the deserted front entrance that had separated us and linked us together,
her steps short and easy, steps with which she proposed only to mark
the passage of time, absentmindedly crossing the trembling of the
bass drum, the daring of the clarinet, the beginning of night, and the
weak unobtrusive smells the night gave off in anticipation of death.

The next day, in the morning, I thought that Vazquez had lied or
exaggerated, or that the woman wasn't in Santa Maria any more. I
came into town on the first bus to have the strings changed on my
racket, to let Hans know that he would rather die than tell anyone
that he had cut my hair on a Monday morning when the barbershop
was closed—both of us whispering, surrounded by shining metal
and mirrors in the half-darkness—to buy pipe tobacco and walk
down to the port.

The woman wasn't there and she didn't come; the ferry arrived
with only a few passengers aboard, some sacks of wheat or corn, an
old discolored bus. I smoked as I walked along—and later as I sat on
the dock, my legs hanging down over the water. Sometimes, out of
the corner of my eye, I spied the movement on the paving stones and
at the gate of the red customs house; I could not figure out what it
would be best to be doing or thinking should the woman and the
little flight bag, and perhaps the wool overcoat, come up and take me
by surprise from behind. The ferry whistled and left the dock at one
o'clock sharp. Still I waited, hungry, the pipe making me sick. The

sacks and the bus had remained on the dock. My father was writing an editorial "Do We Need to Import Wheat?" (on the traditional fertility, recently come to an end, of the fields of Santa Maria) or "Valuable Contribution to Local Transportation" (on the forward-looking work decisively undertaken by our municipal government).

Tiny, almost resting on the horizon, the ferry had come to a halt. I began climbing toward the city. I no longer remembered the woman with the flight bag, no longer felt love or curiosity because of the signal, the allusion she had posed in the air between us, between the corner of the Berna and that of *El Liberal*. Desperate and hungry, swallowing the phosphorous taste of the pipe, I was composing: "An unprecedented measure, inexplicably approved by the authorities who govern us, has just permitted the landing of twenty-seven and a half bushels of wheat at the port of Santa Maria. With the same freedom of judgment that we have demonstrated when we applauded the public works being carried out by the new city council, we must today raise our unimpeachable voice in protest."

From Nueva Italia I called mother and told her that I would eat in town to be able to get to school on time. I was sure that the woman had been rebuffed or dissolved by the idiocy of a Santa Maria symbolized with precision by my father's articles: "A true affront, we do not hesitate to say, committed by the members of the council against the austere and self-sacrificing workers of the surrounding communities who, for generation after generation, have fertilized the enviable wealth we enjoy."

When we got out of class, Tito insisted on going to have a glass of vermouth at the Universal (he didn't want to go to the Plaza for fear of running into his father) and on having me believe a story he told of how he had slept with his second cousin, the teacher. He gave plausible details, ably answered my questions; it was clear that he had been preparing the confession for a long time. I turned serious, sad, indignant.

"Look," I said, staring him fiercely in the eye, "you have to marry her. There's no excuse: even if your cousin doesn't want to. If what you're telling me is true, you have to marry. In spite of everything: even if the poor girl has elbows as thick as thighs, even if her mouth frowns like that of an old spinster."

Tito started smiling and shaking his head and was about to tell me that it was all a joke when I got up and made him blush from fear, from doubt.

"I don't want to see you, I can't see you until you've gotten engaged. Pay for the drinks because it was your invitation."

I was only sorry for about three steps, as I crossed the sidewalk in front of the bar, as I hid my notebooks and the English textbook in the pocket of my raincoat. Pudgy, rosy, presumptuous, servile, perhaps now with tears in his eyes, my friend the fool. The weather continued damp, warm at street corners, uncertain in the shade of patios, hot after I had walked two blocks. While going down toward the port, I felt happy in spite of myself, started humming the unnamed march that crowns the bandstand in the square, imagined an aroma of jasmine, remembered a very distant summer when the gardens bombarded the city with tons of jasmine flowers; I discovered, almost stopping for a moment, that I had a past.

I saw her from the landscaped heights of the promenade: her silhouette growing beyond the jetty as she advanced toward the mist over the water, a mist that sometimes exhibited and sometimes veiled the bag and the winter coat. She went back and forth while I smoked a pipe; sometimes she stopped on the great stones of the dock by the shore, looking at the fog and the distant barren site of the pink ruins of the Latorre Palace. I was sure that she was not waiting for anything, that she could feel my presence. The skiffs moored and then went back out into the river, but she did not move her head to discover the sources of the whistles, did not spy on the blurry groups of passengers. She was there, small and hard, looking at the great whitish cloud that lay over the waves, inventing surprises, encounters. It was starting to turn dark and cool when she got tired and turned halfway around, looking to see whether everything was still in order before coming straight across the dock.

I followed her as far as the hotel, believing that she—without turning around, without looking at me—could feel my presence a half-block behind and that I was useful to her, helped her climb the streets, helped her live. She walked as if asleep, without noticing anything, as she had done the previous afternoon as she passed by the Berna and Sunday and the nostalgic music that Filipaldi was conducting in the square with nothing more than the motion of his furious eyes. But now I saw her stop at every shop window for two blocks around the square: she looked, her right shoulder against the glass, barely turning her head, spending exactly thirty seconds in front of each one, her profile indifferent to the aggressive lights that went on and off, unconcerned whether they displayed slips, packets of yerba mate, fishing rods, tractor parts.

Finally she entered the Plaza; I kept on walking as far as the Club, put tobacco in my pipe, looked at the fog that was beginning to be torn apart by a cold wind right above the square, and then went back. She was sitting on one of the stools at the bar, next to a tiny glass that she was looking at without touching, her hands protecting the bag on her lap. I sat down next to a window, far from the bar, and started looking over my notebook. She stayed quiet, withdrawn, hypnotized by the spot of gold in the glass. Perhaps she could see me in the mirror; perhaps she had seen me ever since I had gone to the port with a pipe between my teeth and a recently discovered past. I read in the notebook: "Why, thou wert better in thy grave than to answer with thy uncovered body this extremity of the skies." And it was true that she was watching me in the mirror, because when I raised my eyes she had no need to turn her head before grasping the little glass with her fingers, getting down off the stool, and coming in a straight line that she traced by some miracle through the tables, clasping the liquid carefully to her chest, the bag held effortlessly away from the invisible movement of her knees.

She sat down and placed the glass in the exact center of the table; since the waiter had not yet served me, nobody could know whether it was hers or mine. I was watching her with eyes lowered and began to make the acquaintance of her face, to be filled with apprehension as I hid the English notebook. There she was, her wool cap—old, fringed, badly knitted—slipping carelessly over one ear, quiet and serious, as if meditating before making up her mind once and for all, as if it were essential that everything begin with a parody of meditation. I discovered that all that really mattered about her body—despite my hunger, and Tito's, and that of all the greedy cowards who were our friends—was her round face, dark, young, and exhausted, her eyelids sunken toward her cheeks, her large mouth chafed. Afterward she drank down the contents of the glass in one gulp, watching me, and was already smiling at me when she set it on the table: a constant furious smile, at once as helpless and possessive as a gaze, as if she were also looking at me with her teeth, the thin red line, the down and the wrinkles that surrounded them.

"May I call you by your first name?" she asked me. "We made the date for this afternoon years ago. Right? It doesn't matter when, because as you can see we couldn't forget it and here we are, right on time."

The face and the voice besides. When the waiter came, she ordered another drink and I nothing; I set to work on my pipe, blushing, letting myself go, sure that all explanations were unnecessary. The face, always, and that voice that went on like her feet, free and unawares, convincing, without the need for pauses.

But all of this is a prologue, because the real story only began a week later. My visit to the doctor, Diaz Grey, is also a prologue; I wanted him to introduce me to the traveling salesman of some laboratory that had been established. The salesman had a half dozen bags full of drug samples on the second floor of the hotel, on the same hallway where the woman's room was. My conversation with the salesman, and his solemn cynicism, his silk shirt with the sleeves rolled up, his damp little mouth were enough to humiliate, painlessly, the phrases I had set to memory, which I tried lazily to repeat one day at noon in his messy room. Before telling me yes, he lay there in bed laughing, almost noiselessly, in his socks, puffing on a cigar, recounting dirty memories. We went downstairs together, and he explained to the manager that I would be coming to his room every afternoon to help him type copies of some reports. "Give him a key," he said, and squeezed my hand hard, serious, as befits a man his age, with a strange pride in his small happy eyes.

I did not want to tell my parents a different lie; I repeated the story of the typed reports the salesman had asked me for, without thinking of the money that I would have to be paid and show for it. Every afternoon, as soon as classes were over—and sometimes earlier, when I could escape—I would enter the hotel, greet whoever was at the front desk with a smile, and go up the elevator or the stairs. The salesman—Ernesto Maynard was what the labels on the sample packages said—was visiting the drugstores up and down the coast; for the first few days, I spent a long time examining the tubes and bottles, reading the promises and instructions on the flyers printed on tissue paper, dominated by their impersonal, sometimes obscure, guardedly optimistic style. Afterward, standing by the door, I would listen to the silence in the hallway, the sounds of the bar and the city. It happened.

The woman always pretended to be asleep and would wake up with a slight start, mumbling a man's name, each time a new one, dazed by the remains of a dream for which neither my presence nor any reality could compensate. I was hungry and my hunger was constantly reborn; it was impossible for me to imagine myself without it. Nevertheless, the satisfying of this hunger, and its complications, whether carefully planned or inevitable, soon turned, for the woman and for me, into a price we both had to pay.

The real story began on an icy evening, when we could hear it raining and each of us was still, curled up, oblivious to the other. There was a narrow stripe of yellow light on the bathroom door, and I imagined the solitude of the streetlights on the square and along the promenade, the vertical threads of the rain in the still evening. The story began when she suddenly said, without moving, when her voice climbed up in the darkness to a spot two feet above us: "It doesn't matter that it's raining; even if it rains for a hundred years, it's not rain. It's water falling, but not rain."

There, or even earlier, was the big invisible smile on the woman's face; she didn't speak until the smile was completely formed and filled her face.

"No more than water falling, and people have to give it a name. That's why they call falling water rain in this miserable little town or city, but it's a lie."

I had no way of suspecting what was starting, not even when the word Scotland came along; the voice fell, soft and uninterrupted, upon my face. She explained to me that rain is only what falls without use or meaning.

"The castle was in Aberdeen, and it was so old that the wind roamed through the hallways, rooms, and staircases. There was more wind there than in the night outside. And the wind—after piling us for two days against a fireplace as tall as a man—finally made us go over to the broken windows. So we didn't talk: there we were morning to night, filling the room, each of our noses pressed against the glass windowpane, as still as the stone figures in a church. That's how it was until the third day, I think, when MacGregor announced that it had stopped raining, that it would start snowing, that the roads would be closed and that each of us was free to decide whether that would be better than the rain or worse."

This was the first story; she told it again several times, usually because I asked for it when I was tired of the heat of India or the campsite at Amatlan. I thought, perhaps there's nobody on earth who knows how to lie like this. Or perhaps no one hunted foxes before the time she burst out laughing, her head shaking, struggling weakly against a memory of faded shame, and suddenly tied her horse to a tree and hid with a lord or sir or younger brother of a lord in some ruined hut, to roll around on the inevitable pile of leaves, while outside, in the trite landscape of cold splendor that she had just created—there, beside me, effortlessly, with an impersonal, divine pleasure—the first fox hunt had shaken the earth with a frenzy she recalled and directed with lofty, faded words: pomp, dog team, dress coat, glade, tracker, needless violence, a small brown death.

And at the heart of each lie was the woman, each story was herself, beside me, beyond doubt. I no longer cared to read or dream; I was sure that when I took the trips I was planning with Tito, the landscapes, the cities, the distances, the whole world would show me faces without meaning, portraits of absent faces, irreparably bereft of any true reality.

There was always the hunger; but listening to her was my own

private vice, the most intense, the richest. Nothing could be compared with the astonishing power she had shown me, the gift of
wavering between Venice and Cairo for a few hours before the conversation, impenetrable, astutely vulgar amid the twelve poor boys
who watched disconcerting words being formed on the blackboard
and on the lips of Mr. Pool; nothing could replace the eager returns I
had only to whisper and request for them to be granted, never the
same, changed, ever more perfect.

We had gone from New York to San Francisco for the first time,
and what she was describing to me disillusioned me because it so
resembled a liquor advertisement that had appeared in one of the
foreign magazines sent to the newspaper office—a meeting in a
hotel room, the enormous bare windows open to the sunlit marble
city—and the anecdote was almost a copy of the one about the
Bolivar Hotel in Lima. We had just "howled with cold on the East
Coast and, believe it or not, less than a day later, there we were
swimming in the ocean"—when the man appeared.

He was short and squat, and I only wanted to gather the few
things that are even today sufficient to construct and sustain him:
the wide brows, the shiny, worn collar of his shirt, the latest cut of
his lapels. Perhaps also, though less essential, his small, stubborn
half-moon of a smile, his hairy hands resting on the table like things
brought to put on display, to exert pressure, never to be forgotten
after he had left. They were sitting near the dining room, at seven in
the evening. She was leaning over the glasses and the ashtray, a column of smoke cutting her face in half; beneath the man's dark
brows, his face had a placid flush, the hesitancy to interrupt an exalted statement of praise.

I took the elevator and went to lock myself into Maynard's room;
lying on the bed, smoking my pipe, I listened to the noises in the
hallway, read a story about dramatic yet partial victories over Par-
kinson's disease, and learned that chronic anemia is characteristic
of blue-eyed blonds. Until all of a sudden it occurred to me that
she might come upstairs in the company of the man, her quick
steps, ignorant of the floor and the destination, accompanied by
deep, slow, masculine heels. I went downstairs. They were at the
table and were still thinking about the same things, her face turned
toward the darkened brows, his eyes watching the hands resting on
the tablecloth.

I crossed the square, not jealous, just sad and resentful, inventing
forebodings of disaster. I turned on Urquiza and went as far as the
hardware store. Sitting on a ladder, covered to his ankles in iron gray
or dust gray overalls, the employee had a wooden box on his lap and

was examining screws to see if the bore went to the left or the right. When he was done smelling them, he classified them. The old lady behind the counter, a black shawl over her shoulders, was solemn, mean, much more nearsighted than the week before.

"Tito is studying upstairs." She did not answer my greeting, did not invite me in, sat there looking at me as if she suspected that it was my fault that her gray hair made me sick. So I had to waste a smile, a sparkle, a special form of candor with two tiny spots of insolence in the eyes. She struggled a little. "Why don't you go up?"

"It's only for a moment, thanks. I want to ask him for some notes."

I crossed the patio, saw Tito's sister ironing behind a door. The cold was still. A black cat silently avoided my kick and my spit. Tito hid the magazine he was reading under the pillow and made signs of complicity and friendship before delving into the closet and showing me a bottle of rum.

"What I don't have is more than one glass."

He was happy, pudgy, worried. Majestic, a bit melancholy, I gestured assent, shared his saliva, sank an elbow into the old blotter on his desk, slowly lit my pipe.

"I was rereading the poem," he said, raising the filthy glass decorated with flowers, bought to hold toothbrushes or herbal tea. "And no matter what you say, it isn't bad. There's lots of smoke here. Would you mind if I open the window?"

In Santa Maria, when night falls, the river disappears, receding without a wave into the darkness like a carpet being rolled up. Rhythmically, the countryside invades on the right flank (we are all at that moment facing north), occupies us and the riverbed. I guess the lonely night on the water or at its bank may offer memory, nothingness, or the will for a future; in contrast, the night on the vast plain, prompt and invincible, only allows us to meet up in the present with our lucid selves.

"That's no poem," I said sweetly. "You make your father believe that you are studying and shut yourself in to read a dirty magazine that I lent you myself. It's not a poem, it's the explanation why I had a reason to write a poem and couldn't do it."

"I tell you it's good," he said, tapping lightly on the table with his fist, rebellious, excited.

When night comes, we are left without a river and the sirens that echo in the port turn into the mooing of lost cows; the storms offshore sound like a dry wind in a wheat field hitting folded bales. May each man be alone and examine himself until he rots, without memory or tomorrow, examine that face without secrets for all eternity.

"And your sister is going to marry the employee in the hardware store, not this year, of course, but when your old man has no other choice than to give him a room. And one day you will sit behind the counter, not to challenge the employee on your sister's behalf, as would be right and poetic, as I would do, but to avoid their robbing you between the two of them."

He offered me the glass with a tolerant, generously cynical smile. I had a drink while I sought to recall what had made me come up to the attic to see him, my friend. I drew a match up to the wheezing of the pipe. I had come to think, under the protection of Tito's lack of understanding, that I was not jealous of the man with the eyebrows and the pearl; that she had not looked at me and could not look at me with that avid need to humiliate that I had sensed when I crossed the bar; that I was really only afraid of losing adventures and geographies: of losing the drunken picnicker in Naples, where she made love to the sound of mandolins; the studio in Sao Paulo where she somehow helped a repentant man with a huge mouth correct the architecture of the temperate and torrid zones. Not fear of solitude, fear of the loss of a solitude I had inhabited with a feeling of power, with a sort of good fortune, that my days could never give me back or make up for.

There was the next afternoon, with no trace of the man, without either of us referring to the failed meeting of the day before. (It also formed part of my pleasure to avoid the obvious questions: why she was in Santa Maria, why she went to the dock with the bag.) Perhaps that afternoon she was more protective, more demanding, more thorough. The only thing I know for sure is that she was not present, was not named, did not embrace any man in the long story about the Rhine, about a boat that traveled during bad weather from Mainz to Cologne. And the other beliefs are uncertain: the intention of her smile in the twilight, the alarming intensity of the cold, the timid love with which she drew out the details of the voyage, her desire to suppress what was essential, to confuse the meanings. In any case, she only gave me things I already knew by heart: a ferry on a river, dauntless blond people, the constantly frustrated hope of a final disaster.

Also, in any case, as I got dressed, as she put on my cap and quickly tried to rearrange my conviction about the stupidity of the world, I forgave her failure, was working on a style of forgiveness that would reflect my turbulent experience, my wearied maturity.

I remember her, hair uncombed, agreeing, letting me go away, helping me to go, bidding farewell to my skinny body, my awkwardness, my ears.

And so, just as in saying goodbye to the woman on the eve of a stormy voyage on the Rhine, I was separating myself from my mother, I encountered my father the next day, at six in the evening. He was sitting at the bar, watching the entrance with a keen reddish glance, sure that he would trap me when I went by, a bit drunk, calling himself Ernesto Maynard. He had only to move a thumb to get me to come over.

"How are you?" I said with my roughest voice; I sat down beside him, set the books and notebook in order on my lap, accepted the drink he ordered.

We drank in silence, slowly. Later he put a hand on my shoulder, just lightly, without imposing himself, without pity. I will remember him with love for many years yet, chewing on his cigar at my side, putting it down to look with small satisfied eyes at the length and heat of the ash, heavy and self-confident, his coarse, simple head seeking for the formula that would not wound too much but that at the same time would contain the sense of bitterness that fortifies and teaches.

"Well, she decided to leave. I know the whole story. I, holed up in a hotel room or traveling up and down the coast, convincing doctors, dentists, pharmacists, and folk healers. I can sell anything, I've always known it, ever since I was younger than you are; it's a gift. Working hard. But no rumor ever got away from me. I guess they're there even before they take shape: all the cuckolds, all the abortions, all the embezzling. She left this morning or, to be more precise, didn't return since last night. She left a note behind asking them to hold onto her trunk, that she'll be back to get it and pay the remainder of the bill, some three hundred pesos. Nothing except the trunk; and it must be full of rocks, or old clothes, or bills from other hotels. And I also knew that at a quarter past six you would arrive at the hotel. I waited for you to tell you, without beating around the bush, that the woman is not coming back and that it doesn't matter that she's not coming back. And that it's not possible for you to live like all those poor fellows who buy shirts, or whose wives buy them shirts, in La Moderna and who choose their suits from the Gath y Chaves catalog. Hoping for women or business deals to happen, or not hoping for anything anymore. You must get out. Maybe some day you'll thank me."

I thanked him and left, really knowing for the first time that I had no one to be with. That night I tried to put the world back together, each place she had given me, each tale. I stopped thinking about her face as soon as light glowed through the window.

And it was also no use asking for a loan of the money. I went to

the bank in the morning and left five pesos in my savings account; I
went to Salem's and pawned the watch I had inherited from my
brother (mute and melodramatic, my sister-in-law had taken it from
my dead brother's wrist). Before noon I was standing before the hotel
cashier, full of money, of power, of a strange need for humiliation
and exhaustion. I explained that the woman had sent three hundred
pesos to me to recover the trunk; they gave me a receipt and made
me sign another one: "For Carmen Mendez." I arranged with Tito to
carry the trunk to the garage of the hardware store while his parents
were asleep. During the whole day I was thinking about Dr. Diaz
Grey, imagining that I was doing all of this for him, because of the
vague prestige that behaving like a gentleman gave him in the town—
short, well dressed, exiled, slightly exaggerating the lameness that
forced him to rely on a cane.

So it was that, exhausted and proud, twenty-four hours after the
woman left Santa Maria, I shut myself up with Tito in the garage,
and we opened the bottle, conversing about wedding nights and the
repercussions of deaths, sitting on the trunk, hitting it gently with
our heels. When the bottle was half-empty and he asked me not to
talk about his sister's body, I broke the lock and we started pulling
out dirty clothes that were no good anymore (without perfume,
smelling of use, of sweat and enclosure), old magazines, English
books, and an album with a leather cover and the initials C. M.

Squatting, matured, trying to handle my pipe with obvious pride,
I saw the photographs in which a woman—less young and more
gullible as I furiously turned the pages—galloped in Egypt, smiled at
golfers on a Scottish meadow, hugged movie actresses at a nightclub
in California, had forebodings of death at the Rouen blizzard, making
real and defaming each of the stories that she had told me, all the
afternoons I had loved her and listened to her.

# Hell Most Feared

The first letter—the first photograph—was delivered to him at the newspaper office between midnight and press time. He was pounding on his typewriter, a bit hungry, a bit sick from all the coffee and tobacco, surrendered with a kind of familiar happiness to the flow of the phrase and the orderly arrival of the words. He was writing: "It is worth noting that the officials saw nothing suspicious or even out of the ordinary about the decisive victory of Play Boy, who was able to take advantage of the wintry field and shoot off like an arrow at the decisive moment," when he saw the red and ink-stained hand of Politics come between his face and the typewriter, offering him the letter.

"This is for you. They always get our mail mixed up. Not even one damn invitation to the clubs, and later they come crying when election time grows near and the space they are granted never seems like enough to them. And it's already midnight and *you* tell me how I'm supposed to fill up my column."

On the envelope were his name, Racing Department, *El Liberal*. The only odd things were the pair of green stamps and the Bahia postmark. He finished the article just as they came up from the typesetter to ask him for it. He was tired and happy, almost alone in the huge space of the city desk, thinking about his last sentence: "We insist again, with the objectivity which for years has marked our statements: we owe our existence to the fans." At the back of the room, the black clerk was looking through envelopes in the archives, and the older woman from the Society Page was slowly taking off her gloves in her glass booth, when Risso carelessly opened the envelope.

It contained a three-by-five photograph: a dark picture, taken in insufficient light, hate and sordidness filling the dark edges, forming

uneven wide borders like a relief, like drops of sweat around an an-
guished face. He looked with surprise, not fully understanding, discovering that he would give anything to forget what he had seen.

He stuffed the photograph in his pocket and was putting on his
overcoat when Society Page came out, cigarette in hand, from her
glass booth, a sheaf of papers in her hand.

"Hi," she said, "look at me, at this hour, and the party just ended."

Risso looked at her from above. Her light-colored dyed hair, the
wrinkles on her neck, the double chin that sank round and pointy
like a little belly, the small, rather exaggerated, touches of color that
decorated her clothing. "She's a woman, even she is. Only now am I
noticing the red scarf around her neck; the purple nails on her old,
tobacco-stained hands; the rings and bracelets; the dress she was
given in exchange by a designer, not a lover; the endless, perhaps
somewhat twisted, heels; the sad curve of her mouth; the almost
frantic enthusiasm she thrusts on her smiles. Everything will be
easier if I can convince myself that she too is a woman."

"It seems like something thought of and planned for a lark. When
I come in you are on your way out, almost as if you were running
away from me. It's cold as hell outside. They leave me the material
they promised, but without even a name or a note. Guess, make a
mistake, publish some fantastic rubbish. I don't know the names of
anyone but the lucky couple, thank God at least for that. Excess and
bad taste, that's what there was. They entertained their friends with
a glittering reception at the home of the bride's parents. But nobody
gets married on Saturday anymore. Get ready, the wind is cold as
hell out on the street."

When Risso married Gracia Cesar, we all gathered in silence, ignoring pessimistic predictions. At that time, she contemplated the in-
habitants of Santa Maria from the tall signs of the Sotano, the Repertory Theater, from walls that looked old because it was the end of
autumn. Sometimes intact, sometimes with a mustache drawn in or
scratched at by vengeful fingernails or by the first rain, she had her
head half-turned to watch the street, alert, a bit defiant, a bit excited
by the hope of convincing and being understood. Revealed by the
shininess of the retouched eyes of the enlargements from Orloff Stu-
dios, you could read in her face that she gave her whole life over to
the farce of love, to the determined and single-minded quest for
pleasure.

All of which was fine (he must have thought), desirable and necessary, and coincided with the result of multiplying the number of
months that Risso had been a widower by the sum total of the

countless Saturday afternoons he had discreetly repeated the polite gestures of waiting and familiarity in the brothel by the shore. A glow, that of the eyes in the poster, was linked with the frustrated skill he showed, tying yet another sad, new, black tie before the portable oval mirror in the brothel bedroom.

They got married and Risso thought it sufficient to keep on living the way he always had but devoting himself to her, without thinking about it, almost without thinking about her, the fury of her body, the mad search for absolutes that possessed him during the long nights.

She thought of Risso as a bridge, an escape, a beginning. She had kept her virginity intact through two engagements (one with a director, one with an actor), perhaps because for her the theater was a craft as well as a game and she thought that love should be born and grow separate from it, uncontaminated by what one does to earn money and oblivion. With one, then with the other, during their dates in the town squares, on the promenade or in the café, she was condemned to feel the tedium of rehearsals, the effort to get into the part, the attention to her voice and hands. She always saw her own face a moment before making any expression, as if she could look at it or touch it. She acted brave and skeptical, taking stock constantly of her farce and of the other's, the sweat and the theatrical makeup that covered them, inseparable, signs of the age.

When the second photograph arrived, from Asuncion and with a man who was obviously not the same one, Risso was afraid, above all, of not being able to stand an unknown feeling that was neither hate nor pain, that would die with him without ever having a name, that was linked to injustice and fate, to the primal fears of the first man on earth, to nihilism and the beginning of faith.

The second photograph was delivered to him by Police Desk one Wednesday night. Thursday was the day he always spent with his daughter, from ten in the morning until ten at night. He decided to tear up the envelope without opening it and put it away, and it was only on Thursday morning, while his daughter was waiting for him in the boardinghouse living room, that he permitted himself a quick glance at the photograph before tearing it up and flushing it down the toilet: in this one, too, the man was facing the other way.

But he had looked at the photograph from Brazil many times. He kept it for almost a whole day; in the early morning he imagined that it must be a joke, a mistake, some passing silliness. Already, many times, he had woken up from a nightmare, smiling abjectly and gratefully at the flowers on the wallpaper of his room.

He was lying in bed when he took the envelope out of his jacket and took the photograph out of the envelope.

"Well," he said aloud, "that's right, that's all right, that's the way it is. It isn't important; even if I didn't see it, I'd know what's going on."

(When she took the picture with the self-timer, when she developed it in the darkened room, beneath the encouraging red glow of the lamp, she probably anticipated this reaction by Risso, this challenge, this refusal to give himself over to anger. She also anticipated, or barely desired, with slight, ill-recognized hopes, that he would discover a message of love in the obvious offense and the astonishing humiliation.)

He sheltered himself again before looking: "I am alone and freezing to death in a boardinghouse on Piedras Street, in Santa Maria, in the wee hours, alone, regretting my solitude as if I had sought it out, proud as if I deserved it."

In the photograph the headless woman was ostentatiously digging her heels into the edge of the sofa, waiting impatiently for the dark man, made enormous by the unavoidable foreshortening; she was sure that she had no need to show her face to be recognized. On the back the neat handwriting read: "Greetings from Bahia."

In the night that followed the second photograph, he thought he could understand the whole evil and even accept it. But he knew that there, beyond his reach, lurked an act of will, persistence, the organized frenzy with which the revenge was being carried out. He measured its excess, felt himself unworthy of so much hatred, of so much love, of such a desire to cause pain.

When Gracia met Risso she could guess many things about the present and the future. She glimpsed his solitude when she looked at his chin and at a button of his jacket; she guessed that he was embittered but not beaten and that he needed a release but could not admit it. Sunday after Sunday she watched him in the square, before the show, carefully observing his sad, impassioned expression, the greasy hat he had forgotten on his head, the large, lazy body he was letting go to fat. She thought of love the first time they were alone together, or of desire, or of a hope of lessening the sadness in the man's cheeks and temples with the touch of her hand. She also thought of the town, in which the only possible and prudent course was giving up in time. She was twenty and Risso was forty. She set herself the task of believing in him, discovered intensity in his curiosity, told herself that you really are alive only when each day brings some surprise.

During the first few weeks, she shut herself in to laugh alone, devoted herself to fetishistic worship, learned to distinguish moods by their smell. She learned to discover what was behind the voice, the silences, the tastes, and attitudes of the man's body. She loved Risso's daughter and modified her face, praising her resemblance to her father. She did not leave the theater because the city government had just begun to help support it and the Sotano now provided her with a reliable salary, a world apart from her home, from her bedroom, from the frantic and indestructible man. She did not seek to distance herself from lust; she wanted to rest and forget it, to let lust rest and forget. She made plans and followed them, confident of the infinity of the universe of love, sure that each night would give them a different, freshly created surprise.

"Anything," Risso insisted, "absolutely anything can happen to us, and we will always be happy and in love. Anything: be it created by God or by ourselves."

Actually, he had never had a woman before and thought he was creating what was in fact being imposed on him. But it wasn't she who was imposing anything on him. She, Gracia Cesar, Risso's creation, was separated from him so as to complement him, like air from a lung, like winter from the wheat.

The third photograph took three weeks to arrive. Also, it came from Paraguay and did not arrive at his house but instead at the boarding-house, and the maid brought it to him at the end of an afternoon. He was waking up from a dream in which he had been advised to defend himself from fear and madness by keeping any future photograph in his wallet and turning it into an incident of his life, something impersonal and inoffensive, by means of a hundred absentminded glances a day.

The maid knocked on his door, and he saw the envelope hanging from one of the slats of the blinds; he began to feel its vile qualities, its pulsating threat, filtering into the twilight, filling the dirty air. He was watching it from his bed as if it were a poisonous insect squashed while awaiting a brief distraction, some propitious mistake.

In the third photograph she was alone, pushing back the shadows of a badly lit room with her whiteness, her head thrust painfully back toward the camera, her shoulders half-covered by her loose, full, manelike hair. She was now as unmistakable as if she had had her picture taken in some studio, posing with the most tender, meaningful, and oblique of smiles.

Now he, Risso, felt only a powerless pity for her, for himself, for all those who ever loved in the world, for the truth and error in their beliefs, for the simple absurdity of love, for the complex absurdity of love created by men.

But he tore up this picture also and discovered that it would be impossible for him to look at another one and stay alive. Yet, in the magic sphere where they had begun to understand one another and to converse, Gracia no doubt realized that he would tear up the photographs as soon as they arrived, each time with less curiosity, with less remorse.

In that magic realm, all of the urgent men, whether vulgar or shy, were no more than obstacles, inevitable steps in the ritual act of choosing the most gullible and inexperienced man in the street, restaurant, or café who would lend himself to her designs without suspecting anything, with a comic sort of pride during the exposure, facing the camera and the shutter release, the least unpleasant of those who would buy a memorized spiel worthy of a traveling salesman.

"It's just that I never had a man like you, so unique, so different. And, thanks to my life in the theater, I never know where I will be tomorrow, whether I will ever see you again. I want at least to look at you in a photograph when we are far apart, when I miss you."

And after this conversation, which usually went smoothly, she thought about Risso or deferred her thoughts for the next day, carrying out the task she had set herself, arranging the lights, preparing the camera, and turning on the man. If she was thinking about Risso, she evoked some remote event, reproaching him again for not having hit her, for having sent her off forever with a clumsy insult, an intelligent smile, a comment that lumped her together with all other women. And without understanding—showing that he had never understood, despite all the nights and conversations.

Without getting her hopes up, she bustled sweatily around the inevitable sordid and muggy hotel room, measuring distances and lights, correcting the position of the man's numb body. Using any excuse, lure, drunken lie, she forced the man of the hour to turn his cynical, suspicious face toward her. She tried to smile and to tempt him, aping the affectionate clucking noises you make to newborn infants, calculating the passage of the seconds, at the same time calculating the intensity with which the picture would allude to her love for Risso.

But since she was never able to discover this, since she didn't even know whether the photographs reached Risso's hands, she began to intensify the testimony of the pictures and turn them into documents that had little to do with them, Risso and Gracia.

She even went so far as to allow and require that the faces drawn by desire, dulled by the old masculine dream of possession, confront the camera aperture with a hard smile, a shamefaced insolence. She found it necessary to slip down on her back and sink herself deeper into the picture, allowing her head, her short nose, her huge, unflinching eyes to descend from the void beyond the photograph and form part of the filthiness of the world, the crude and deceptive photographic vision, the satires on the love she had sworn to send regularly to Santa Maria. But her real mistake was changing the addresses on the envelopes.

The first separation, six months after the wedding, was welcome and overly distressing. The Sotano—now the Santa Maria Municipal Theater—went on tour to Rosario. There she fell once again into the old hallucinatory game of being an actress among actors, of believing what was happening on stage. The audience was moved, applauded or resisted being won over. The programs and reviews appeared on time, and people accepted the game and helped it go on until the end of the evening, speaking of what they had seen and heard, of what they had paid to see and hear, conversing with a certain desperation, with a sort of earnest enthusiasm, about the acting, the sets, the speeches, and the plots.

So the game, the remedy, alternately moody and exhilarating, initiated when she slowly approached the window looking out on the fjord and, trembling, whispered to the whole theater: "Perhaps . . . but I too have a life full of memories that remain closed to others," a line also accepted in Rosario. Cards were always laid on the table in response to those she put down, the game was structured, and soon it was impossible for her to distance herself and look at it from the outside.

The first separation lasted exactly fifty-two days, and during them Risso tried to continue exactly the same life that he had had with Gracia Cesar during the six months of married life. Always going to the same cafe at the same hour, to the same restaurant, seeing the same friends, rehearsing moments of silence and solitude on the promenade, walking back to the boardinghouse, obediently suffering through the anticipation of their meeting, brow and mouth stirring with the excessive images born of idealized memories or of ambitions impossible to realize.

He went ten or twelve blocks, alone and slower now, through nights fanned by warm and chilly winds, along the uneasy edge that separated spring from winter. They gave him a chance to measure his need and his helplessness, to know that the madness he was part of at least had the grandeur of being without a future, of not being the means to anything.

As for her, she had believed that Risso gave a theme to their common love when he whispered, prostrate with a fresh feeling of surprise, dazed: "Anything can happen and we will still be happy and in love."

The phrase was no longer a judgment, an opinion; it expressed no desire. It was dedicated and imposed on them, it was a verification, an ancient truth. Nothing that they did or thought could lessen the madness, the inescapable and changeless love. All human possibilities could be made use of and everything was destined to nourish it.

She believed that beyond them, outside the room, lay a world bereft of all meaning, inhabited by beings who did not matter, filled with events without value.

So she only thought about Risso, about the two of them, when the man began waiting for her at the stage door, when he invited her and took her along, when she began taking off her clothes.

It was the last week in Rosario, and she saw no need to mention it in her letters to Risso, for the event was not separated from them and at the time had nothing to do with them, because she had acted like a curious, alert animal, with a certain degree of pity for the man, with some scorn for what she was adding to her love for Risso. And when she returned to Santa Maria, she preferred to wait until Wednesday evening—because Risso didn't go to the paper on Thursday—until a timeless night, until an early morning exactly like the twenty-five they had lived through together.

She began telling about it before taking off her clothes, with the simple pride and tenderness of having invented a new caress. Leaning on the table, in shirtsleeves, he closed his eyes and smiled. Afterward he made her undress and asked her to repeat the story, now standing up, walking barefoot on the carpet and almost without moving forward or sideways, her back to him, her body rocking as she stood on one foot, then on the other. At times she saw Risso's long sweaty face, his heavy body leaning on the table, his shoulders shielding his glass of wine, and at times she only imagined them, absentminded, in her zeal for fidelity in the tale, for the joy of reliving that odd intensity of love she had felt for Risso in Rosario, next to the man whose face she had forgotten, next to nobody, next to Risso.

"Good; now you can get dressed again," he said, with the same astonished, hoarse voice that had said over and over that anything was possible, that everything would belong to them.

She examined his smile and put her clothes back on. For a while the two of them sat looking at the designs on the tablecloth, the stains, the bird-shaped ashtray with a broken beak. Then he finished dressing and went out, devoting his Thursday, his day off, to conversations with Dr. Guiñazu, to convincing him of the urgent need to approve divorce laws, to block all talk of reconciliation in advance.

Afterward there was a long unhealthy period during which Risso wanted to have her back and at the same time hated the pain and loathing of every imaginable new encounter. Later he decided that he needed Gracia, and now a bit more than before. That reconciliation was necessary and that he was inclined to pay any price for it so long as his will was not involved, so long as it was possible to have her again at night without saying yes to her even with his silence.

He started spending his Thursdays once more going out with his daughter and listening to the list of predictions that had come true which the grandmother always made to enliven the after-dinner conversations. He had vague, cautious news of Gracia, began imagining her as if she were an unknown woman whose gestures and reactions had to be guessed or deduced, as if she were a woman who remained intact and alone amid people and places, destined to be his and be loved by him, perhaps at first sight.

Almost a month after the start of the separation, Gracia gave out differing addresses and left Santa Maria.

"Don't worry," Guiñazu said. "I know women well and was expecting something like this. This confirms the abandonment of the home and simplifies our course of action, now made easier by an obvious delaying maneuver, further evidence of the defendant's folly."

It was a damp start of spring, and often Risso came home at night from the newspaper or the café on foot, calling the rain names, reviving his suffering as if blowing on a coal, pushing it farther away to see it better and still not believe it, imagining acts of love he had never experienced so as to be able instantly to set himself the task of remembering them with a desperate greed.

Risso had destroyed the last three messages without looking at them. Now, both at the paper and at the boardinghouse, he constantly felt like a rat in its hole, like an animal that hears the hunters' shots echoing at the door of its lair. He could only save himself from death and from the idea of death by forcing himself into stillness and ignorance. Curled up, his whiskers, snout, paws were twitching; he could only hope for the other's fury to be used up. Without allowing himself words or thoughts, he felt forced to begin to understand, to confuse the Gracia who sought out and chose men and poses for the photographs with the girl who, many months before, had planned dresses, conversations, makeup, gestures of affection for his daughter to win over the widower devoted to grief, a man who earned a small salary and who could only offer women an astonished but loyal lack of understanding.

He had begun to believe that the girl who had written long and overstated letters during the brief separations the summer of their courtship was the same one who sought his despair and annihilation when sending him the photographs. And he thought too that the lover who, in the hopeless stubbornness in bed, always manages to breathe the dark smell of death is condemned (for his own sake and for hers) to seek annihilation, the final peace of nothingness.

He thought about the girl who used to walk on the promenade hand in hand with two girlfriends in the afternoon, dressed in the ample inlaid dresses of stiff cloth that his memory invented and imposed, and who glanced across the overture of the *Barber of Seville* that capped the Sunday band concert to look at him for a moment. He thought of that bolt of lightning by which she turned her furious expression into a proposal and a challenge, showing him directly the almost virile beauty of a pensive and capable face, in which she chose him, dazed by bereavement. And, little by little, he came to admit to himself that the same woman—naked, a little heavier now, with a certain expression of aplomb and self-knowledge—was the one sending him photographs from Lima, Santiago, and Buenos Aires.

He even thought, why not, why not accept that the photographs, elaborately prepared and promptly mailed, were all born of the same love, the same capacity for looking back, the same inborn loyalty.

The next photograph arrived from Montevideo; it was not sent to the paper or the boardinghouse. And he was never to see it. He was leaving *El Liberal* one night when he heard the hobbling of old Lanza chasing after him down the steps, the trembling cough behind him, the innocent and deceitful phrase of the prologue. They went to eat at the Bavaria. And Risso could have sworn afterward that he knew that the unkempt, bearded, sick man, who during the after-dinner conversation puffed again and again on a cigarette moistened by his sunken mouth, who did not want to look him in the eye, who recited obvious comments about the news that UP had sent the paper that day, was impregnated with Gracia, with the frantic absurd perfume prepared by love.

"From one man to another," Lanza said with resignation. "Or from an old man who has no happiness left in life except the uncertain one of staying alive. From an old man to you, and I don't know, because one never knows, who you are. I know some facts and have heard comments. But I no longer have any interest in wasting time believing or doubting. It's all the same to me. Each morning I verify that I'm alive, with no bitterness and no feeling of gratitude. I drag a sick leg and my arteriosclerosis through Santa Maria and around the newspaper office; I remember Spain, correct the proofs, write, and sometimes talk too much. Like tonight. I received a dirty photograph, and there's no doubt about who sent it. I can't guess why I was chosen. On the back it reads: 'To be donated to the Risso collection,' or something like that. It reached me on Saturday, and for two days I wondered whether to give it to you or not. I decided that the best thing was to tell you about it, because sending that picture to me is an act of madness without extenuating circumstances and perhaps it would do you good to know that she is crazy. Now you know. I want only to ask your permission to tear up the picture without showing it to you."

Risso told him to do so; that night, while watching the light of the streetlamp on the ceiling of his room until daybreak, he understood that the second misfortune, the revenge, was essentially less serious than the first one, the act of infidelity, but at the same time much harder to stand. He felt his long body exposed like a nerve to the pain of the air, helpless, beyond hope of finding rest.

The fourth photograph that was not addressed to him was thrown on the table by his daughter's grandmother the following Thursday. The girl had gone to take a nap, and the picture had been put back inside its envelope. It fell between the seltzer bottle and the candy bowl, long, traversed and colored by the reflection of a bottle, displaying eager letters in blue ink.

"I'm sure you understand that after this—" the grandmother stuttered. She was stirring her coffee and looking at Risso's face, searching his profile for the secret of universal filth, the cause of her daughter's death, the explanation for so many things she had suspected without having the nerve to believe them. "You understand," she repeated with fury, her voice comic and aged.

But she didn't know what he needed to understand, and Risso didn't understand either, no matter how hard he tried, staring at the envelope that had stopped in front of him, one edge resting on his plate.

Outside the night was heavy, and the open windows of the city mixed the mysteries of the lives of men, their desires and habits, with the milky mystery of the sky. Rolling over in bed, Risso believed he was starting to understand, that understanding, like some sickness, like a feeling of well-being, was taking place within him, free of his intellect and will. It was simply taking place, from the contact of his feet with his shoes up to the tears that reached his cheeks and neck. Understanding was taking place within him, and he was not interested in knowing what it was that he understood; he remembered or saw weeping and stillness, the stretched passivity of the body in the bed, the bulging clouds in the window, past and future scenes. He saw death and friendship with death, the proud scorn for rules all men had agreed to live by, the true surprise of freedom. He tore the photograph to pieces on his chest, never taking his eyes from the whiteness in the window, slowly and carefully, afraid of making noise or interrupting something. Afterward he felt a new air stirring, perhaps one breathed in his childhood, filling the room and extending with a clumsy slowness through the streets and the buildings, all unprepared for it, an air awaiting him, offering him refuge for the following day and those after.

Since early that morning, he had made the acquaintance of indifference, of motiveless happiness, of the acceptance of solitude, as if of cities that had seemed inaccessible to him. And when he woke up at noon, as he loosened his tie and belt and wristwatch, as he walked sweating to the window, toward the putrid smell of a storm, he was invaded for the first time by a paternal fondness for men and for everything that men had done and built. He had resolved to discover Gracia's address, to call her or to go live with her.

That night at the paper he was a slow, happy man, acting with the clumsiness of a newborn infant, filling his quota of pages with the absentmindedness and mistakes that one is accustomed to forgive in a newcomer. The big piece of news was Ribereña's inability to run at San Isidro, because we are in a position to inform our readers that the good fortune which the stud Gorrion has enjoyed heretofore has become uncertain today due to pain in his hindquarters, evidence of an inflammation of the tendon the name of which clearly expresses the origin of the disease that troubles him.

"When you recall that he covered racing," Lanza recounted, "you try to explain that feeling of bewilderment, comparing it to that of the man who gambled his whole paycheck on a tip he had been given, confirmed in turn by the trainer, the jockey, the owner, and even the horse. Because even though, as we all know, he had the strongest possible motives for feeling pain and taking all of the capsules of sleeping pills in all of the drugstores in Santa Maria all at once, what he showed me no more than a half hour earlier was nothing but the reasoning and the attitude of someone who has been swindled. A man who had been safe, out of danger, but is no longer, and who cannot explain to himself how it could happen, what mistake of reckoning produced the failure. But at no moment did he call the bitch who was scattering the filthy pictures all over the city the bitch that she was, and he did not even accept the way out I offered him, insinuating, without quite believing it myself, that the bitch—in heat and naked, as she preferred to let it be known, or on stage observing the ovarian problems of other bitches made famous by world drama— might very possibly be completely out of her mind. Nothing. He had made a mistake, not in marrying her but at some other moment he refused to mention. The fault was his alone. Our conversation was unbelievable and frightening because he had already told me that he was going to kill himself and he had already convinced me that it was useless, even grotesque and useless all over again, to try and argue with him to save him. And he spoke to me coldly, without accepting my requests that he get drunk. He had been mistaken, he insisted; he, not that damned slut who had sent the picture to the little girl, there in the convent school. Perhaps thinking that the mother superior would open the envelope, perhaps desiring that it reach the hands of Risso's daughter intact, sure this time of finding the one place where Risso was truly vulnerable."

*for Dorothea Muhr—forgotten dog of happiness*

# The Image of Misfortune

## 1

At dusk, despite the high wind, I was in shirtsleeves, leaning on the rail of the hotel porch, alone. The light made the shadow of my head reach as far as the edge of the sandy trail through the bushes that links the highway and the beach with the cluster of houses.

The girl appeared, pedaling along the road, only to be immediately lost from sight behind the A-frame cabin, vacant but still adorned with the sign in black letters above the mailbox. It was impossible for me not to look at the sign at least once a day; though lashed by rain, siestas, and the sea wind, it showed a proud face and a lasting glow, and stated: "My Rest."

A moment later the girl appeared again along the sandy margin surrounded by thickets. She held her body erect on the seat, moving her legs at a slow, easy pace, her legs wrapped with calm arrogance in thick gray wool socks, tickled by the pine needles. Her knees were amazingly round and mature considering the age of the rest of her body.

She braked the bicycle right beside the shadow of my head, and her right foot, seeking balance, released the pedal and came to rest in the short dead grass, all brown now, on the shadow of my body. All at once she pulled the hair from her forehead and looked at me. She was wearing a dark sweater and a pink skirt. She looked at me calmly and attentively as if her brown hand, pulling the hair away from her eyes, were sufficient to hide her examination of me.

I calculated there were sixty feet between us and less than thirty years. Leaning on my forearms I held her gaze, changing the position of the pipe in my mouth, looking steadily toward her and her heavy bicycle, the colors of her thin body set against a backdrop of a landscape of trees and sheep sinking into the calm of the evening.

Suddenly sad and irritated, I looked at the smile the girl offered my exhaustion, her hair stiff and messy, her thin curved nose moving as she breathed, the childish angle at which her eyes had been stuck onto her face (which had nothing to do by now with her age, which had been formed once and for all and would remain that way until death), the excessive space left for the sclerotic membrane lining the eye. I looked at the glow of sweat and fatigue gathered together by the last or perhaps first light of sunset, covering and highlighting the coming darkness.

The girl laid her bicycle gently down on the bushes and looked at me again, her hands touching her hips, the thumbs sunk below the waist of her skirt. I don't know if she was wearing a belt; that summer all the girls were using wide belts. Then she looked around. Now she was facing sideways, her hands joined behind her back, without breasts as yet, still breathing with an odd shortness of breath, her face turned toward the spot in the afternoon where the sun would set.

Suddenly she sat down on the grass, took off her sandals, and shook them; one at a time she held her bare feet in her hands, rubbing the short toes and moving them in the air. Over her broad shoulders I watched her shake her dirty reddish feet. I saw her stretch out her legs, take out a comb and a mirror from the large monogrammed pocket on the lap of her skirt. She carelessly combed her hair, almost without looking at me.

She put her sandals back on and got up, then stood for a moment banging on the pedals with swift kicks. Repeating a sharp quick movement, she turned toward me, standing alone by the porch railing, still as ever, looking at her. The smell of honeysuckle was starting; the light from the hotel bar made pale splotches of light on the grass, the areas of sand, and the round driveway that circled the terrace.

It was as if we had seen each other before, as if we knew each other, as if we had fond memories. She looked at me with a defiant expression while her face slipped off into the meager light; she looked at me with the defiance of her whole scornful body, of the shiny metal of the bicycle, of the landscape with the A-frame cabin and the privet hedges and the young eucalyptus with milky trunks. For a moment that's all there was; everything that surrounded her became a part of her and her absurd pose. She climbed back on her bicycle and pedaled off beyond the hydrangeas, behind the empty benches painted blue, ever more quickly through the lines of cars in front of the hotel.

2

I emptied my pipe and watched the sun dying through the trees. I already knew what she was, perhaps too well. But I didn't want to name her. I thought of what was awaiting me in the hotel room around dinnertime. I tried measuring my past and my guilt with the rod I had just discovered: the profile of the thin girl looking toward the horizon, her brief, impossible age, the pink feet a hand had hit and squeezed.

By the door of my room, I found an envelope from the management with the biweekly bill. When I picked it up, I caught myself bending over to smell the honeysuckles' perfume barely floating in the room, feeling expectant and sad, without any new reason I could point to. I lit a match so as to reread the framed *Avis aux passagers* on the door, then lit my pipe again. For several minutes I stood there, washing my hands, playing with the soap; I looked at myself in the mirror above the washstand in almost total darkness, until I could pick out my thin, badly shaven, white face, perhaps the only white face among the guests in the hotel. It was my face; all the changes of the last few months had no real importance. I realized that the custom of playing with the soap had begun when Julian died, perhaps the very night of the wake.

I went back to the bedroom and opened the suitcase, after pushing it out from under the bed with my foot. It was a stupid ritual, but a ritual; however, perhaps it would be better for everyone if I stuck faithfully to this form of madness until using it up or getting used up myself. Without looking, I sorted things out, separated clothes and two little books, and found the folded newspaper at last. I knew the story by heart; it was the fairest, the most profoundly mistaken, and the most respectful of any of the ones published. I pulled the armchair up to the light and began not reading, just looking at, the big black headline across the top of the page, now starting to fade: FUGITIVE TREASURER KILLS SELF. Underneath was the picture, the gray spots forming the face of a man looking at the world with an expression of astonishment, his mouth almost smiling under a mustache that slanted down at the edges. I remembered the sterility of having thought about the girl, a few minutes earlier, as if she might be the beginning of some melody that would resound elsewhere. This place, my place, was a private world, narrow, irreplaceable. No friendship, presence, or dialogue could find a place there, apart from that ghost with the listless mustache. Sometimes he allowed me to choose between Julian and the Fugitive Treasurer.

Anyone would admit the possibility of having influence on, or of doing something for, one's younger brother. But Julian was—or had been until a few days more than a month before—a little more than five years older than I was. Nonetheless, I should write nonetheless. I may have been born, and continued to live, to spoil his condition as an only child; I may have forced him, by means of my fantasies, my aloofness, and my scant sense of responsibility, to turn into the man he became: first into the poor devil proud of his promotion, then into a thief. Also, of course, into the other, into the relatively young dead man we all looked at but whom only I could recognize as my brother.

What has he left me? A row of crime novels, some childhood memories, clothes I cannot use because they are too tight and too short. And the photo in the newspaper beneath the long headline. I looked down on his acceptance of life. I knew he was a bachelor for lack of spirit. How many times would I pass, almost always by chance, in front of the barbershop where he went for a shave every day. His humility irritated me and it was hard for me to believe in it. I was aware of the fact that a woman visited him punctually every Friday. He was very affable, incapable of bothering anyone, and from the time he was thirty, his clothes gave off the smell of an old man. A smell that cannot be defined, that comes from God knows where. When he doubted something, his mouth formed the same grimace as our mother's. Had circumstances been different he would never have been my friend; I would never have chosen him or accepted him as that. Words are pretty, or try to be, when they point toward an explanation. From the first, all these words are useless, at odds with one another. He was my brother.

Arturo whistled in the garden, jumped over the railing, and came straight into the room, dressed in a bathrobe, shaking sand from his hair as he crossed toward the bathroom. I saw him rinse in the shower and hid the newspaper between my leg and the back of the chair. But I heard him shout: "The ghost, same as always."

I did not answer and once again lit my pipe. Arturo came out of the bathroom whistling and closed the door on the night. Sprawled on the bed, he put on his underwear and then continued dressing.

"And my belly keeps growing," he said. "I barely had any lunch, swam out to the breakwater. Result: my belly keeps growing. I would have bet anything that of all the men I know, this wouldn't have happened to you. Yet it happens, and happens hard. About a month ago, right?"

"Yes. Twenty-eight days."

"You've even counted," Arturo continued. "You know me well. I say it without any disrespect. Twenty-eight days since that wretch shot himself, and you—you, no less—go on playing with feelings of remorse. Like some hysterical spinster. Because not even all spinsters would behave like this. It's unbelievable."

He sat on the edge of the bed drying his feet and putting on his socks.

"Yes," I said. "If he shot himself, he was apparently none too happy. Not so happy, at least, as you are at this moment."

"It's maddening," Arturo went on. "As if you had killed him. And don't ask me again . . ." He stopped for a moment to look at himself in the mirror, "Don't ask me again whether in one of the seventeen dimensions you are guilty of the fact that your brother shot himself."

He lit a cigarette and lay down on the bed. I stood up, put a pillow over the rapidly yellowing newspaper, and began walking around in the heat of the room.

"As I told you, I'm leaving tonight," Arturo said. "What do you intend to do?"

"I don't know," I answered softly, with some feeling of indifference. "For the moment I'll stay here. The summer will last for a while yet."

I heard Arturo sigh and listened as his sigh turned into a whistle of impatience. He got up, throwing his cigarette in the toilet.

"It so happens that my moral duty is to kick you a few times and take you with me. You know that everything is different there. When you get very drunk, on toward dawn, completely distracted, then it will be all over."

I shrugged my shoulders, just my left shoulder, and recognized a gesture that Julian and I had inherited, not chosen.

"I'm telling you again," Arturo said, poking a handkerchief in his lapel pocket. "I'm telling you, insisting over and over, with a bit of anger and with the respect I mentioned earlier. Did you tell your unfortunate brother to shoot himself to escape from the trap? Did you tell him to buy Chilean pesos and change them into liras and then turn the liras into francs and the francs into Swedish crowns and the crowns into dollars and the dollars into pounds and the pounds into yellow silk slips? No, don't shake your head. Cain in the depths of the cave. I want a yes or a no. Although I don't really need an answer. Did you advise him (which is all that matters) to steal? Never. You're incapable of that. I told you so, many times. And you'll never know whether that's a compliment or a reproach. You didn't tell him to steal. And so?"

I sat down on the armchair again.

"We already talked about all that so many times. Are you leaving tonight?"

"Sure, on the bus at nine something. I have five days off and have no intention of spending them getting healthier and healthier only to waste it all right afterward on the office."

Arturo chose a tie and began knotting it.

"It's just that it doesn't make sense," he said once more in front of the mirror. "I admit that I too have shut myself in with a ghost one time or another. The experiment always turned out badly. But with your own brother, the way you're doing now . . . A ghost with a wiry mustache. Never. The ghost isn't your brother, that much we know. But now it's the ghost of nothingness, that's all. This time it came from misfortune. It was the treasurer of a cooperative who wore the mustache of a Russian general."

"Won't you be serious for this one last time?" I said in a low voice. I wasn't asking him for anything: I just wanted to keep my promise, and even today I don't know to whom, or even what promise.

"The last time," said Arturo.

"I see the reason well enough. I didn't tell him, didn't make the least suggestion, that he should use the Cooperative's money for the currency exchange business. But one night, just to encourage him or so his life would be a little less boring, I explained to him that there were things that could be done in this world to make money and spend it, something other than picking up a check at the end of the month . . ."

"I know," Arturo said, sitting down on the bed with a yawn. "I swam too hard; I'm not up for such things anymore. But it was the last day. I know the whole story. Now explain to me—and I would like to remind you that the summer is coming to an end—what good can you hope to do by staying shut in up here? Explain to me why it's your fault if the other guy did something stupid."

"Something is my fault," I mumbled with my eyes half-closed, my head resting on the armchair; my words were sluggish and choppy. "It's my fault that I was enthusiastic, that I lied maybe. It's my fault that I spoke for the first time to Julian of something we cannot define, something we call the world. It's my fault that I made him feel, though I can't say believe, that if he took risks that thing I called the world would be his."

"And so what," Arturo said, looking at his hair in the mirror at the far end of the room. "Brother. All of that is just complicated idiocy. Well, life is also just complicated idiocy. One of these days this phase of yours will pass; when that happens come visit me. Now get dressed and let's go have a drink before dinner. I have to leave early. But, before I forget, I want to leave you with one last argument. Maybe it will be good for something."

He touched my shoulder and looked me in the eye.

"Listen," he said. "In the middle of all this happy complicated idiocy, did your brother Julian use the money properly, did he use it in exact accordance with the silly things you had told him?"

"Him?" I asked with surprise, getting up. "Please. When he came to see me, it was already too late. At first, I'm almost certain, he made good buys. But he got frightened right away and did unbelievable things. I know few of the details. It was something like a combination of bonds and foreign currency, of casinos with racehorses."

"You see?" Arturo said, nodding his head. "A certificate of irresponsibility. I give you five minutes to get dressed and meditate on that. I'll wait for you in the bar."


3


We had a drink while Arturo tried to find a woman's picture in his wallet.

"It's not here," he said finally. "I lost it. The picture, not the woman. I wanted to show it to you because there was something unique about her that few people saw. And before you went crazy you understood such things."

And, I thought, there were memories of childhood that would surge up and become clear in the next days, weeks, or months. There was also the deceitful, perhaps deliberate, deformation of memory. In the best possible case, it was a choice I had not made. I would see the two of us, in a moment of recollection or in nightmares, dressed in ridiculous clothes, playing in a damp garden, or hitting one another in a bedroom. He was older but weaker. He was tolerant and kind, had accepted the burden of my faults, lied sweetly about the marks my blows had made on his face, about a broken cup, about coming home late. It was strange that it all had not yet begun during the month of fall vacation at the beach; perhaps, without meaning to, I was holding back the torrent with the newspaper articles and the evocation of the last two nights. During one of them Julian was alive, on the next he was dead. The second night was of no importance, and all the interpretations of it had been mistaken.

It was his wake; they had just hung his jaw back on his head; the bandage around his head grew old and yellow before dawn. I was very busy offering drinks and comparing the similarity of the regrets. As he was five years older than I, Julian had turned forty some time before. He had never asked life for anything of importance, or perhaps only for this: that he be left in peace. As in childhood, he came and went, asking permission. His residence on earth, unsurprising but long, stretched out by me, had not been any use to him, not even to become known. All the whispering and listless people, drinking coffee or whiskey, agreed to judge and feel sorry for the suicide as a sort of mistake. Because with a good lawyer, after a couple of years in jail . . . And besides, everyone found the ending out of proportion and grotesque in relation to the crime as they understood it. I thanked them and nodded; afterward I wandered around the hall and the kitchen, carrying drinks or empty glasses. Without any information to help me, I was trying to imagine what the cheap tart who visited Julian every Friday or every Monday (days when there were few clients) must be thinking. I pondered the invisible, never revealed truth of their relationship. I asked myself what her judgment would be, attributing an impossible degree of intelligence to her. She who each day endured the fact of being a prostitute, what could she think about Julian, who accepted the idea that he was a thief for a few weeks but who could not, as she could, endure the idea that the fools who inhabit and form the world might learn of his slip? But she did not come at any point during the night, or at least I did not recognize a face, an insolence, a perfume, a meekness that could be identified as hers.

Without stirring from the bar stool, Arturo had bought the bus ticket and seat reservation—9:45.

"There's time to spare. I can't find the picture. Today there's no use talking anymore. Bartender, another round."

I already said that the night of the wake was of no importance. The one before was much briefer and more difficult. Julian could have waited for me in the hallway of the apartment. But he was already thinking about the police and chose to wander around in the rain until light appeared in my window. He was soaked—he was born to use an umbrella and this time he had forgotten it—and he sneezed various times, begging pardon, joking, before sitting down next to the electric heater, before using my house. All of Montevideo knew the story of the Cooperative, and at least half of the newspaper readers desired, absentmindedly, that nothing more be discovered about the treasurer.

But Julian had not waited an hour and a half in the rain to see me, to say goodbye with words announcing the suicide. We had a few drinks. He accepted the alcohol without display, without resistance:

"Now in any case . . ." he mumbled, laughing almost, shrugging one shoulder.

Nonetheless, he had come to say goodbye to me in his own way. Memory was unavoidable: thoughts of our parents, of the now demolished house and garden of our childhood.

He moistened his long mustache and said worriedly, "It's strange. I always thought you knew and I didn't. Since I was a child. And I don't think it's a problem of character or intelligence. It's something else. There are people who instinctively find their way in the world. You do and I don't. I always lacked the necessary faith." He stroked his unshaven jawbones. "But neither is it a case of my having had to adjust to deformities or vices. There was no handicap, or at least I never knew of one."

He stopped and emptied his glass. When he raised his head— the head I have been looking at on the front page of a newspaper every day for the last month—he showed me his healthy, tobacco-stained teeth.

"But," he continued as he stood up, "your strategy was very good. You should teach it to someone else. The failure is not yours."

"Sometimes it works out and other times it doesn't," I said. "You can't go out in this rain. You can stay on here forever, as long as you want."

He leaned on the back of the armchair and was making fun of me without looking at me.

"In this rain. Forever. As long as you want." He came up to me and grasped my arm. "Forgive me. There will be trouble. There is always trouble."

He had already gone. He was bidding me farewell with his presence, cowering as always, with his generous, well-trimmed mustache, with a reference to everything dead and dissolved which the blood tie could (can) revive for a couple of minutes at a time.

Arturo was speaking of swindles at the races. He looked at his watch and asked the bartender for a last drink. "But with a little more gin, please," he said.

Then, not listening to him, I caught myself linking my dead brother with the girl on the bicycle. I didn't want to remember his childhood or his passive goodness, nothing in fact except his impoverished smile, his body's meek posture during our final conversation (if I could give that name to what I allowed to happen between us when he came to my apartment, soaked to the skin, to say goodbye to me in his own way).

I knew nothing about the girl on the bicycle. But then, all of a sudden, while Arturo was speaking of Ever Perdomo or the poor promotion of tourism, I felt my throat penetrated by a whiff of the old, unfair, almost always mistaken feeling of pity. What was clear was that I loved her and wanted to protect her. I could not guess from what or against what. Angry, I sought to save her from herself and from all danger. I had seen her unsure of herself and defiant; I had seen her face turn into a haughty image of misfortune. Such an image might last but is usually crushed in a premature way, out of all proportion. My brother had paid for his excess of simplicity. In the case of the girl—whom I might never see again—the debts were different. But, by very different paths, both of them coincided in their anxious approach to death, to the definitive experience. Julian, by inertia; she, the girl on the bicycle, by trying to do everything in a great hurry.

"But," Arturo said, "even if they show you that all the races are fixed, you go on betting just the same. Hey, now it looks to me like it's going to rain."

"For sure," I answered, and we went into the dining room. I saw her right away.

She was near a window, breathing in the stormy air of the night, with a lock of dark, wind-ruffled hair hanging down over her eyes and forehead, and areas of light freckles—now, beneath the unbearable flourescent light of the dining room—on her cheeks and nose, while her childish, watery eyes absentmindedly looked at the shadow of the sky or at the mouths of her table companions, with strong, thin bare arms reaching out from under what could be considered a yellow evening gown, a hand over each shoulder.

An old man was sitting next to her and was talking to a woman sitting across the table, a young woman whose fleshy white back faced us, a wild rose in her hair above one ear. And when she moved, the little white circle of the flower would cover the girl's absent profile, then would uncover it again. When the woman laughed, tossing her head toward the shiny skin on her back, the girl's face would be left alone against the night.

While talking with Arturo, I looked at the table, trying to guess the origin of her secret, the sensation that she was something extraordinary. I wanted to remain quiet forever beside the girl and take charge of her life. I saw her smoke as she drank her coffee, her eyes now fixed on the old man's slow mouth. Suddenly she looked at me as she had earlier on the path, with the same calm, defiant eyes, accustomed to contemplating or imagining disdain. With an inexplicable feeling of desperation, I felt the girl's eyes on me, pulling mine in the direction of the long noble young head, then escaping from the tangible secret only to plunge into the stormy night, to conquer

the intensity of the sky and scatter it, impose it on the young face
that observed me, still and expressionless. The face which let flow
the sweetness and adolescent modesty of scarlet freckled cheeks in
the direction of my serious and exhausted grown man's face, for no
purpose, unconsciously.

Arturo smiled, smoking.

"Et tu, Brute?" he asked.

"What?"

"The girl on the bicycle, the girl in the window. If I didn't have to
leave at this very moment . . ."

"I don't understand."

"That one, the one in the yellow dress. Hadn't you seen her
before?"

"Once. This afternoon, from the porch. Before you came back
from the beach."

"Love at first sight," Arturo agreed. "Intact youth, scarred experience. It is a pretty story. But, I must confess, there is someone who
tells it better. Wait."

The waiter came up to clear the plates and the fruit bowl. "Coffee?" he asked. He was small, with a dark monkey face.

"OK," Arturo smiled, "what passes for coffee. They also say 'miss'
to the girl in yellow by the window. My friend is very curious; he
wants to know something about the girl's nocturnal excursions."

I unbuttoned my jacket and sought out the girl's eyes. But her face
had turned to one side, and the old man's black sleeve cut diagonally
across the yellow dress. Right then the hairdo of the woman with
the flower leaned forward, covering the freckled face. All that was
left of the girl was a bit of her dark brown hair, metallic-looking at
the top of her head where the light was reflected. I remembered the
magic of her lips and her glance; *magic* is a word I cannot explain,
which I use now because I have no other choice, not the slightest
possibility of substituting another one.

"Nothing bad," Arturo continued with the matter. "The gentleman, my friend, is interested in cycling. Tell me, what happens at
night when daddy and mommy, if that's who they are, are asleep?"

The waiter rocked back and forth smiling, the empty fruit bowl
raised to shoulder height.

"That's right," he said finally. "Everybody knows. At midnight
the young lady rides off on her bicycle; sometimes she goes to the
woods, other times to the dunes." He had managed to look serious,
repeating without malice: "What else can I tell you? I don't know
anything else, no matter what anyone says. I never watched. That
she returns with her hair mussed up and without makeup. That one

night I was on duty and I ran into her and she put ten pesos in my hand. The English fellows who are staying at the Atlantic talk a lot. But I won't say anything because I didn't see it."

Arturo laughed, patting the waiter's leg.

"There you have it," he said, as if he had scored a victory.

"Excuse me," I asked the waiter. "How old do you think she is?"

"The young lady?"

"Sometimes, this afternoon, she seems like a child to me; now she seems older."

"This much I know for certain, sir," the waiter said. "According to the register she is fifteen. Her birthday was a few days ago. So, two cups of coffee?" He leaned over before leaving.

I tried to smile at Arturo's merry look; at the corner of the table-cloth, my hand trembled as it held the pipe.

"In any case," Arturo said, "whether it works out or not, it is a more interesting program than living shut up with a ghost with a mustache."

When she got up from the table, the girl turned to look at me again, from a higher angle now, one hand still wrapped in the napkin—for a moment, while the air from the window tossed the stiff hair on her forehead—and I stopped believing what the waiter had said and what Arturo accepted as the truth.

In the hallway, carrying his suitcase, his overcoat over his arm, Arturo patted me on the shoulder.

"One more week and we'll see one another again. I'll go to the Jauja and meet you at a table savoring the flower of knowledge. Well, happy cycling."

He went out into the garden and then toward the group of cars parked across from the terrace. When Arturo had crossed the lighted area, I lit my pipe, leaned on the railing, and smelled the air. The storm seemed far-off. I went back to the bedroom and lay there, sprawled on the bed, listening to the music that wafted in endlessly from the hotel dining room, where perhaps they had already started dancing. I held the warmth of my pipe in my hand and went slipping into a heavy dream of a grimy, airless world where I had been condemned to go forward, with enormous effort and no desire to do so, my mouth open, toward an entrance where the intense light of the morning was shining indifferently, always out of reach.

I woke up in a sweat and went to sit down again in the armchair. Neither Julian nor the memories of childhood had appeared in the nightmare. I left the dream forgotten on the bed, inhaled the air that was blowing in the window from the storm, pulled the paper out from under my body and looked at the headline, smelled the heavy, hot smell of a woman. Almost without moving, I saw Julian's faded picture. I dropped the paper, turned out the bedroom light, and jumped over the railing onto the soft earth of the garden. The wind was making thick zigzags and wrapped around my waist. I decided to cross the lawn as far as the patch of sand where the girl had been sitting that afternoon. Her gray socks riddled by the pine needles, then their bare feet in her hands, the skinny buttocks flattened on the ground. The woods were off to my left, the dunes to the right; everything was black and the wind struck my face. I heard steps and immediately saw the luminous smile of the waiter, the monkey face next to my shoulder.

"Bad luck," the waiter said. "She's gone."

I felt like striking him but quickly calmed my hands, scratching at the pockets of my raincoat. I stood panting, facing the noise of the sea, still, my eyes half-closed. "What you can do is wait for her when she comes back. If you give her a good scare . . ."

I slowly unbuttoned the raincoat without turning around; I took a bill out of my pants pocket and gave it to the waiter. I waited until the sound of his footsteps disappeared in the direction of the hotel. Then I bent my head down—my feet held firm on the spongy ground and the grass where she had sat—sunken in that memory (the girl's body and movements in the seemingly so distant afternoon), protected from myself and my past by an indestructible aura of belief and hope without object, breathing the hot air where everything was forgotten.

4

I saw her all of a sudden, under the excessive autumn moon. She was walking by herself along the shore, dodging the rocks and the bright puddles that were growing ever larger, pushing her bicycle, no longer wearing the comical yellow dress, with tight pants and a sailor's jacket on instead. I had never seen her wear those clothes, and her body and footsteps had not had time to become familiar to me. But I recognized her immediately and crossed the beach almost in a straight line toward her.

"Night," I said.

A while later she turned to look me in the eye; she stopped and turned her bicycle toward the water. She looked at me attentively for a time, and there was already something solitary and helpless about her when I greeted her again. This time she answered me. On the deserted beach her voice shrieked like a bird. It was an unpleasant and alien voice, utterly separate from her, from the beautiful face, so sad and thin; it was as if she had just learned a language, some dialogue in a foreign language. I reached out to hold the bicycle. Now I was looking at the moon and she was protected by the shadow.

"Where were you going," I said, then added: "Baby."

"Nowhere in particular," her strange voice uttered laboriously.

I thought of the waiter, of the English boys at the Atlantic; I thought of everything I had lost forever, through no fault of my own, without anyone consulting me.

"They say . . ." I said. The weather had changed: it was no longer cold or windy. Helping the girl hold up the bicycle in the sand beside the pounding sea, I had a sensation of solitude that no one had ever allowed me to feel before: solitude, peace, and trust.

"If you don't have anything better to do, they say that very nearby there is a boat that's been turned into a bar and restaurant."

The hard voice repeated with mysterious joy, "They say that very nearby there is a boat that's been turned into a bar and restaurant."

I heard her struggle with her shortness of breath; after a rest she added, "No, I don't have anything to do. Is that an invitation? And like this, with these clothes on?"

"Yes. Like that."

When she turned away I saw her smile; she was not making fun of me, she seemed happy and unaccustomed to happiness.

"You were at the next table with your friend. Your friend left this evening. But one of my tires burst as soon as I left the hotel."

She irritated me with her recollection of Arturo; I took the handlebar from her, and we began walking along the shore toward the boat.

Two or three times I spoke some idle phrase, but she didn't answer. The heat and air of a storm were increasing again. I felt the girl growing sad at my side; I spied her firm steps, the resolute erectness of her body, the boyish buttocks hugged by the ordinary trousers.

The boat was there, pointed toward land, all its lights off.

"There is no boat, no party," I said. "I beg your pardon for having made you walk all this way for nothing."

She had stopped to look at the tilted freighter under the moon. She stayed like that for a while, her hands behind her back as if she were alone, as if she had forgotten about me and the bicycle. The moon was going down toward the watery horizon or was coming up from there. All of a sudden the girl turned and came toward me; I did not let the bicycle fall. She took my face in her rough hands and moved it until it was facing the moon.

"What?" she said hoarsely. "You spoke. Once more."

I could hardly see her but I remembered her. I remembered many other things for which she could serve effortlessly as a symbol. I had begun to love her, and sadness was beginning to leave her and fall on me.

"Nothing," I said. "There's no boat, no party."

"No party," she repeated. I glimpsed a smile in the darkness, white and brief as the foam of the little waves that lapped a few yards down the beach. She suddenly kissed me; she knew how to kiss and I felt her warm face damp with tears. But I did not release the bicycle.

"There's no party," she said again, now with lowered head, smelling my chest. The voice was more confused, almost guttural. "I had to see your face." Once again she raised it toward the moon. "I had to know that I was not mistaken. Does that make sense?"

"Yes," I lied; then she took the bicycle from my hands, climbed on, and made a large circle on the wet sand.

When she came around next to me, she rested a hand on the back of my neck, and we returned toward the hotel. We avoided the rocks and made a detour toward the woods. It was not her doing, or mine. She stopped next to the first pine trees and let the bicycle drop.

"Your face. Once more. I don't want you to get angry with me," she begged.

I obediently looked toward the moon, toward the first clouds that were appearing in the sky.

"Something," she said in her strange voice. "I want you to say something. Anything."

She put her hand on my chest and stood on tiptoe to bring her girlish eyes nearer my mouth.

"I love you. And it's no good. It's just another kind of misfortune," I said after a while, speaking with almost the same slowness as she did.

Then the girl mumbled "poor thing" as if she were my mother, with her strange voice, now tender and protective, and we began to go crazy with kisses. We helped one another undress her to the extent necessary, and I suddenly had two things I did not deserve: her face shaped by weeping and happiness beneath the moon and the disconcerting certainty that she had never been penetrated before.

We sat down near the hotel on the dampness of the rocks. The moon was covered up. She began throwing pebbles; sometimes they fell in the water with a loud sound, other times they barely went beyond her feet. She did not seem to notice.

My story was grave and definitive. I told it with a serious masculine voice, resolving furiously to tell the truth, unconcerned whether she believed it or not.

All the facts had just lost their meaning; from now on they could only have the meaning she desired to give them. I spoke, of course, of my dead brother. However, since that night, the girl had turned into the central theme of my story, even going back in time to become a principal obsession in the previous days. From time to time I heard her move and tell me yes with her strange malformed voice. It was also necessary to refer to the years that separated us, to feel excessively sad about it, to feign a disconsolate belief in the power of the word *impossible,* to display a certain degree of discouragement in the face of the inevitable struggles. I did not want to ask her any questions; her affirmatives, not always uttered during the right pauses, did not demand confessions. There was no doubt that the girl had freed me from Julian and from many other failures and complications that Julian's death represented or had brought to the surface; there was no doubt that I, since a half hour earlier, needed her and would continue to need her.

I accompanied her almost to the hotel door, and we parted without telling each other our names. As she drew away I thought I noticed that the two bicycle tires were full of air. Perhaps she had lied to me about that, but nothing mattered any more. I didn't even see her go into the hotel; just the same, I went into the shadow parallel to the hallway outside my room; I continued laboriously toward the dunes, wanting to think of nothing, at last, and to wait for the storm.

I walked along the dunes and then, already some distance away, returned toward the eucalyptus grove. I walked slowly through the trees, between the twisting wind and its cry, beneath thunderclaps threatening to rise up from the invisible horizon, closing my eyes against the stinging sand that was blowing in my face. Everything was dark and—as I had to repeat several times afterward—I saw no bicycle lamp, were anyone to use one on the beach, nor did I see the burning cigarette tip of anyone walking or resting on the sand, seated on the dry leaves, leaning against a trunk, with legs drawn up, tired, damp, happy. That was the way I was, and although I did not know how to pray, I wandered around giving thanks, refusing to accept the way things were, incredulous.

I finally reached the end of the trees, a hundred yards from the sea, just opposite the dunes. I felt cuts on my hands and stopped to suck on them. I walked toward the noise of the surf until I felt the damp sand of the shore underfoot. I did not see, I repeat once more, I saw no light, no movement in the shadow; I heard no voice breaking or deforming the wind.

I left the shore and began climbing up and sliding down the dunes, slipping on the cold sand that trickled into my shoes, pushing aside the bushes with my legs, almost running, angry and with a sort of joy that had pursued me for years and was now within reach, excited as if I would never be able to stop, laughing in the midst of the windy night, running up and down the little peaks, falling to my knees and relaxing my body until I could breathe without pain, my face turned toward the storm that was coming off the water. Afterward it was as if all of my discouragement and renunciation had given me chase; for hours I looked, unenthusiastically, for the path that would take me back to the hotel. Then I encountered the waiter and I repeated the act of not speaking to him, of putting ten pesos in his hand. The man smiled and I was so tired that I thought he had understood, that all of the world understood and for all time.

Half-dressed, I fell back to sleep on my bed as if on the sand, listening to the storm that had finally decided to break, knocked by the thunderclaps, sinking thirstily into the angry noise of the rain.

5

I had just finished shaving when I heard fingers knocking on the glass of the door that opened onto the porch. It was very early; I knew that the nails of those fingers were long and painted fiery colors. Still carrying my towel, I opened the door. It was unavoidable: there she was.

Her hair was dyed blond and perhaps it had been blond when she was twenty. She wore a tailor-made herringbone suit that the years and the frequent washings made cling to her body. She carried a green umbrella with an ivory handle that had perhaps never been opened. Of the three things, I had guessed at two of them—correctly, to be sure—in the course of my brother's life and of his wake.

"Betty," she said as she turned around, with the best smile she could put on.

I pretended that I had never seen her, that I did not know who she was. It was just a sort of compliment, a twisted form of tact that no longer interested me.

I thought, this was, and will never again be, the woman whose blurry image I saw behind the dirty windows of a neighborhood cafe, touching Julian's fingers during the long prologues to the Fridays or Mondays.

"Excuse me," she said, "for coming so far to bother you and at this time of day. Especially at these moments when you, the best of Julian's siblings . . . Even now, I swear to you, I cannot accept that he is dead."

The light of the morning made her look older; she must have looked different in Julian's apartment, even in the cafe. To the end, I had been Julian's only sibling, not the best or the worst. She was old and it seemed easy to soothe her. I too, despite everything I had seen and heard, despite the memory of the night before on the beach, had not fully accepted Julian's death. It was only when I raised my head and held out my arm to ask her into my room that I discovered that she was wearing a hat and that she decorated it with fresh violets surrounded by ivy leaves.

"Call me Betty," she said, choosing to sit on the armchair where I hid the newspaper, the picture, the headline, the sordid (yet not utterly sordid) article. "But it was a matter of life or death."

No trace remained of the storm, and the night might well not have happened. I looked at the sun in the window, the yellowish splotch that was heading for the rug. Nonetheless it was certain that I felt different, that I breathed the air with eagerness, that I felt like walking and smiling, that indifference—and also cruelty—seemed to me possible forms of virtue. But all of that was confused and I could only understand it a bit later.

I drew my chair up near the armchair and offered my excuses to the woman, to that outmoded form of slovenliness and unhappiness. I took out the newspaper, struck several matches, and let the burning paper dance out over the porch rail.

"Poor Julian," she said behind me.

I went back to the center of the room, lit my pipe, and sat down on the bed. I suddenly discovered that I was happy and tried to calculate how many years separated me from the last time I had felt happiness. The smoke of the pipe irritated my eyes. I lowered it to my knees and sat there happily, looking at the trash there on the armchair, the mistreated filth that lay half-conscious in the fresh morning.

"Poor Julian," I repeated. "I said it many times during the wake and afterward. Now I'm fed up, enough is enough. I was waiting for you during the wake and you didn't come. But, please understand, thanks to the anticipation I knew what you were like; I could have met you on the street and recognized you."

She observed me, disconcerted, and smiled again. "Yes, I think I understand."

She was not very old, though far from my age or Julian's. But our lives had been very different, and what was lying there on the arm-chair was nothing but fat, a wrinkled baby face, suffering, veiled ran-cor, the grease of life stuck forever to her cheeks, to the corners of her mouth, to the wrinkled dark circles under her eyes. I felt like hitting her and throwing her out. But I sat there quietly, began smok-ing again and speaking to her with a sweet voice.

"Betty. You gave me permission to call you Betty. You said it was a matter of life or death. Julian is dead, out of the picture. What is it then, who else?"

She sprawled back on the armchair covered in faded cretonne, on a cover with hideous huge flowers, and sat there looking at me as if at a possible client: with the inevitable quota of hatred and calculation.

"Who dies now?" I insisted. "You or me?"

She relaxed her body and was preparing a touching expression. I looked at her, admitted that she could be convincing, and not just to Julian. Behind her the autumn morning stretched without a cloud, the little offering of glory to mankind. The woman, Betty, twisted her mouth and composed a bitter smile.

"Who?" she said, speaking in the direction of the announcement on the door. "You and me."

"I don't think so; the business is just beginning."

"There are IOUs with his signature and no money to back them up, and they're coming into court now. And there is the mortgage on my house, the only thing I possess. Julian assured me that it was no more than an offer, but the house, my little house, is mortgaged. And it has to be paid off right away. If we want to save something from the disaster. Or if we want to save ourselves."

By the violets on her hat and the sweat on her face, I had foreseen that it was inevitable that sooner or later on this sunny morning I would listen to some such phrase.

"Yes," I said, "you may be right, maybe we have to join together and do something."

For many years I had not derived so much pleasure from a lie, from sham and iniquity. But I had turned young again and didn't owe any explanations even to myself.

"I don't know," I said cautiously, "how much you know about my guilt, about my part in Julian's death. In any case, I can assure you that I never advised him to mortgage your house, your little house. But I am going to tell you everything. I was with Julian about three months ago: one brother eating in a restaurant with his older brother. And it was a matter of brothers who did not see one another more than once a year. I think it was somebody's birthday—his, our dead mother's. I don't remember and it isn't important. The date, what-ever it was, seemed to dishearten him. I spoke to him about specula-tion, about some exchange of foreign currency, but I never told him to steal money from the Cooperative."

She had let the time go by with the help of a sigh and stretched her high heels toward the rectangular patch of sun on the carpet. She waited for me to look at her and then smiled once again; now she looked as if it was somebody's birthday—Julian's or my mother's. She was tenderness and patience, wanted to help me get through without stumbling.

"Kid," she mumbled, her head leaning on one shoulder, the smile brandished against the limit of tolerance. "Three months ago?" she snorted while raising her shoulders. "Kid, Julian was stealing from the Cooperative for the last five years. Or four. I remember. You spoke to him, dear, about some deal with dollars, right? I don't know whose birthday it was that night. And I'm not being disrespectful. But Julian told me the whole story and I couldn't stop laughing hys-terically. He didn't even think about the dollar deal, whether it was a good idea or not. He stole and bet on the horses. For the last five years, since before I met him."

"Five years," I repeated, chewing on my pipe. I got up and went over to the window. There was still water on the weeds and the sand. The fresh air had nothing to do with us or with anybody.

In some hotel room upstairs, the girl must have been sleeping peacefully, sprawled out, beginning to stir amid the insistent despera-tion of dreams and hot sheets. I imagined her and kept on loving her, loving her breathing, her smell, the references I imagined to the memory of the previous night, to me, that might fit into her morn-ing slumber. I returned heavily to the window and looked without revulsion or pity at what destiny had located in the armchair of my hotel room. She was arranging the lapels of the tailored jacket, which was perhaps not herringbone after all; she smiled at the empty air, waited for me to return, for my voice. I felt old, with little strength left. Perhaps the obscure dog of happiness was licking my knees, my hands; perhaps it was something else altogether: that I was old and tired. But, in any case, I felt the need to let time pass, to light the pipe again, to play with the flame of the match, with its sputtering.

"As far as I'm concerned," I said, "everything's fine. It's true that Julian did not use a revolver to make you sign a mortgage applica-tion. And I never signed an IOU. If he forged the signature and was able to live that way for five years—I think you said five—then you had quite something, you both had something. I look at you, think about you, and it doesn't matter to me at all that they take away your house or bury you in jail. I never signed an IOU for Julian. Unfortunately for you, Betty—and the name does not seem particularly apt to me, I don't think it fits you—no danger or threats will work for you. We cannot be partners in anything, and that is always a sad thing. I think it's especially sad for women. I would be very grateful to you if you left right away, if you made no fuss, Betty."

I went outside and continued insulting her in a low voice, searching for defects in the wondrous autumn morning. Very far away, I heard the apathetic cursing she directed at my back. I heard, almost immediately, a door slamming. A blue Ford appeared near the cluster of houses.

I was small and all of that seemed undeserved to me, organized by the poor uncertain imagination of a child. Since adolescence I had always displayed my defects; I was always right, inclined to converse and argue without reserve or silence. Julian, on the other hand—and I began to feel sympathy and some very different form of pity for him—had deceived us all for many years. This Julian I had only become acquainted with after his death was laughing softly at me ever since he began to confess the truth, exhibiting his mustache and his smile in the coffin. Maybe he was still laughing at all of us a month after his death. But it was useless for me to invent rancor or disillusionment.

Above all, I was irritated by the memory of our last conversation, by the gratuitous nature of his lies, and could not understand why he had come to visit me, considering all the risks, to lie for one last time. For, though Betty provoked only my pity or contempt, I believed her story and felt sure of the unending filth of life.

The blue Ford sputtered its way up the hill, behind the cabin with the red roof; it left the road and crossed parallel to the porch until reaching the hotel door. I saw a policeman get out in a faded summer uniform and an extraordinarily tall, thin man in a suit with thick stripes on it and also a young blond man dressed in gray, no hat, smiling at every phrase, holding a cigarette to his mouth between two long fingers.

The hotel manager went slowly down the staircase and approached them, while the waiter from the night before came out from behind a column on the stairs in shirtsleeves, his dark brown hair shining. They all spoke with few gestures, almost without moving the position of their feet. The manager took a handkerchief from the inner pocket of his jacket, wiped his lips with it, and put it back, only to pull it out again a few seconds later with a rapid movement, squeeze it, and rub his mouth with it. I went inside to confirm that the woman had gone; when I came out on the porch again, paying attention to my own movements, to the lethargy with which I wanted to live, to assume each pose as if trying to caress everything that my hands had made, I felt happy in the morning air, felt that other days might be waiting for me somewhere.

I saw that the waiter was looking at the ground and that the four other men had raised their heads and that their faces revealed an absentminded observation of me. The young blond man tossed away his cigarette; then I began to part my lips into a smile and, nodding my head, greeted the manager, and just after, before he could answer, before he could bow, staring up at the porch, wiping his mouth with the handkerchief, I raised a hand and repeated my greeting. Then I went back to my room to finish getting dressed.

I passed quickly through the dining room, watching the guests have breakfast, and then decided to have a gin, just one, at the bar; I bought cigarettes and went down the stairs to the group that was waiting at the bottom. The manager greeted me again, and I noticed that his jaw was trembling a little. I uttered a few words and heard them talking; the young blond man came up to me and touched my arm. They were all in silence, and the blond and I looked at each other and smiled. I offered him a cigarette, and he lit it without taking his eyes off my face; then he stepped three steps back and looked at me again. Perhaps he had never seen the face of a happy man; such was my case also. He turned his back on me, walked over to the first tree in the garden, and leaned there beside some man. All of that had some meaning, and without understanding, I found I agreed and nodded my head in assent. Then the very tall man said: "Shall we go to the beach in the car?"

I walked forward and got in the front seat. The tall man and the blond sat down in the back seat. The policeman slowly got into the driver's seat and started the car. Right away we were riding quickly through the calm morning; I could smell the cigarette the young man was smoking, could feel the silence and stillness of the other man, the will at work in that silence and stillness. When we got to the beach, the car stopped by a pile of gray rocks that separated the road from the sand. We got out, crossed the rock wall, and went down toward the sea. I walked beside the blond youth.

We stopped by the shore. The four of us were silent, our ties whipped by the wind. We lit cigarettes once more.

"The weather seems uncertain," I said.

"Shall we go?" the young blond answered.

The tall man in the striped suit stretched out one arm until he touched the young man's chest and said in a thick voice: "Notice. From here to the dunes. Two blocks. No more, no less."

The other nodded in silence, shrugging his shoulders as if it were of no importance. He smiled again and looked at me.

"Let's go," I said, starting to walk toward the car. When I was about to get in, the tall man stopped me.

"No," he said. "It's over there, on the other side."

In front of us there was a shed made of bricks stained with the dampness. It had a corrugated tin roof and dark letters painted above the door. We waited while the policeman came back with a key. I turned to see the midday sun close at hand over the beach; the policeman took off the open lock, and we all went into the shadow and the unexpected cold. The rafters were a shiny black, softly painted with tar, and bits of burlap were hanging from the ceiling. When we walked in the gray twilight, I felt the shed grow bigger as every step moved us farther from the long table made of sawhorses in the middle of the room. I saw the form stretched out, wondering who teaches the dead the posture of death. There was a little puddle of water on the ground, dripping from one corner of the table. A barefoot man, his shirt open to his ruddy chest, came up, clearing his throat, and put one hand on a corner of the plank table, his short index finger covered instantly by the shiny water that had not yet dripped off. The tall man stretched out one arm and, pulling on the canvas, uncovered the face that was lying on the planks. I looked at the air, at the man's striped arm, still stretched out against the light of the door, holding the ringed edge of the canvas. I looked once more at the bareheaded blond and made a sad grimace.

"Look at this," the tall man said.

Then, little by little, I saw that the girl's face was bent backward, that it looked as if the head—purple, with spots of a reddish purple atop a more delicate bluish purple—would roll away at any moment were anyone to speak too loudly, were anyone to step hard on the floor, were time simply to pass.

From the back, invisible to me, someone was beginning to recite in a hoarse common voice, as if speaking to me. Who else?

"The hands and feet, the skin whitened a bit and folded at the edges of the fingers and toes, also exhibit a small amount of sand and mud under the nails. There is no wound or scarring on the hands. On the arms, particularly on the forearms near the wrists, there are various superimposed ecchymoses on the transversal, the results of violent pressure on the upper limbs."

I didn't know who it was, I didn't have any desire to ask questions. I had the lone defense, I repeated to myself, of silence. Silence for us. I went closer to the table and touched the stubborn bones of the forehead. Perhaps the five men were waiting for something more, and I was prepared for anything.

The idiot, back at the end of the shed, was now listing in his vulgar voice: "The face is stained with a bluish bloodlike liquid that has flowed out of her mouth and nose. After having washed her carefully, we recognize extensive flaying and ecchymosis and the marks of teeth sunken into the flesh. Two similar marks exist below the right eye, the lower lid of which is deeply bruised. Besides marks of violence obviously made while the subject was still alive, on the face numerous contusions are visible on the skin, scoring, without redness or ecchymosis, a simple drying of the skin produced by the rubbing of the body on the sand. There is a clot of blood on either side of the larynx. The tegumenta have begun to decay, but vestiges of contusions or ecchymosis are visible in them. The interior of the trachea and of the bronchial tube contains a small amount of a cloudy (though not foamy) dark liquid mixed with sand."

It was a good answer; everything was lost. I leaned over to kiss her forehead and then, out of pity and love, the reddish liquid that was bubbling out of her lips.

But the head with its stiff hair, the squat nose, the dark mouth stretched in the shape of a sickle, the edges pointing down, limp, dripping, remained there without moving, the size of the head unchanging in the dark air smelling of bilge, as if harder each time my eyes passed over cheekbones and forehead and chin that refused to hang open. They, the tall man and the blond, spoke to me one after another, as if they were playing a game, banging away with the same question. Then the tall man let go of the canvas, sprang up, and shook me by the lapels. But he didn't believe in what he was doing—it was enough to look at his round eyes—and when I smiled at him out of fatigue, he quickly showed me his teeth and with hatred opened his hand.

"I understand, I guess, that you have a daughter. Don't worry: I will sign whatever you want without even reading it. The funny part is that you have made a mistake. But that doesn't matter. Nothing, not even this, really matters."

I paused before the violent light of the sun and asked the tall man in a proper voice, "I may be overly curious and I beg pardon—do you believe in God?"

"I will answer, of course," the giant said, "but first, if you don't mind, and not for the record of the proceedings, just, as in your case, out of simple curiosity . . . Did you know that the girl was deaf?"

We had stopped halfway between the renewed summery heat and the cool shade of the shed.

"Deaf?" I asked. "I was indeed with her last night. She never seemed deaf to me. But that's neither here nor there. I asked you a question; you promised to answer it."

The lips were too thin to call the grimace the giant made a smile. He looked at me again without disdain, with sad surprise, and crossed himself.

# Sad as She

*Dear Sad:*

*I understand, despite the inexpressible and innumerable ties that bind us together, that the moment has come for us to thank one another for the intimacy of the last few months and say goodbye. You have all the advantages; I accept my guilt, responsibility, and failure. I try to excuse myself—only for the benefit of the two of us, of course—by invoking the difficulties involved in vacillating for so many pages. I also accept the happy moments as well deserved. In any case, forgive me. I never saw your face directly, never showed you mine.*

*J. C. O.*

Years before, many years perhaps, or perhaps confused with the day before during the few moments of happiness, she had been in the man's room. An easily imagined bedroom, a bathroom that was falling apart and filthy, a shaky elevator—that was all she remembered of the house. It was before the marriage, only a few months before.

She wanted to go, desired something to happen—the most brutal, the most insubstantial and disappointing thing—anything useful to her solitude and ignorance. She was not thinking about the future and felt capable of denying it. But a move that had nothing to do with her old pain made her say no, defend herself with her hands and with the rigidity of her thighs. She only received, and accepted, the taste of the man stained by the sun and the beach.

At dawn, already disentangled and far away, she dreamed she was walking alone at night, perhaps some other night, almost naked in her short nightshirt, carrying an empty suitcase. She was condemned to desperation; she slowly dragged her bare feet along deserted tree-lined streets, her body erect, almost defiant.

The disillusionment, the sorrow, the assent given to death, were only tolerable because, by some whim, the taste of the man came back in her throat at every cross street where she asked for and demanded it. The painful steps continued, ever more slowly, toward the silence. Then, half-naked, wrapped in the shadows, the simulacrum of silence, a distant pair of headlights, she stopped and noisily inhaled the air. Carrying the light suitcase, savoring the memory, she continued walking back.

Suddenly she saw the huge moon rising amid the dirty gray and black cluster of houses; it was more silvery at every step, and the bloodred edges that had marked it were swiftly dissolving. Step by step, she understood that she was not advancing with the suitcase toward any destination, any bed, any room. By now the moon was monstrous. Almost naked, her body erect and her little breasts piercing the night, she kept on walking so as to sink into the enormous, still-growing moon.

The man was thinner every day and his gray eyes were losing color, getting watery, far now from curiosity and entreaty. It had never occurred to him to cry, and his thirty-two years had at the very least taught him the futility of emotional release, of all hope of understanding.

He looked at her without frankness or untruthfulness every morning, across the wobbly, cluttered breakfast table she had set up in the kitchen for the joys of summer. Perhaps it was not only his fault, perhaps it's useless to try to find out whose fault it was, whose fault it continued to be.

She watched his eyes on the sly—if watching is the name for her reserve, the cold lightning glance, her calculation. Without giving anything away, the man's eyes became bigger and lighter every time she looked, every morning. But he did not try to hide them; he only wanted, without being rude, to deflect what the eyes were condemned to ask and to say.

He was thirty-two, and from nine to five he would go back and forth in a series of offices in a huge building. He loved money, so long as it was plentiful, much as other men feel attracted by tall fat women, tolerating the fact that they are old, not caring about that. He also believed in the joy of tiring weekends, in health that rained down on all from heaven, in fresh air.

He was here or there, knowing ahead of time that he was in control of any form of happiness, of temptation. He had loved the small woman who fed him, who had given birth to a baby who cried incessantly on the second floor. Now he looked at her with surprise: at times she was something baser, more abject, more dead than an unknown woman whose name never reached us.

At the irregular breakfast hour, the sun came in through the tall windows; the smells of the garden mixed at the table, quickly fading, like the easy beginning of a suspicion. None of them could deny the sun, the spring: in the last instance, the death of winter.

A few days after the move, since nobody had thought yet of turning the wild tangle of the garden into a gravelike succession of fish tanks, the man got up in the early morning and waited for dawn. At the first light he nailed a tin can to the araucaria and measured the distance with the tiny revolver inlaid in mother-of-pearl that was hanging from his hand. He raised his arm and heard only the frustrated little bangs of the firing pin. He went back into the house in a bad mood, with an exaggerated sense of having made a fool of himself; carelessly, without respecting the woman's sleep, he threw the weapon in a corner of the closet.

"What's going on?" she mumbled to the man who had started undressing for his bath.

"Nothing. Either the bullets are no good (I bought them less than a month ago, they cheated me) or the revolver is finished. It belonged to my mother or my grandmother; the trigger is loose. I don't like the fact that you're here alone at night with nothing to defend yourself. But I'm going to do something about that today."

"It doesn't matter," the woman said while walking barefoot to fetch the child. "I have good lungs and the neighbors will hear me."

"I know," the man said, laughing.

They looked at one another with affection and jest. The woman waited for the sound of the car and then fell asleep again with the child at her breast.

The servant came in and out and it was impossible to figure out why. The woman was used to it, no longer believing in the pleading look she had glimpsed so many times in the man's eyes, as if the look, the expression, the damp silence mattered no more than the color of the iris, the slant of the eyelids. For his part he was incapable now of accepting the world: neither business nor the nonexistent, so frequently forgotten daughter, forgotten with a raw insistent hard frequency, different despite the premeditated drinking sprees, the unavoidable business deals, the company, and the solitude. It was also likely that neither she nor he fully believed in the reality of the nights, in their brief, predictable moments of happiness.

They could expect nothing of the hours they spent together, but they did not accept that imperfection. He kept on playing with the cigarette and the ashtray; she spread butter and jam on toast. Those mornings he would not even really try to look at her; he did no more than show her his eyes, just as an almost indifferent beggar, lacking confidence in his ability to convince anyone, might exhibit a sore or a stump.

She was speaking of the remains of the garden, of the suppliers, of the rosy baby in the room upstairs. When the man tired of waiting for her sentence, the impossible word, he would move forward and kiss her on the forehead, leaving orders for the workers who were building the fish tanks.

Every month the man confirmed that he was richer, that his bank accounts were growing without the slightest effort or purpose. He could not settle on a sufficiently ambitious use for the new funds.

Until five or six in the afternoon he would sell parts for cars, tractors, all kinds of machinery. But after four he would use the telephone, patient and without feelings of resentment, to protect himself against anguish, to guarantee that he would have a woman in his bed or a table in a restaurant. He resigned himself to very little, to what was strictly necessary: a smile, a caress on the cheeks that might be confused with tenderness or understanding. And of course later the acts of love, scrupulously paid for with clothes, perfume, useless things. The vice, the power, the whole night, were also paid for with resignation to shifting, silly conversations.

When he came back in the early morning, she smelled vulgar smells impossible to disguise and spied at his bony face that searched (always mistakenly) for peace. The man did not bring home anything to tell her. He looked at the line of bottles on the chest of drawers and chose one of them at random. Sunk in an armchair, sluggish, with one finger stuck between the pages of a book, he drank, facing her silence, facing her pretense of sleep, facing her still eyes fixed on the ceiling. She did not cry out; for a while she tried to understand without condescension, hoping to show him part of the pity she felt for herself, for life and its ending.

In the middle of September, at first almost imperceptibly, the woman began to find consolation, to believe that existence simply is, like a mountain or a stone: we do not invent it, neither of them was inventing it.

No one, nobody at all, can know how or why this story began. What we are trying to tell started one quiet autumn afternoon when the man's shadow covered the last sunny patches in the garden and he stopped to look around, to smell the grass, the last flowers of the ill-formed wild bushes. He was motionless for a while, his head leaning to one side, his arms hanging down as if they were dead. Later he went forward as far as the pyracantha hedge and from there began measuring the garden with controlled, regular paces of about a yard each. He walked from south to north, then from east to west.

She watched him from behind the upstairs curtains; anything out of the ordinary could mean the birth of hope, the confirmation of misfortune. The child was screaming in the late afternoon; nobody could say for sure whether he was already dressed in pink, whether he had been dressed that way from birth or even before.

That Sunday night, the saddest day of the week, standing in the kitchen, the man said, while stirring a cup of coffee: "So much land and it's no good for anything."

She spied on his ascetic face, his misunderstood, dissolved torment. She saw a new and threatening languor, the birth of the will.

"I always thought," the woman said, understanding as she spoke that she was actually lying, that she had not had the time or the desire to think about it, understanding that words had lost all their meaning. "I always thought about fruit trees, about flower beds laid out according to some plan, about a real garden."

Although she had been born there, in the old house some distance from the water of the beaches that old Petrus had baptized, under some pretext or another. She had been born, had grown up there. And then the world came looking for her, she did not understand it completely, protected and deceived as she was by the capricious unkempt shrubs, by the mystery (equally mysterious in light and in shadow) of old trees all twisted and intact, by the innocent, tall, ordinary grass. She had a mother who bought a lawn mower, a father who always promised during dessert after dinner every night that he would start the work the next day. He never did. He would oil the lawn mower for hours at a time or would lend it to a neighbor for months.

But the garden, the deformed imitation of a forest, remained untouched. So the little girl learned that there is no word like tomorrow: never, nothing, permanence, and peace.

As a little girl she discovered the loving joke of the bushes, the grass, of the nameless twisted trees; laughing, she discovered that they were threatening to invade the house, only to retreat a few months later, shrunken and satisfied.

The man drank his coffee and then sat there moving his head slowly and resolutely. He paused or let the pause come and stretch out.

"Near the picture windows we can leave a corner to sit down and drink cool drinks when the summer returns. But the rest of the garden, all of it, must be covered with concrete. I want to build fish tanks. Rare varieties, difficult to raise. There are people who make a lot of money that way."

The woman knew that the man was lying; she didn't believe that he was truly interested in money, didn't believe that anyone could cut back the old trees, so useless and sick, or kill the unkempt grass, the flowers whose names she did not know: pale, quickly fading, depressed flowers.

But the men, the three workers, came up to talk one Sunday morning. She looked at them from the upper floor; two were standing, surrounding the almost horizontal garden chair from which instructions were being issued, questions about price and schedules; the third, squatting, wearing a beret, fat and placid, was chewing on a stalk.

She remembered it until the very end. The oldest one, the boss, stooped over, with abundant white hair, his hands hanging down, halting for a moment with his back turned to the wrought-iron gate. Without surprise, he contemplated the ravaged trees, the vast surface of confused weeds. The other two moved forward, unnecessarily burdened with scythes and shovels, with picks and a perplexity that made their legs ever more clumsy. The youngest and largest, who was also the laziest, kept on chewing on a stalk that ended in a little rose-colored flower. It was a Sunday morning and spring was shaking the leaves of the garden; she watched the men, hoping she was mistaken, the baby's mouth at her breast.

She knew the man's resentment, his desire to hurt her. But all of that had been discussed so many times, understood to the extent that one can expect to understand oneself and the other; she did not think possible such an act of revenge, the destruction of the garden and of her own life.

Sometimes, when both of them accepted the dream of having forgotten, the man would find her knitting in some part of the garden and would start in again without any preface: "Everything's all right, everything's as dead as if it had never happened." His thin, obsessive face avoided looking at her. "But why did he have to be born a boy? So many months had passed buying pink wool, and the result was this: a male child. I'm not crazy. I know it's all the same in the end. But a girl could have ended up being yours, exclusively yours. This little beast, however . . ."

She sat still for a while, calmed her hands, and then finally looked at him. Thinner, his light-colored eyes bigger than ever, sitting with legs apart at her side, desolate and mocking. He was lying; they both knew that the man was lying, but understood it in different ways.

"We have already spoken so much about this," the woman said in a bored voice. "I have had to listen to you so many times . . ."

"That's possible. Although not so many times as I felt like coming back to the topic. He is a boy, he bears my name, I support him and will have to educate him. Can we move some distance away, look at it from the outside? Because, in this case, I am either a gentleman or a poor devil. And you, a sharp little tart."

"Shit," she said softly, without hatred, without giving any sign to whom she was speaking.

The man looked again at the darkening sky, the sure signs of spring. He turned and started walking toward the house.

Perhaps the whole story had come from this, something at once simple and terrible. The choice depends on whether one wants to think about it or prefers to be distracted. The man only believed in misfortune and fortune, in good or bad luck, in everything happy or sad that can befall us unexpectedly whether we deserve it or not. She wanted to know something more; she was thinking about destiny, about mistakes and mysteries; she accepted her guilt and finally ended up admitting that being alive is sufficient guilt for us to accept the penalty, recompense, or payment. All the same, when all is said and done.

Sometimes the man would wake her up to speak to her about Mendel. He would light his pipe or a cigarette and would wait long enough to assure himself that she was resigned and listening. Perhaps he was waiting for a miracle in his soul or in that of his naked wife, anything that could be exorcised and might give them peace or some equivalent deception.

"Why with Mendel? You could have chosen from among so many better men; there are so many who would bring me less shame."

He wanted to go back to listening to the story of the woman's encounters with Mendel, but actually he would also draw back, fearful of learning everything once and for all, determined, finally, to save himself, not to know the reason why. His madness was modest and its limits could be respected.

Mendel or anyone else. It didn't matter. It didn't have anything to do with love.

One night the man tried to laugh.

"And yet, it was written. Because things have gotten complicated, or harmonious, to the extent that today I can send Mendel to jail. Mendel, not anyone else. A forged paper, a signature he had drawn. And I am not moved by jealousy. He has a wife and three children who are completely his. A house or two. He still seems happy. It's not jealousy but envy. That is hard to understand. But I personally get nothing out of destroying all of that, whether I destroy Mendel or not. I wanted to do it long before the discovery, even before I knew it was possible. You know, I imagine the possibility of pure envy, without any concrete motives, without resentment. Sometimes, once in a while, I think it possible."

She did not answer. Curled up to keep out the first chill of dawn, she was thinking about the child, waiting for the first cry of hunger. He, however, was waiting for the miracle, the resurrection of the pregnant girl he had met, being resurrected himself, the resurgence of the love they had believed in or had been resolutely building for months (without deliberate deception), abandoned when they were so close to happiness.

The men began working one Monday, unhurriedly sawing down the trees they hauled off at the end of the day in a ramshackle old truck, gasping, all bent. Several days later they began mowing the flowering plants, the grass that had grown tall and straight. They were not on any sort of regular schedule; perhaps they had been contracted for the whole of the job, all at once, ignoring the nuisance of daily wages, absences, and malingering. In any case, they never showed any sign of hurrying.

The man never spoke about what was happening in the garden. He continued thin and quiet, smoking and drinking. Now the concrete was spreading over the earth and its memories—white, now grayish.

Then, at the end of breakfast one day, resentful and heedless, the man put out his cigarette in the bottom of his cup, and almost smiling, as if he fully understood the impact of his words, he said slowly, without looking at her, "It would be good if you could watch the work of the well diggers. Between the baby's bottles. It doesn't look to me like the cement work is moving forward."

From that moment on the three workers turned into well diggers. Now they were bringing great pieces of glass to use to make the fish tanks, huge, arrayed with deliberate asymmetry, out of proportion to whatever kind of creatures he might want to raise there.

"Yes," she said. "I can speak with the old man. I'll go to the spot where the garden was and watch them work."

"The old man," the man jested, "does he know how to speak? I think he directs the others just by moving his hands and eyebrows."

She began going down to the concrete every day, in the morning and in the afternoon, taking advantage of the irregular hours the workers chose to follow. Perhaps it could also be said of her that she was resentful and heedless.

She walked slowly, taller now on the smooth, hard floor, disconcerted, moving at a slant, restoring the old twists and turns, the lost shortcuts that once existed through the trees and flower beds. She looked at the men, watching them construct the huge fish tanks. She smelled the air, awaiting the solitude of five in the afternoon, the daily ritual, the conquest of the absurd, now turned almost into a custom.

First it was the incomprehensible excitement of the well in itself, the black hole that was sinking into the earth. That would have been enough for her. But she soon discovered the two men working at the bottom, their torsos naked. One, the one who had been chewing on the stalk, was carelessly moving his enormous biceps; the other one, tall and thin, slower, younger, aroused pity, the desire to help him, to wipe his sweaty forehead with a cloth.

She did not know how to go away and lie to herself in solitude.

The old man was smoking, perched uncomfortably on a trunk. He looked at her impassively.

"Are they working?" she asked, not really interested.

"Yes, ma'am, they're working. Exactly what they have to do each day, each shift. That's why I'm here. For that, and for other things I can guess. But I am not God. I only barely foresee the future, and help when I can."

The well diggers greeted her by slightly moving their cordial and taciturn heads. Once in a great while, they were able to find some topic of conversation, some pretext that would bounce around for a few minutes. She and the pair of well diggers, the calm giant who always wore his beret and chewed on a stalk that no longer could be pulled from the uprooted garden, and the other one, so young and thin, made foolish and sick by hunger. But the old man did not talk; he could spend the entire day standing still or sitting on the ground rolling cigarettes, one after another.

They kept on digging, measuring, and sweating, as if some part of all of that could matter to her, as if she were alive or were capable of taking part. As if she had once been the owner of the vanished trees and the dead lawns. She spoke of anything at all, with exaggerated courtesy and respect, the form of sadness that helps bind people together. She spoke of anything and always left her phrases unfinished, waiting for five in the afternoon, waiting for the men to depart.

The house was surrounded by a hedge of pyracantha. They were trees by now, about nine feet tall, although the trunks preserved a youthful slenderness. They had been planted very close together but had found a way of growing without getting entangled, leaning on one another, their thorns intertwined.

At five in the afternoon the well diggers imagined the sound of a bell, and the old man raised his arm. They threw their tools in the cool shade of the shed, put away their things, greeted her, and then left. They walked, the old man in front, the beast with the beret and the stooped thin one in back, so that the clouds and what was left of the sun might notice their respect for hierarchies. The three of them walked slowly, smoking calmly, reluctantly.

From upstairs, her back turned to the uproar in the cradle, the woman would spy on them to make sure. She would wait quietly for ten or fifteen minutes. Then she would go down to what had once been her garden, avoiding obstacles that no longer existed, her heels clicking on the cement that reached as far as the pyracantha hedge. Of course, she did not always try the same place. She could walk through the large iron gate that the well diggers and the imaginary visitors used; she could escape through the garage door, which always remained open while the car was out.

But without conviction, in fact without any desire, she would choose the useless, bloody game with the pyracantha, against them, shrubs or trees. For no reason or purpose, she would seek to find a way through the trunks and the thorns. She would pant for a time, opening her hands. She would always end up in defeat, accepting it, saying yes to herself with a frown, a smile.

Afterward she would cross the twilight, sucking on her hands, looking at the sky of the newborn spring, the tense sky bearing the promise of future springs when her son would run around. She would cook, would take care of the baby, and with an ill-chosen book would start waiting for the man on one of the flowered armchairs or lying in bed. She would hide the clocks and wait.

But each night the man's return was the same, easy to confuse with another. On toward October she happened to read: "Imagine to yourselves the growing pain, the desire to flee, the impotent revulsion, the submission, the hatred." The man hid the car in the garage, crossed the concrete, and climbed upstairs. He was the same as ever; the sentence she had just read was not enough to change him. He would walk back and forth in the bedroom, his key ring rattling, telling her simple or complicated stories about his day at work, lying to her, at times during the pauses leaning his face with its prominent cheekbones and widening eyes. As sad as she was, perhaps.

That night the woman let herself go, asked for what they had not done for the last few months. Everything that might make them happy or help them forget was welcome, sacred. Beneath the small half-hidden light, the man ended up falling asleep, almost smiling, soothed. Reviving, sleepless, she discovered without surprise or sorrow that since childhood she had not had any other true or solid happiness apart from that granted her by the green shades of the garden, now snatched away. Nothing more than that, those changing things, those colors. And she was thinking, until the baby cried out again, that he had guessed that, that he wanted to deny her the only thing that truly mattered to her. To destroy the garden, to keep on looking at her gently, his light-colored eyes lined by dark circles, to play with an indirect, ambiguous smile.

When the noises started in the morning, the woman looked at the ceiling with her mouth open, thinking from time to time of the first part of the Hail Mary. Nothing else, because she couldn't accept the word death. She recognized that she had never been deceived, accepted that she had been right about the perplexities, fears, doubts of childhood: life was a mixture of imprecisions, cowardice, diffuse lies, not all of which were always intentional.

But, even now and with ever greater force, she remembered the feeling of deceit that began at the end of her childhood and was attenuated during adolescence thanks to desires and hopes. She had never asked to be born, had never desired that the perhaps momentary, fleeting, routine union of a couple in bed (mother, father, afterward and forever) bring her into the world. And, above all, she had not been consulted about the life she had been forced to get acquainted with and to accept. Had there been just one question beforehand, she would have rejected with horror the intestines and death, the need for a word to communicate with others and seek their understanding.

"No," the man said when she brought the breakfast from the kitchen. "I don't plan on doing anything to Mendel. Not even to help."

He was dressed with an odd degree of care, as if he had not gone to his office but to some party. While looking at the new suit, the white shirt, the brand-new tie, she spent several minutes remembering and believing in her memory; that was how he had been for her during their engagement. She found herself dazed and incredulous, relieved of anguish and years.

The man moistened a piece of bread in the sauce and pushed the plate away. The woman saw a new look shine in his eye—timid, scrutinizing her from across the table—or perhaps she imagined it.

"I am going to burn Mendel's check. Or I can give it to you. In any case, it's a matter of days. Poor fellow."

She had to wait a while. Then she was able to move away from the

fireplace and went over to sit down across from the thin man, patient, not suffering, waiting for whatever might happen.

When she heard the sound of the car die away in the distance on
the highway, she went up to the bedroom. Right away she found the
useless little revolver with mother-of-pearl inlays on the handle. She
looked at it without touching it. Outside her, summer had not arrived either, although spring was advancing furiously and the days,
the little things, could not or would not have wanted to hold still.

In the afternoon, after the ritual with the thorns and the lazy
trickles of blood on her hands, the woman learned to whistle with
the birds and discovered that Mendel had disappeared together with
the thin man. It was possible that he had never existed. She was left
with the baby upstairs, and it was no help in lessening her solitude.
She had never been with Mendel, had never met him or seen his
short muscular body; she had never found out about his tenacious
masculine will, about his easy laughter, about his carefree involve-
ment with joy. The gash on her forehead was dripping slowly now,
and the blood was running down her nose.

The baby cried and she had to go upstairs. The old man was smoking, sitting on a rock, so quiet, so nonexistent, that it seemed as if he
was part of what he was sitting on. The other two were out of sight
at the bottom of the well. Upstairs, she comforted the baby and saw
the man's wrinkled suit on the floor. She poked around, looking at
incomprehensible papers full of numbers, money, a document. At
last, the letter.

It was written in a feminine hand, very clear and handsome, impersonal. It was less than two pages long, and the signature had an
incomprehensible meaning: *Masam*. But the sense of the letter, the
accumulation of silliness, of promises, of phrases aspiring at once to
wit and talent, was very clear. "She must be very young," the woman
thought, without pity or envy. "That was how I wrote, how I wrote
to him." She found no photographs.

Below *Masam* the man had written in red ink: "She must be six-
teen and will come naked over and under the earth to be with me as
long as this song and this hope last."

She never became jealous of the man or felt capable of hating him;
maybe she did hate life a bit, her own lack of understanding, the
vague tricks that the world had played on her. For weeks they kept
on living the same as always. But he did not take long to sense the
change, to perceive that rejection and forgiveness were turning into
something gentle and remote, free of hostility.

They said things but did not really converse. She would impassively underline the sparks of entreaty that sometimes leapt from the man's eyes. "It is as if he had died several months ago, as if we had never met, as if he were not here beside me." Neither of them had anything to hope for. The phrase would not come; they averted their eyes. The man played with the cigarette and the ashtray; she spread butter and jelly on the bread.

When he would return at midnight, the woman would stop reading, pretending to sleep, or would speak about the work in the garden, about the shirts that had not been washed properly, about the baby and the price of food. He listened to her without asking any questions, lacking curiosity, without bringing any true story to tell her. After a while he would take a bottle from a cupboard and drink into the wee hours, with or without a book.

In the summer night air, she would spy on his pointed profile, on the back of his head, where some unexpected gray hairs had appeared a few days earlier, where his hair was starting to thin out. She stopped feeling sorry for herself and felt sorry for the man instead. Now, when he came back, he would refuse to eat. He would go to the cupboard and drink through the night until dawn. Lying on the bed, he would sometimes speak with a strange voice, addressing neither her nor the ceiling; he would tell of happy and unbelievable things, would make up people and actions, simple or doubtful circumstances.

She made up her mind one night when the man arrived very early; he did not want to read or get undressed, and smiled at her before speaking. "He wants to aid the passing of time. He will tell me a lie as big as he feels is necessary. Something absurdly encrusted in our lives, in the deathly story we are living." The man brought a glass that was less than half full and offered her one that was full. He knew, had known for years, that she would not touch it. He had not given her time to slip into bed, had surprised her sitting on the large armchair where she was looking at a book from time to time, at words she knew by heart: "Imagine to yourselves the growing pain, the desire to flee, the impotent revulsion, the submission, the hatred."

The man sat down facing her, listened to the routine news, nodded in silence. When a deadly pause was approaching, he said, in words something like this: "The old man. The one who collects money, smokes, carelessly oversees the workers. He studied for a year in the seminary, studied architecture for several months. They mention a trip to Rome. With what funds, the poor devil? I don't know how much later, several years in any case, he chose to reappear in these parts, in the city. He was disguised as a priest. Without boasting, he would lie, confusing and misleading. He was able to stay, no one knows how, for two days and two nights at the seminary. He tried to get help to build a chapel. With an obstinance that bordered on fury, he would unfold and display bluish plans. Finally, they threw him out again, despite the fact that he offered to take charge of the expenses, to raise the necessary money on his own.

"Perhaps it was then, not before, that he disguised himself with the cassock and went knocking from door to door asking for help. Not for himself but for the chapel. It seems that he succeeded in convincing people with his fervor and with the vague story of his failure. He had astutely deposited the money he received in an escrow account as he went along. That way when the real priests intervened, they could do nothing except resign themselves to a fine (which he didn't pay) and a few days in jail. Afterward, nobody could keep him from devoting himself to building houses. He put the roofs on many of the horrors that surround us here in Villa Petrus, and the people call him 'the builder.' I don't know whether this story is true or false. Who would waste time finding out?"

"And if it's true?" she mumbled over her glass.

"In any case, it's not our story."

She turned in bed. She thought about anyone who was alive or had performed the incomprehensible ritual of living, about anyone who was living or had been living centuries before; her questions could only be answered with the usual silence. Man or woman, it was all the same. She thought about the gigantic well digger, about anyone at all, about compassion.

"As long as he fulfills . . ." he began to say; then the telephone rang and the man got up, thin and agile, slowing his long steps. He talked in the dark hallway and then returned to the bedroom with an almost furious expression of annoyance.

"It is Montero, from the office. He had stayed behind to balance the books and now . . . now he tells me there is something strange, that he needs to see me right away. If you don't mind . . ."

She had no need to look him in the face to understand, to remember that she had known from the start the reason for the incongruous story of the old man; that he had spoken and she had listened so that together they could await the telephone call, the confirmation of the meeting.

"But Am, Masam," the woman uttered, barely smiling, feeling that pity was rising without her getting her share of it. She drank down the contents of her glass in one gulp and got up to bring the bottle and place it on the little table at her side.

The man did not understand, held firm without understanding or responding.

"But if you think I should stay . . ." he insisted.

The woman smiled again while looking straight at the curtain, which was slowly moving in the window.

"No," she answered. She filled her glass again and leaned over to drink without spilling anything, without using her hands.

The man remained standing for a while, silent and still. Then he returned to the hallway in search of a hat and coat. She quietly awaited the sound of the car; then, almost happy at the very center of solitude and silence, she sat shaking her head, bewildered, and poured some more cognac in her glass. She was determined, certain by now that it was inevitable, suspecting that she had desired it from the moment she saw the well and, down in the well, the torso of the man who was digging, the huge white arms effortlessly maintaining the work rhythm. But she could not give up her feelings of mistrust; she could not convince herself that she was the one who was choosing, thought that someone, that others or something had decided for her.

It was easy, as she had known for some time. She waited in the garden, in what remained of the garden, knitting without much interest as always, until the beast came out of his cave, took a pitcher of water, and went off looking for the hose to refresh himself. She signaled to him and brought him over. By the garage, she ventured silly questions. They did not look at each other. She asked if plants and flowers, bushes or herbs, any sort of green vegetal form would ever grow there again.

The man squatted down, was scraping with his dirty worn fingernails at the patch of sandy dirt in front of him.

Quick and whispering and willful, without having heard him, her hands linked behind her back, looking at the cloudy threatening sky, the woman ordered: "After they leave. And don't tell anybody. OK?"

Impassive, aloof, without understanding, the man touched his temple and agreed with his heavy voice.

"Come back at six and come in through the gate."

The giant left without saying goodbye, slow, swaying. The old man was listening to the angels announcing that it was five o'clock and telling him to depart. That afternoon she left the pyracantha in peace; slowly, as if walking in her sleep, repentant and incredulous, she climbed the stairs and saw to the child. Then, from the window, she set herself to watching the road, looking at the deepening blue of the sky. "I'm crazy, or I was crazy and still am, and I like it," she repeated to herself with an invisible smile of joy. She was not think-

ing of revenge, of getting even; she was thinking just a little, super-
ficially, of her distant, incomprehensible childhood, of a world of lies
and disobedience.

The man came to the gate at six, with the stalk he had already
chewed on decorating one ear. She let him walk for a while, very
slowly, on the concrete that covered the murdered garden. When the
giant stopped, she went running down—her heels drumming quickly
and rhythmically on the stairs—and approached him, smaller than
ever, until almost touching the huge body. She could smell his
sweat, contemplated the stupidity and suspicion in the blinking
eyes. Standing on tiptoe, with a bit of rage, she extended her tongue
to kiss him. The man panted and twisted his head to the left.

"There's the shed," he proposed.

She laughed softly for a moment; she was looking calmly at the
pyracantha, as if she were bidding it farewell. She had slapped the
man's wrist.

"Not in the shed," she finally answered, sweetly. "Very dirty, very
uncomfortable. Either upstairs or not at all." She led him as if he
were a blind man up to the door, helped him climb the stairs. The
child was asleep. Mysteriously, the bedroom was still the same, un-
conquered. It was still filled with the wide, reddish bed, the few
pieces of furniture, the liquor cabinet, the restless curtains, the
same decorations, flowerpots, paintings, chandelier.

Indifferent, distant, she let him talk about the weather, gardens,
and harvests. When the well digger was finishing his second drink,
she took him up to the bed and gave him other orders. She had never
imagined that a naked man, a real man, her man, could be so re-
markable and so terrifying. She recognized desire, curiosity, an old
feeling of well-being that had slumbered for years. Now she watched
him approach; she began to be aware of her hatred for the other's
physical superiority, her hatred for maleness, for those who give
orders, for those who have no need to ask useless questions.

She called the well digger and took him to her, smelly and obedient. But it was impossible, over and over again, because they had
been created in ways that were definitively, inescapably, capriciously
different. The man moved away, grumbling, with his throat clogged
and hateful: "It's always like that. It's always that way for me," he
said sadly, remembering, without a trace of pride.

They heard the child cry. Without words, without violence, she
made the man dress, told him lies while she caressed his cheek covered with stubble.

"Some other time," she murmured in farewell and consolation.

The man went out again into the night, perhaps chewing on a stalk, trampling on his anger, his ancient, unfair failure.

(As for the narrator, he is only allowed to make guesses about time. At dawn he can repeat the forbidden name of a woman in vain. He can ask for explanations; when he wakes up he is allowed to fail, to wipe away tears, mucus, and curses.)

Perhaps it happened the next day. Perhaps the old man, his thin face even older than he was, free of any expression, waited longer than that. Three days, let's say. Until he saw her walking around what had been the garden, between the house and the shed, hanging handkerchiefs from a line.

He lit a thin cigarette and, before moving, whispered ill-humoredly to the workers, "I want to find out if they are going to pay us for the next two weeks in advance."

Very slowly, almost groaning, he managed to pry himself loose from his seat and went limping toward the woman. He found her without hope, more childish than ever, almost as freed from the world and its promises as he was himself. The seminarian architect looked at her fraternally, with pity.

"Listen, ma'am," he asked. "I don't need an answer. From you, I don't even need words."

Laboriously he pulled a handful of newly opened roses from his pants pocket, amazingly small, common ones, with broken stems. She took them without a moment's hesitation, wrapped them in a damp rag, and kept on waiting. She did not waver; the old man's tired eyes only awakened a desire to weep that she had suppressed because it had nothing to do with her present life, with her at all. She did not say thanks.

"Listen, my daughter," the man asked again. "This, the roses, are so that you will forgive or forget. It's all the same. It doesn't matter, we don't want to know what we are talking about. When the flowers wilt or you have to throw them out, think about the fact that whether we like it or not we are all brethren in Christ. No doubt they have told you many things about me, even though you live alone. But I am not crazy. I watch and endure."

He lowered his head in farewell and departed. Exhausted by his monologue he started listening in the quiet, stormy afternoon air for the prelude to the five o'clock bell.

"Let's go," he told the well diggers. "It seems there won't be an advance payment."

After several nights of vacillating between waiting and hoping for nothing in particular, one night, before subjecting herself to a dull book and indomitable dreams, she heard the noise of the car in the garage, the slight whistle cautiously climbing the stairs. Ignorant, decidedly innocent about so many things, the man was whistling "The Man I Love."

She watched him move, frowned at him in greeting, accepted the glass that was offered her.

"Did you go to the doctor?" the woman asked. "You promised. Or did you swear?"

The bony profile smiled without turning, happy to give her something.

"Yes. I went. It's nothing. An emaciated naked man standing before a placid fat man. The routine of the X rays and lab tests. A fat man in a lab coat, a not excessively clean one perhaps, who did not believe in his little hammer, in his stethoscope, in the instructions he was writing down. No, nothing is wrong as far as they can see."

For the first time, she accepted another brimming glass. She moved her fingers to get a cigarette. She was laughing and stiffened her body to suppress a cough. The man looked at her, surprised, almost happy. He stepped forward to sit on the bed, but she slowly moved away from the sheets, from the fatherly caress. She still had half a lighted cigarette and kept on smoking cautiously.

She was standing with her back to him when she said, "Why did you marry me?"

The man looked for a while at her thin form, at the unruly hair on the back of her head; then he walked away from her, toward the armchair and the table. Another glass, another cigarette, quick and sure. The woman's question had aged him, marking wrinkles, spreading randomly in all directions like ivy on a wall. But he had to gain time, because the woman, although they never discovered it, although no one ever found out, was more intelligent and more unhappy than the thin man, her husband.

"You had no money, that's not the reason," the man tried to joke. "The money came later, through no fault of mine. Your sister, your brothers."

"I already thought of that. Nobody would have guessed. And besides, money doesn't interest you. What occurs to me sometimes is worse than that. So I insist: why did you marry me?"

The man smoked for a while in silence, nodding to her, stretching his bloodless lips over the glass.

"Everything?" he finally asked, feeling cowardice and pity.

"Everything," the woman said, getting up from the bed to see his hardened, determined head grow weak.

"Nor did I do it because you were expecting Mendel's son. There was no pity, no desire to help my neighbor. So it was very simple. I loved you, I was in love. It was love."

"And it's gone," she affirmed from the bed, almost shouting. But, inevitably, she was also asking.

"With such cunning and dissembling and treachery. It's gone; I couldn't say whether it was a matter of weeks or months or whether it preferred to disappear little by little, gently. It's so hard to explain. Assuming that I knew, I mean. Here, at the beach resort that Petrus invented, you were the girl. With or without the shifting fetus. The girl, not quite a woman, who could be contemplated with melancholy, with the frightful feeling that it's no longer possible. Hair falls out, teeth rot. And, above all, knowing that your curiosity was just beginning and mine was ending. It's possible that my marriage to you has been my last real act of curiosity."

She kept on waiting, in vain. Finally she got up, put on a bathrobe, and faced the man across the table.

"Everything?" she asked. "Are you sure? I beg you. And if necessary I'll get down on my knees . . . For this little past that we help one another to trample on, never agreeing, both free; this past upon which, shoulder to shoulder for reasons of space, we squat down to relieve ourselves."

The man, with the cigarette hanging from this thin mouth, turned toward her, and the vertebrae cracked in his neck. Without pity or surprise, dulled by custom, she found herself looking at his cadaverous face.

"Everything?" the man joked. "More than that?" He spoke with his glass raised, to lost times, to what he thought he was. "Everything? Perhaps you don't understand. I spoke, I think, of the girl."

"Of me."

"Of the girl," he insisted.

The voice, the confusion, the careful slowness of the movements. He was drunk and close to doing something rude. She smiled, invisible and happy.

"That's what I said," the man continued, slow, vigilant. "The girl every normal guy looks for, invents, meets, or is persuaded that he has met. Not the one who understands, protects, spoils, helps, straightens and improves things, supports, counsels, directs, and administers. None of that, thanks very much."

"Me?"

"Yes, now; and all the goddamn rest of it." He leaned on the table to get up to go to the bathroom.

She took off her bathrobe and the nightshirt that looked like it belonged to a girl in an orphanage and waited for him. She waited for him until she saw him come naked and clean from the bath, until he caressed her in a vague way. Then, lying beside her in bed, he began breathing like a child, peacefully, without memory or sin, sunken in the unmistakable silence in which a woman drowns her grief, her suppressed exasperation, her atavistic feeling of injustice.

The second well digger, the listless thin one, the one who seemed not to understand life or ask it for a meaning, a solution, turned out to be easier, even more hers. Perhaps because of the man's way of being, perhaps because she had him many times.

After five she would cut herself on the pyracantha, closing her eyes. She would slowly suck on her hands and wrists. Ungainly, hesitant, without understanding, the second well digger would arrive at six and let himself be taken to the shed that smelled of sheep and enclosure.

Naked, he turned into a child, fearful, pleading. The woman used all of her memories, all of her sudden inspirations. She got used to spitting at him and slapping him; between the corrugated iron wall and the ceiling, she discovered an old, forgotten whip, all dried up.

She enjoyed calling him like a dog, with a whistle, snapping her fingers. One week, two or three weeks.

Nevertheless, each blow, each humiliation, each penance and joy plunged her deeper into the fullness and sweatiness of summer, into the culmination that could only continue as decline.

She had been happy with the boy, and sometimes they cried together, each of them ignorant of why the other was doing so. But, inevitably and slowly, the woman had to return from desperate sexuality to the need for love. It was better, she thought, to be alone and sad. She did not see the well diggers again; she would go down at dusk, after six, and would cautiously approach the trees of the hedge.

"Blood," the man would say when he woke her up on his return in the wee hours; "blood on your hands and face."

"It's nothing," she would answer while waiting for sleep to return. "I still like playing with the trees."

One night the man came back to awaken her; he served himself a glass while loosening his tie. Sitting on the bed, the woman heard his laugh and was comparing it with a clear, fresh, irrepressible sound she had heard years before.

"Mendel," he said finally. "Your wonderful, irresistible friend Mendel. And, in consequence, my bosom friend. He was arrested yesterday. And not because of my papers or documents but because it had to end like this."

She asked for a glass without soda and drank it down at once.

"Mendel," she said without surprise, unable to understand, to guess.

"And I," the man mumbled with a tone of truth, "not knowing the whole day whether I should do the judge the favor of submitting the filthy papers or whether I should burn them."

So, right in the middle of the summer, came the afternoon foreseen so long before, when she had her wild garden and no well diggers had come to destroy it.

She walked through the garden that was being covered with concrete and threw herself, with a technique that was old and familiar by now, upon the pyracantha and pain.

She bounced off of soft and tame places, as if the plants had suddenly turned into rubber sticks. The spines no longer had the strength to hurt her and were slowly dripping with a sort of milk, a thick, sluggish, lazy, whitish liquid. She tried some other trunks and they were all the same: tractable, inoffensive, oozing.

At first she was in despair but she ended up accepting it; she was in the habit. It was already after five and the workers had gone. Picking some flowers and leaves as she went by, she stopped to pray beneath the immortal araucaria tree. Someone was crying, from hunger or from fear, upstairs. With a mangled flower in her hand, she began climbing the stairs.

She nursed the child until she felt him fall asleep. Afterward she crossed herself and walked, dragging her feet a little, toward the bedroom. She burrowed into the chest of drawers and almost at once, amid shirts and underwear, succeeded in finding the useless, impotent Smith and Wesson. It was all a game, a ritual, a prologue.

But she started praying again, while looking at the bluish sheen of the weapon, repeating the first half of the Hail Mary twice; she slid down until falling on the bed, reconstructing the first time, letting herself go, crying, seeing that night's moon once more, submissive, like a child. The icy barrel of the dead revolver passed her teeth, leaned against her palate.

Back in the child's room, she stole the hot-water bottle. In the bedroom, she wrapped the Smith and Wesson in it, waiting patiently for the barrel to acquire a human temperature for her anxious mouth.

Without shame she admitted the farce she was committing. Then she listened, unhurriedly, without fear, to the three failed blows of the firing pin. For a few seconds, she listened to the fourth shot of the bullet that tore into her brain. For a while, without understanding, she was back at the first night with the moon, believing that she could feel the melting taste of the man in her throat, so much like

fresh grass, like happiness or summer vacation. Stubbornly, she advanced to each intersection of the fragmented dream and brain, to
each moment of exhaustion while climbing the endless slope, half-
naked, bent over by the suitcase. The moon kept on growing larger.
Piercing the night with her little breasts bright and hard as zinc, she
kept on walking until sinking into the huge moon that had waited
for her steadily for years, not so many years.

# New Year's Eve

When the whole city discovered that midnight had finally arrived, I was alone and in almost total darkness, looking at the river and the lighthouse from the coolness of the window where I was smoking, determined to discover some memory that would move me, some reason to feel sorry for myself and angry at the world, to contemplate the lights of the city, off to my left, with some sort of exciting hatred.

Earlier I had finished the drawing of the two children in pajamas who were astonished in the morning by the invasion of horses, dolls, cars, and scooters on their shoes by the chimney. In accordance with the agreement, I had copied the figures from an ad published in *Companion*. The hardest part was drawing the idiotic expression of the parents, who were spying from behind a curtain, and preventing myself from using my sable brush and crimson ink to write in big fuzzy letters across the picture: "Hip hip for happiness."

But instead I was able to devote the forty minutes that separated me from the New Year, from my birthday and Frieda's promised return, to painting a new sign for the bathroom in green letters. The old one was faded, spotted with soap and toothpaste. Besides, it had been made with horrid italic letters, with the calligraphy used for the signs that idiots hang in their houses: *"Small House, Big Heart,"* *"Welcome,"* *"Young Ship, Old Captain."*

The present I had bought Frieda awaited her, wrapped in sky-blue paper next to her glass, the bottle of rum, the little plate with glazed fruit, almond nougat, and nuts at the place where she always sat at the table. I had also bought a cigar and a packet of razor blades so she could cut her hair. Although we had only been living together for a few months, these presents were traditional at the anniversaries we honored or invented. She thanked me for them with occasionally convincing insults of a surprisingly obscene nature, promising re-

venge, but always ending with acceptance of my goodwill, my es-
teem, and my careless understanding. Her presents, on the other
hand, were jobs, forms of earning not very much money, schemes to
help me forget that I was living on hers.

On Saturday nights when there were lots of people, when she was
starting to get drunk, Frieda would go sit down on the toilet, and for
a few minutes or a quarter of an hour, as long as nobody went looking for her, she would sit still, with her panties down by her knees,
eagerly cutting the hair that covered her forehead with a razor blade,
her alert birdlike face fixed on the little sign tacked between the
medicine cabinet and the sink, the same one I was doing over to surprise her, with the verses from Baudelaire that say: "Thank you, oh
my God, for not having made me a woman or a black or a Jew or a
dog or a dwarf." Nobody who used the toilet could get away without
repeating that prayer.

But this New Year's Eve we had decided—or had wrapped ourselves in lies until committing ourselves—to be alone and try to be
happy. She had promised to leave everything—her dance students,
the clients at the dressmaker's, unexpected propositions—to be
alone with me before midnight. I didn't have many things to give up
in return; the last night of the year someone, some member of the
sinister tribe, would dedicate to watching the old man's head rock
back and forth until daybreak.

It was not happiness but it required the least effort. Frieda would
arrive (but she did not arrive) before midnight. We would eat something and would devote ourselves to getting drunk like experts,
stretching things out so as not to ruin them; I would ask questions,
feigning an interest in the subject, encouraging her to repeat her
monologue about her childhood and adolescence in Santa Maria, the
story of her expulsion, the capricious, always shifting evocations of
the lost paradise.

Perhaps, toward the end of the night, we would make love on the
large bed, on the rug in the first room, or on the balcony. It didn't
matter to me whether we did or not, but I had never known a woman
so capable of constant surprises or so disposed to confess everything.
When she was drunk she felt compelled to talk; going to bed with
her when she was in that state was like possessing dozens of women
at once and finding out everything about them. Besides, maybe she
would accept the idea of celebrating the New Year by lying on her
back on the floor or the mattress.

I was smoking in the window, drinking something with lots of
water in it, when the horns and shots began ringing out. It was impossible for me to think of myself, so I thought of Maria Eugenia and

of my son Seoane, forced myself to suffer and accuse myself, remembered anecdotes that made no sense to me.

Everything, quite simply, had been or was that way, though it could have easily turned out another way, though one might imagine each person would give a different version. And, once and for all, I not only could not be the object of pity but was not even believable. Everybody else existed and I watched them live, and the love I devoted to them was nothing but the putting into practice of my love for life.

Already midnight had been forgotten in Montevideo. The lights across the bay in Ramirez were beginning to thin out, and the dancing partners in the Park Hotel must have been coming and going on the beach when the New Year really started. Someone pounded an African drum once more, deep, lonely, unbroken, somewhere in the direction of the barracks, and made the words sound confused.

But I could recognize Frieda's voice, unsure of herself, surrendering, losing energy. She was shouting "Himmel!"; I crossed the apartment, quietly went down the brick staircase in the dark toward the garden and the entrance.

There was no light there except what filtered in from the Proa. But I could see her, standing firm between two dry flower beds, athletic, rocking energetically, while some runt born to consumptive parents, dark and wearing a skirt, the head rendered incredibly large by the labor of a cheap hair stylist, was berating her: ". . . cause you bitch, cause if you think you're just going to play with me, cause if you go with me you don't go with nobody else." She was slapping Frieda's face and Frieda was taking it; then she began hitting her methodically with her purse, over and over.

I sat down on a step and lit a cigarette. "Frieda can squash her just by moving her arm," I thought. "Frieda can kick her into the river with just one blow."

But Frieda had chosen to start the year that way: with her hands on her buttocks, exaggerating the breadth of the shoulders of her tailor-made suit, allowing herself to be slapped and enjoying it, answering the blows with the purse with her hoarse cries of "Himmel!" that seemed to ask for more blows.

When that trash got tired of hitting her, they both cried and left the garden for the street. I saw them stop, out of breath, and then walk holding onto each other. Then I went upstairs to turn all the lights on and offer Frieda a good reception for the New Year.

I had her under the luxury of a standing lamp, or she was just there in the armchair, her blond hair covering her forehead, her mouth twisted by depravity and bitterness, her right eyebrow raised as always and now curving over a black eye. With her lips broken and bleeding, refusing to let me attend to them, she forced me to enter the New Year speaking of Santa Maria. Her family had thrown her out and sent her money every month because ever since she was fourteen, she had devoted herself to drinking, behaving scandalously, and making love with all of the sexes imagined by divine wisdom.

I say this in homage to her, who proved more catholic every Sunday and who filled our apartment every Saturday, late every Saturday night, with women who were ever older, more surprising, and abject. She spoke about her provincial childhood and about her family of German immigrants, who were completely to blame for the fact that now, in Montevideo, she had no alternative to drinking and repeating the scandal and the dissolute love. She spoke until dawn that New Year's Day about failed dates and the faults of others, drunk even before she arrived, rubbing the eye now swollen almost completely shut, enjoying the pain from her split, swollen lips.

"It seemed to me," she said smiling, "you're not going to believe me, it seemed to me that I saw Seoane at the corner."

"At this hour? Besides, he would have come up to see me."

"Perhaps he didn't come to see you."

"Yes, sweetheart," I said.

"Not to visit you. Perhaps to spy on your house, to see if you were going in or out."

"That could be," I agreed, because I didn't like talking about Seoane with Frieda, and perhaps not with anybody else either.

She was speaking (like all women) about an ideal Frieda, marveling at the unending triumph of injustice and misunderstanding, seeking out and naming those at fault, though without hating them.

She did not mention the inexplicable repugnance that had been beating her face with a purse. I was already used to her need to find lovers, each dirtier and cheaper than the last. Since time lacks importance, since simultaneity is a detail that depends on the whims of memory, I could easily evoke nights when the apartment where Frieda allowed me to live was filled with numerous women she had brought in from the street, from the bars by the port, from the Victoria Plaza. Some of them were pretty and well dressed, with only a few jewels, with bangles, with dark dresses adorned with pearls.

But lately there had been a run of insolent, dirty mestizas, with foul language and cigarettes hanging from their mouths. Frequently, the angry dialogues kept me from sleeping, and I would jump out of bed and walk around the apartment chomping on a cigarette as if on an olive branch, dodging the women with some difficulty whether crouching on the floor, sitting on the table, sprawling on the sofa, kneeling in the kitchen, changing in the bathroom, catching the sun or the moon on the red tiles of the balcony.

"Herrera paid up," Frieda said. "He did the right thing: that way the year gets off to a good start and may bring him luck."

The bills had fallen from my chest onto the table. I picked them up without removing the rubber band that held them together; they were a hundred pesos each.

"Did he pay it all?" I asked.

Frieda started laughing and then sucked on her split lip.

"Give me a drink and a smoke. That poor fool. But it's so wonderful letting things go, letting them do whatever they want to you, never even suspecting who you are. Let go until all of a sudden someone realizes that it's all over; then you stop putting up with it all, taking pleasure in giving in, and eagerly, even happily, committing the greatest horror in the world. In revenge: not from pride or from a desire to get even, but because all at once pleasure consists of hitting instead of being hit. Right?"

"I understand," I said. As I listened to her, I let the roll of bills dance around in my hand.

"Are you going to help me? When the time comes, I mean, if it comes."

"Of course." I put the money in my pants pocket, filled the glass with rum and gave it to her, put a cigarette in her mouth and lit a match. "Whenever you want. Did he pay or not? I mean, did he pay it all, once and for all?"

Frieda sat up, laughing hysterically, and then slipped down on her side, sprinkling the floor with spit.

"I think that that filthy woman . . ." She held her ribs, then put on a childish face to listen to what was left of the night. "That—that filthy bitch got me in the groin with her knee. It's nothing. I don't know whether it's true, I don't know whether next week, when he is playing with his children and their presents for Three Kings' Day, I should appear and ask for more money. And Herrera's money doesn't matter to me. You know, you already put it away. What matters to me is fucking him over—that's the nature of my relationship with him and that's how it has to remain."

"Frieda," I said in a very loud voice. She stirred in the armchair and then raised her head. She was drunk, had a childlike smile, tears were beginning to fall. I put the money on the table, taking care that it not roll away. "This is wrong. We have to call an end to the business with Herrera."

She shrugged her shoulders and was looking at me as if she loved me, with such a sad, surprised smile, while her tongue moved slowly to lick her tears.

"Whatever you like," she said. "Give me another drink, let's celebrate the New Year."

# The Stolen Bride

Nothing was going on in Santa Maria. It was autumn; there was just the brilliant sweetness of a dying sun going out, slowly and punctually. All the variety of townspeople of Santa Maria were watching the sky and the earth stop before accepting the sufficient folly of work.

Without a break, nothing happened during the summer I suffered in Santa Maria until March fifteenth began without violence, soft as the sanitary napkins that women carry concealed in their purses, soft as paper, as silky tissue paper being wiped between buttocks.

That fall nothing happened in Santa Maria until the hour arrived—inexplicable or accursed or fateful or definite or unavoidable—the happy hour of lying, and the yellow light slipped in between the cracks of the Venetian lace.

Moncha, they told me this story had already been written and (less importantly) was also lived by another Moncha in the South liberated and destroyed by the Yankees, in some uncertain place in Brazil, in a county of an England that also holds the Old Vic.

I said it doesn't matter, Moncha, because it's just a matter of a letter of love or affection or respect or loyalty. I think you always knew that I loved you and that the words that come before and after these are weakened because they spring from pity. Mercy, if you prefer. I'm telling you, Moncha, in spite of everything. Many will be called to read them but only you, and now, are chosen to listen to them.

Now you are immortal, and across the many years that you too perhaps recall, you succeeded in avoiding wrinkles, fanciful varicose designs on swollen legs, the pitiable clumsiness of your little brain, old age.

It's just a few hours since I drank coffee and anisette, surrounded by witches who would only pause in their conversations to look at you, Moncha, to go to the bathroom, or to swallow their snot behind a handkerchief. But I know more than that, and even better, I swear to you that God approved your deceit and also found a way of rewarding it.

They tell me, besides, that if I persist, I should begin at the end, go back to your incomprehensible journeys on all fours when you were a year old, skip over the terror you felt during your first menstrual period, return to the ending with mystery and trickery, go back to when you were twenty and to the trip—move immediately to your unlucky, harrowing first abortion.

But you and I, Moncha, have agreed, consistently and frequently, on the need not to lend credence to the scandal, so I prefer to talk about you from the beginning that really matters until the greeting and farewell. You will thank me, will laugh at my memory, won't move your head when you hear what I perhaps should not tell you. As if you were already prepared to know that words are more powerful than deeds.

No, it was never that way for you. At bottom, you never understood words that did not voicelessly announce money, safety, something that would allow you to rest the abundant buttocks of your thin body on a recent widow's wide, docile armchair.

This is not a love letter or an elegy; it is a letter of having loved and understood, from the none too memorable beginning to the repeated kisses of your yellow feet, strangely dirty yet odorless.

Moncha, once more: I remember with clarity that whole regiments saw you naked and used you. That you opened yourself without any other violence than your own, that you kissed in the middle of the bed, that they all did almost the same thing to you.

Now the ladies are arriving to see you in a new yet definitive nakedness, to wash you with old sponges and an intense Puritanical stubbornness. Your feet are still emaciated and dirty.

Compared with your mouth, smooth and generous for the first time, nothing that I might tell you from memory is of any importance. Comparing it with the smell that penetrates and surrounds you, nothing matters. I less than everything, of course; I who am smelling the first timid, almost pleasant, hint of your decay. Because I was always old in relation to you and you inspired no possible desire in me except the desire some distant day to write you a conclusive love letter, just a brief note, a string of words that would tell you everything. The unforeseeable brief letter, I insist, would watch you go by, grotesque and pitiful, along the streets of Santa Maria, or would find you grotesque and pitiful, impassive, stubbornly insisting on your disguise in the face of the never fully explicit jests of the men on the street corners; silently, I contributed to creating and imposing a respect owed you from time immemorial by virtue of your being a woman and of your carrying your person modestly and unavoidably between your legs.

And it is a lie, because I saw you parade around in front of the church, when Santa Maria was shaken by the first timid and almost innocent brothel. You were young, vigorous and clumsy, tripping over yourself, with an expression of disregard and challenge, coming from behind the billboard which bore the bold yet shy, thin black letters: "We want chaste boyfriends and healthy husbands."

The letter, Moncha, could not be foreseen, but now I invent the fact that I suspected it from the beginning. The letter plotted on an island that is not called Santa Maria, that has an exotic name pronounced with an *f* in the throat (although perhaps it's just called Bisinidem, without any *f* in it), a solitude for us, the tenacious mania of someone obsessed and bewitched.

By cunning, resourcefulness, humility, a love for truth, a desire for clarity and order, I leave behind the first person singular and pretend that I am losing myself in the plural. They all did the same thing.

For it is easy and lazy to use the umbrella of a pseudonym, of a signature without signature: J. C. O. I used it many times.

It is easy to write as if playing, repeating what old Lanza or some other irresponsible person told us about her: a defiant look, a sensual, scornful mouth, the strength of her jaw.

It has already been done once.

But Moncha Insurralde, or Insaurralde, the little Basque woman, went back to Santa Maria. She returned, as they all returned or return, over the years, those who had their final farewell party and who now wander, vegetate, try to survive on the basis of any little solid thing, a square yard of land, so far, so removed from Europe (which is also called Paris), so far from the dream, the great dream. It could be said that they return, reappear. But the truth is that we have them back in Santa Maria and listen to the explanations of their forgettable failures, about how unfair it all is. Irately, they protest in tones ranging from a bass to the scream of a newborn baby. In any case, they protest, explain, complain, disdain. But we get bored, know they will chew with pleasure on their defeat and their embellished memories, falsified of necessity, without any thought-out intention. We know that they have returned to stay and, once again, that they will go on living.

So the key for a narrator who is amiable and patriotic is, must be, an alien and incomprehensible misunderstanding and bad luck, equally alien and incomprehensible. But they return, cry, toss about, make their peace and stay on.

That is why here, in our Santa Maria of today, with its wide highways, so different from before, we have what any great city can and does have, without the need for expropriation proceedings and for a sad but low price. We recognize the relative proportions: ten to one hundred, one hundred to one thousand, one hundred thousand to one million. But in Santa Maria we have (and always will have, with new faces and elbows replacing those who have recently gone) our Picasso, our Bela Bartok, our Picabia, our Frank Lloyd Wright, our Ernest Hemingway, though this last is fat, bearded, and abstemious, a healthy hunter of flies paralyzed by cold.

Many other failures, caricatures who offer to think, clumsy, stubborn copies. We answer yes, we accept, and it seems that we must try to keep on living.

But they all returned, though some of them never traveled anywhere. Diaz Grey came without ever having left us. The Basque Insurralde was here but later appeared among us as if she dropped out of the sky, and we still don't know how; that is why we tell stories.

Ever mysterious, Moncha Insurralde returned from Europe and chose not to speak to any of us, the notables. She locked herself in her house, refused to receive anyone, and for three months we forgot her. Afterward, without seeking publicity, the news arrived from the Club and from the Plaza bar. It was inevitable, Moncha, that opinion should be divided. Some of us did not believe and asked for another drink, a deck of cards, a chessboard, to change the subject. Others of us believed in a dispassionate way and let the already dead afternoons of winter drag themselves along on the other side of the hotel windows, playing poker, waiting with blank faces for the hoped-for and certain confirmation. Others of us knew that it was true, that it floated in between the impossible luxury of understanding and a sealed secret.

The first news made us uncomfortable but brought us hope, flew in as if born in some other world, somewhere totally apart, totally alien. That thing, scandal, would not come to the city, would not brush against the churches, disturb the peace of Santa Maria's homes, especially not the nightly peace of dessert conversation, the perfect hours of peace, digestion, and hypnotism before an absurd but clumsy world, the crass and cheerfully shared foolishness that blinked and stuttered on the television screens.

The pointlessly tall walls around the house of the dead Basque, Señor Insaurralde, protected us from the cry and the vision. The crime, the sin, the truth, and the thin madness could not touch us, did not drag into our midst a thin, trembling silvery mucus, bringing us injury or clarity.

Moncha remained hidden in her house, separated by the four brick walls of unusual height. Besides, guarded by a maid, a cook, a motionless driver, a gardener, male and female peons, Moncha was a remote lie, easy to forget or not to believe in, a distant white legend.

We knew, it was known, that she slept like the dead in the big house, that during the dangerous moonlit nights she wandered around the garden, the orchard, the unkempt lawn, dressed in a wedding gown. She came and went, slow, erect, and solemn, from one wall to the other, from dusk until the moon dissolved into dawn.

And we who were safe, thanks to our ignorance and oblivion, we, all of Santa Maria, were protected by the quadrilateral of high, peaceful, and ironic walls, capable of not believing in the remote, absent whiteness, in the white flash walking beneath the always greater whiteness of the round or horned moon.

The woman was getting out of the four-horse carriage, out of the fragrance of orange blossoms, of Russian leather. The woman, in a garden we now make huge and full of exotic plants, advancing implacable and calm, not needing to turn her steps aside as she walked between the rhododendrons and the rubber trees, not even brushing against the tall trees covered with orchids, not breaking their nonexistent perfume, always hanging weightlessly from the arm of the best man. Until at last the best man, without lips, tongue, or teeth, whispers ritualistic, insincere, and ancient words, free of violence, with just a hint of an unavoidable and elegant male resentment, to give her to the groom in the abandoned garden, in the whiteness of the moon and the wedding dress.

And then, every clear night, slowly, the ceremony of the hand— childlike now, stretched out again, trembling slightly, waiting for the ring. In this other lonely frozen park, she, kneeling next to the ghost, is listening to the endless Latin phrases that slip down from heaven: to love and obey, for richer or for poorer, for better or for worse, in sickness and in health, until death do us part.

All of this was so beautiful and so unreal, repeated without weariness or any real hope on every relentless white night. Shut in by the contemptuous height of the four walls, removed from our peace, our routine.

At that time there were many newer and better doctors, but the Basque woman, Moncha Insaurralde, almost immediately after her return from Europe, before shutting herself inside the walls, called Dr. Diaz

Grey, made an appointment, climbed the two flights of stairs, and smiled dazed and breathless, her hand clutching her chest so as to lift the left breast and make it touch the spot where she thought her heart was, excessively close to the shoulder.

She said she was going to die, said she was going to get married. She seemed (or was) very different. The inevitable Diaz Grey tried to remind her of the time some years before, during the flight from Santa Maria, from the brothel, when she believed that Europe guaranteed her at the very least a change of skin.

"Nothing, there are no symptoms," the girl said. "I don't know why I came to see you. If I were really sick, I would have gone to a real doctor. Pardon me. But someday you will know you are something more than that. My father was a friend of yours. Maybe that's why I came."

She got up, thin yet massive, swaying without being flirtatious, pushing her uneven body with an aging will.

"Still a lovely filly, a purebred mare, with painful bony tumors," the doctor thought. "If I could wash your face and listen to it with a stethoscope, no more than that, your invisible face beneath the violet, red, yellow, black lines that stretch out your eyes without any certain or understandable meaning.

"If I could see you once more defying the imbecility of Santa Maria, without any defense or protection or mask, with your hair hastily tied at the back of your neck, with just that masculine element that makes a woman into a person, without being too much. That ineffable something, that fourth or fifth sex we call a girl.

"Another madwoman, another sweet and tragic madwoman, another Julita Malabia, so soon afterward and in our midst, this one also right in our midst so there's nothing for us to do but put up with her and love her."

She advanced into the examining room while Diaz Grey unbuttoned his lab coat and lit a cigarette; she turned her purse upside down, and out spilled everything, a tube of something, some feminine fetish slowly rolling off. The doctor did not look; he saw only her, wanted only to see her face.

She separated the bills, shuffled them with a gesture of disgust, and put them next to the doctor's elbow.

"Crazy, beyond cure, no chance to ask questions."

"I am paying," Moncha said. "I pay so that you will write me prescriptions, will cure me, will repeat with me: I am going to get married, I am going to die."

Without touching the money, without rejecting it, Diaz Grey stood up, took off his lab coat—so white, so starched—and looked at the twitching profile, the vulgar makeup that now, illuminated by the large window nearby, was changing its astonishing combination of colors.

"You are going to get married," he obediently recited.

"And I am going to die."

"That is not a diagnosis."

She smiled briefly, recovering her adolescence, while starting to stuff things back in her purse: papers, documents, jewelry, perfume, toilet paper, a golden powder puff, candies, pills, a partly eaten cracker, maybe some wrinkled envelope, faded from age.

"But that's not enough, doctor. You must come with me. I have the car down below. It's close by; I'm living in the hotel, for a few days or forever, depending on who wins."

Diaz Grey went and like a father saw everything. While he was looking at the secret he absentmindedly caressed Moncha's restless neck; he touched her elbows, his gestures brushing against one of her breasts.

Diaz Grey saw only a tenth of what a woman would have seen and been able to explain. Silk, lace inserts, lace edging, the sinuous foam on the bed.

"Now do you understand?" the woman said without asking. "It's for my wedding dress. Marcos Bergner and Father Bergner." She laughed, looking at the whiteness curling on the dark bedspread. "The whole family. Father Bergner is going to marry me to Marquitos. We still haven't set the date."

Diaz Grey lit a cigarette while stepping back. The priest had died in his sleep two years before; Marcos had died six months earlier, after a meal and too much to drink, lying on top of a woman. But, he thought, none of that mattered. The truth was what could still be heard, seen, perhaps touched. The truth was that Moncha Insaurralde had come back from Europe to marry Marcos Bergner in the cathedral, blessed by Father Bergner.

He approved and said, caressing her back, "Yes. That's right. I was sure."

Moncha knelt down to kiss the lace, slowly and carefully.

"I couldn't be happy there. We arranged it by mail."

It was impossible that the whole city took part in a conspiracy of lies or silence. But Moncha was surrounded, even before the dress, by lead, cork, silence that prevented others from understanding or even from listening to the deformations of her truth, the truth that we had made, and shaped with her. Father Bergner was in Rome, always returning from color postcards with the Vatican in the background,

constantly going from one room to another, forever saying goodbye
to cardinals, bishops, silk cassocks, an endless parade of youths
dressed as altar boys, cruets, swift spirals of incense smoke.

Marcos Bergner was always on his way back in his fabulously expensive yacht, always tied to the main mast during the inevitable
yet inevitably conquered storms, playing every day or night with the
wheel, maybe a bit drunk, his unforgettable face coming into focus
as he returned, the sea salt and iodine making his face grow, red-
dening his beard, as in the happy ending of an English brand of
cigarettes.

This, the uncertainty about the definite dates of the returns, the certainty beyond doubt or firm evidence of an Insaurralde's word or
promise, a Basque word that fell on or burdened us without any need
to be uttered once and forever, for all eternity. A thought, barely and
perhaps never entirely thought; a yearned-for promise placed in the
world, imposed there, indestructible, always defiant, stronger and
fuller if touched by time or bad weather—rain, wind, hail, moss, and
the furious sun—alone.

So that all of us helped her, without foreboding or remorse, to
sink into the brief first part, the prologue written for the benefit of
those who didn't know. We told her yes, we accepted its urgency and
necessity, perhaps touched her shoulder so that she would get on the
train, waiting, maybe, hoping not to see her again.

And so, urged on to some extent by our goodwill, by our well-
deserved hypocrisy, Moncha, Moncha Insaurralde, or Insurralde,
went to the Capital (in the language of the scribes at *El Liberal*) so
that Madame Caron could transform her silk, lace inserts and lace
edging into a wedding gown worthy of her, of Santa Maria, of the late
Marcos Bergner, dead but forever aboard his yacht, of the late Father
Bergner, dead but forever saying endless goodbyes in the Vatican in
Rome, in the worm-eaten town church we were capable of imagining.

But once again she went to the Capital and returned to us with a
wedding dress that the decaying chroniclers of the social column
could describe in their hermetic, nostalgic style:

*The day of her wedding, celebrated in the Basilica of the Holy
Sacrament, she wore a crepe dress with strass embroidery marking the high waist. A lace roundlet adorned her head and held the
veil of transparent tulle; in her hand she was holding a bouquet of
phalaenoposis. Her marriage was blessed in the Basilica of Our
Lady of Help; the bride wore a princess dress of embroidered silk*

*organdy. She wore her hair high, and the chignon was adorned with little flowers and the top of the veil. In her hand she held a rosary. At San Nicolas de Bari the bride wore a straight-cut dress of a single piece of embroidered cloth, with an open apron that revealed a skirting of satin camellias, a detail repeated on the headdress holding a transparent tulle cloak. Later, at the cathedral of Santa Maria, she wore an original gown all cut from one piece of silk, her long veil of transparent tulle pinned to her hair with mother-of-pearl flowers that continued down the sides of the dress, forming sleeves attached to her wrists; in her hand she held a bouquet of tulips and orange blossoms.*

She went, she knocked, she bounced back, like a football pumped too full of air, not squashed, not yet dead. She left and returned to us, to Santa Maria.

And then we all thought, faced our improbable guilt. She, Moncha, was crazy. But all of us had contributed to her madness with our love, goodness, good intentions, faint jests, our respectable desire to feel comfortable and sheltered, our desire for nobody, not even Moncha, whether crazy or dead or alive or well, no matter how admirably dressed, to deprive us of a few minutes of sleep or of normal pleasures.

We accepted her, finally, and were left with her. God, Brausen, forgive us.

She did not speak to us about hotel ceilings, or about outings in the country, or about monuments, ruins, museums, historic names referring to battles, artists, or the spoils of war. When the wind or light or fancy made her do so, she told us, without our having asked any questions, without beginning or end:

"I had arrived in Venice at dawn. I had hardly slept at all that night, my head resting on the window, watching the light of cities and towns I was seeing for the first and last time pass by, and when I closed my eyes I could smell the strong smell of wood, of leather, of the uncomfortable seats, and could hear the voices that from time to time whispered phrases I could not understand. When I got off the train and left the station, the lights were still on; it was about 5:30 in the morning. I walked half-asleep through the empty streets until reaching Saint Mark's Square, absolutely deserted except for the pigeons and a few beggars lying by the columns. From afar, it was so identical to the pictures on the postcards I had seen, the colors were so perfect, the complicated silhouette of the curved roofs against the rising sun—it was all as unreal as the notion that I was there, that I

was the only person there at that moment. I walked slowly, like a
sleepwalker, and found myself crying and crying; it was as if the solitude, seeing it all so perfect, the way I had expected, had turned it
into a part of me forever, although it was the closest thing to a waking dream that a person could ever have. And later—or was it earlier,
one night in Barcelona—the boy who danced, dressed as a bull-
fighter, with tight red pants, within the circle formed by the tables. I
remember when we went upstairs, to a table that looked out on the
dance floor, and there was almost no one left; and there were the two
boys dancing together, very close, about the same height, brown-
skinned; and the owner offered to find somebody for me, and I got
frightened, not knowing whether he was offering me a man or a
woman. And a street, I don't remember where, old houses painted
some gaudy color, now faded, clothes hanging from one side to the
other of the narrow sidewalk, children in rags, their bare feet slipping on wet cobblestones between stands of fish and octopus, full of
strange colors and forms."

By then, doubtless after the torture of the passing months, when
we called together the notable people to forget Juntacadaveres, the
young man or woman at Barthé's drugstore had grown, was broad
and strong, and only used the ready whiteness of his smile to recall
his shyness of a few years before.

"Barthé played with fire," the silliest one among us once said, remembering when, as he dealt cards at the table at the Club.

We. We knew that yes, Barthé the druggist had played with fire, or
with the healthy animal who had been a child in his time, that he
had played and had ended up getting burnt.

But, it may be worth noting, parenthetically, that the face and
smile of the young man in the drugstore never had the brilliant glow
of cynicism. For no reason, he displayed a goodness, exhibited a
simple acceptance of being located in the world or molding himself
to life, to a world that seemed unlimited to him, to Santa Maria.

One of us, while dealing or receiving cards in the poker game,
spoke of the absent sorcerer, of the solitary sorcerer's apprentice. We
did not make any comments because in poker you're not allowed
to talk.

"I'll take one."

"Not me. I'll pass."

"One more. I'll raise ten."

The police report said nothing and the gossip column of *El Liberal* heard nothing about it. But we all knew; gathered around the
card table or the bar, we knew that Insaurralde, the Basque woman,

so different from everyone, would shut herself in at night in the drugstore—in sight of Barthé's diploma as a pharmacist, high above the counter, beyond any doubt—with Barthé and the young man or woman who was now smiling absentmindedly at everyone and who was in fact, though without visible means, the owner of the drugstore. The three of them inside, and all our seasoned curiosity had to use for guesses and slanders was the blue button by a little illuminated sign: "Emergency Service."

We moved chips and cards, whispering games and challenges, thinking mutely: the three of them, two, and one looking on, two and one says it serves me right, I'm out, I don't see but am always looking. Or, once again, the three of them, and the drugs, liquids or powders hidden in the drugstore belonging to the confused, mistaken, interchangeable owner.

Everything was possible, even what was physically impossible, to us, four old men sitting around a bunch of cards—legitimate tricks, various drinks.

As Francisco, the headwaiter, might have said, each of the four of us had learned, perhaps even before mastering the game, how to hold the muscles of our faces perfectly still for hours at a time, how to maintain an invariable deathly glow in our eyes, to repeat slow, monotone, bored expressions with indifference.

But when we killed off all expression that might transmit joy, discouragement, calculated risks, large or small stratagems, it was necessary or inevitable for our faces to show other things, things we resolved or were accustomed to hiding day by day, for years, from the moment of waking through the hours of work until the time we fell asleep again.

Because very soon afterward we found out, laughing discreetly, shaking our heads with feigned pity, with the pretense of understanding, about the fact that Moncha shut herself in the drugstore with Barthé and the young man. She always dressed as a bride; the boy always displayed his naked torso without remembering the time before; the druggist in slippers suffered from gout and the eternal, ill-defined bad humor of spinsters.

The three of them leaned over Tarot cards, pretending to believe in returns, in sudden changes in luck, in deaths barely avoided, in betrayals that could be foreseen and awaited.

For only a moment: Barthé's soft fat, his expectant, frowning mouth; the growing muscles of the young man who no longer needed to raise his voice to give orders; the unlikely wedding dress that trailed after Moncha between display cases and shelves, before the huge brown flasks with white labels, all or almost all of them incomprehensible.

But the strange Tarot cards were always on the table; irresistibly, they came back to them to be surprised, afraid, or hesitant.

And it must be pointed out, for the benefit or the perplexity of probable future interpreters of the life and passions of Santa Maria, that the two men had stopped belonging to the novel, to the indisputable truth.

Barthé, fat and asthmatic, in hysterical withdrawal, suffering from grotesque explosions tolerated by the others, was no longer a councilman, no more now than the pharmacist's diploma hanging behind the counter stained by the years and the flies, no more than the sporadic leader of one of the ten Trotskyist groups, each consisting of three or four dangerous revolutionaries who, with a menstrual rhythm, drafted and signed manifestos, declarations, and protests on the most diverse and exotic topics.

The young man was nothing but the annoyed, timid cynic who one winter evening came up to the bed of a Barthé frightened by flu, a bad conscience, fear, the beyond, 101 degrees of fever, and recited in clear, cautious words: "Two things, sir, and forgive me. Make me your partner; I have a lawyer here with me. Or else I'm leaving and I'll close the drugstore. And the business is finished."

They signed the contract, and Barthé, to maintain his belief in survival, was just left with the sadness of thinking that things had never been different, that the partnership he had thought about for so long as a belated wedding present had in fact been imposed by extortion, not by the harmonious maturing of love.

So that of the three of them Moncha, despite her partial madness and the death that could only be seen as a detail, a personal characteristic, a way of being, was the only one who remained alert and active, only Brausen knows how long.

Like an insect? Perhaps. One can also accept as equally novel the metaphor of the mermaid pulled without mercy from the sea, patiently enduring the lurches and land sickness in the cave of the drugstore. Definitely, like an insect trapped in the dirty twilight by the strange cards that filtered yesterday and today and displayed the inexorable future in a confusing, contradictory way. The insect, with its shell of a faded white, fluttered weakly around the sad light that fell on the table and the four hands, drawing off to bounce against decanters and glass cabinets, slowly and clumsily dragging its long, silent, quite undeserved tail, designed and made one distant day by Madame Caron herself.

And each night, after closing the drugstore and illuminating the purple lights outside to signal night service, the large white insect would traverse its usual large circles and near horizons before settling down again, rubbing or just touching its antennae, above the promises whispered by the Tarot cards, above the stammering of cards with sacerdotal, threatening faces repeating joys to be reached after tiresome labyrinths, telling of inevitable yet imprecise dates.

And, though it may be of no importance, the half-naked young man was left with a not fully understood feeling of fraternity, and Barthé's remaining old age with an insoluble problem to chew on toothlessly, sunken in an armchair he had moved into, rubbing his thumbs on a belly that had never grown smaller: "She was here and it was as if the house was hers. She walked and poked and rummaged around. The two of us always loved her, because she never stole any poison, which would not have been stealing in any case, and it ended quicker and with less unhappiness."

And then it began happening to us and kept on happening until the end and for a little while thereafter.

Because, we insist, just as Moncha had once returned from the brothel, bumped into Santa Maria, and then went to Europe, so now she was arriving in Europe via the Capital and then coming back to us, to live together with this Santa Maria that, as someone said, wasn't the same anymore.

We could not shelter you, Moncha, in the large gray and green spaces of the avenues; we could not expel so many thousands of bodies, could not reduce the height of the incongruous new buildings to make you feel more comfortable, more at one or in solitude with us. There was very little, just the unavoidable, that we could do against scandal, irony, indifference.

Downtown another wall of concrete or glass was being built every day, much taller and better than we old people who insisted on denying time, on pretending, on believing in the static existence of that Santa Maria where we walked and looked around; and Moncha sufficed for us.

There was something else, something of no importance. With the same naturalness, with the same effort or farce we employed to forget the new and undeniable city, we tried to forget Moncha as we leaned over our glasses and cards, in the Plaza bar, in the chosen restaurant, in the brand-new Club building.

Perhaps someone infused respect or silence with some sharp phrase. We accepted and forgot Moncha and spoke once more of harvests, of the price of wheat, of the still river and its ships—and of what was entering and leaving the holds of the ships—of the rise and fall in the exchange rate, of the health of the governor's wife, the lady, Our Lady.

But nothing was any use, the childish tricks or the recourse to exorcism. Here we were, Moncha's disease, the seventy-five-thousand-dollar illness of the Lady, the first installment.

So we had to wake up and believe, tell ourselves that yes, we had seen it months earlier, that Moncha was in Santa Maria and was the way she was.

We had seen her, knew that she went by in taxis or in a broken-down '51 Opel, that she made futile courtesy calls, commemorating (perhaps with intentional malice) anniversaries that were dead and beyond the possibility of resurrection. Births, weddings, and deaths. Perhaps (but they exaggerate) commemorating the precise day when it was advisable, even good, to forget a sin, a flight, an act of blackmail, some defiled form of farewell, an act of cowardice.

We never discovered if all of this was contained in her memory; we never found a notebook, even a simple almanac with cheerful illustrations that might explain it.

Santa Maria has a river, ships. If it has a river, it has fog; the ships use horns, sirens. They warn, they exist, poor lifeguard, watcher of fresh water. With your umbrella, your robe, your bathing suit, your picnic basket, wife and children—you (in a quickly forgotten moment of imagination or weakness), you can, you could think, you might have thought of the tender, hoarse cry of the baby whale calling its mother, of the hoarse, fearful cry of the mother whale. That's right; that is more or less what happens in Santa Maria when the fog covers the river.

The truth, if we could swear that ghost was among us for three whole months, is that Moncha Insaurralde went out almost every day, always with the smell and appearance of eternity (such as it was) in the wedding gown Madame Caron had made for her in the Capital, with the silk and lace she had brought from Europe for the wedding ceremony with one of the Marcos Bergners she had invented from afar, blessed by an unchangeable Father Bergner, grayish, made of stone. She was the only one still left to die.

All things are this way and not some other, although it may be possible to shuffle four times thirteen when it's all over and things are beyond help.

Various kinds of surprise, rotund affirmations by old people who refuse to surrender, inevitable confusions—all prevent us from assigning an exact date to the day and night of the first great fear. Moncha arrived at the Plaza bar in the wheezing car, made the chauffeur disappear, and advanced as if sleepwalking toward the table for two she had reserved. The wedding gown crossed, was dragged across, the stares; then, for hours, for more than an hour, it was almost quiet facing the emptiness (plates, forks, and knives) before it. She, barely happy and affable, directed questions at the nothingness, her arm still in midair with a serving of food or drink, listening. Everybody noted the breeding, the undeniable signs of good manners she had learned as a child. Everybody saw, in a different way, the yellowing wedding gown, the lace torn, even here and there hanging loose. She was protected by indifference and fear. The best people, if they were there, linked the dress to some memory of happiness, also used up by time and failure.

Neither too early nor too late, the headwaiter himself—for Moncha is named Insaurralde—brought the check, folded on a little plate, and placed it exactly halfway between her and the absent, invisible other, separated from us, from Santa Maria, by an incomprehensible distance of maritime miles, by the hunger of the fish. He asked, was barely there, nodded his fat, impassive, smiling face. He seemed to bless and to consecrate; he seemed used to the role. His summer tuxedo could also convincingly pass for a surplice.

One had to organize secret and solitary pilgrimages to the restaurant where she had dined with Marcos. A difficult, complex task, for it was not a matter of a simple move in space. It required that one first create and sustain a mood that one sometimes felt was gone forever, a spirit fitting the excitement of a date, knowing it would last, enjoyable and unavoidable, until the end of the evening, until the precise hour when one knows for sure that everything in Santa Maria is closed. And more than that: the mood should be sustained beyond closing time, should remain in the silence of the night, engender the sweetness of dreams. Because it must be understood that all the rest, what we people of Santa Maria insist on calling reality, was for Moncha as simple as a physiological act performed by a healthy body. To call the headwaiter at the Plaza, to ask him for a table "not too close or too far away," to announce Marcos's return to him and the consequent festivity, to argue in a provoking way about the possibilities for the meal, demanding Marcos's favorite wine, a wine that no longer existed, that no longer reached us, a wine that had been sold in elongated bottles bearing confused labels.

Aged, unsmiling, Francisco, the headwaiter, calmly played the game on the telephone, never abandoning his old convictions: he repeated that the impossible wine should be served (agreed, without a doubt) at room temperature, not too far, not too close to the point with the ideal, impossible temperature.

The date is written at the bottom and seems definite. Nevertheless, someone, something may swear, forty years after this story is written, that he saw Moncha Insaurralde at the corner of the Plaza. The details of the vision do not matter, nor do the civic advances of Santa Maria celebrated in *El Liberal*. All that matters is that everybody share in seeing her and they find themselves in agreement. Shrunken, with the wedding gown dyed black, wearing a hat, a straw hat with dark ribbons, excessively small even for the style of forty years later, leaning slightly on a thin ebony cane, on the inevitable silver handle, alone and determined in the autumn night (the air so smooth, the mooing sounds of the tugboats on the river so discreet), waiting with patient, ironic eyes for the departure of the occupants of precisely that table, the one located neither too close to nor too far from the front door and the kitchen. And always, in that infinite time that will exist when forty years have passed, the true, promised moment came, the moment when the table was empty and she could advance, coquettishly feigning to lean on the cane, greeting Francisco or Francisco's now adult grandson, going forward toward Marcos's impatience, excusing herself quietly for having been delayed. God was in his heavens and reigned on the earth; Marcos, drunk by now, unfading, forgave her, between jokes and dirty words, placing a little bouquet of the first violets of that middle-aged autumn beside her on the tablecloth.

As arranged, we, the old men, parted. There was no need for words of respect or understanding. Some forgot when necessary; they would have been able to continue for forty years in the shaping of oblivion. They forgot; they did not discover that Moncha Insaurralde wandered the streets of Santa Maria, entered the stores, punctually visited the mansions of the rich and the little houses down along the coast, always dressed in the wedding gown that awaited Marcos's return to be decorated with the prescribed white flowers, hard and fresh.

Some recalled the Basque Insaurralde, also dead and loyal to a memory, in the delirious woman who dragged the inevitable dirt stuck to the tail of her dress, who clung to that dirt. And these people also chose to look after the ghost, to pretend they believed in him, in his wealth and prestige, in what remained of his tender adolescent cruelty still uncovered by ashes.

There was little, for both groups; in any case, they saw and found out much less. They simply saw.

If there is spikenard and jasmine, if there are candles or wax, if there is a light and blank papers on a desk, if there are lines of foam on the river, if there are girls' teeth, if the whiteness of dawn grows atop the whiteness of milk falling hot and white on the cold pail, if there are aged women's hands, hands that never worked, if there is a small line of petticoat for the boy's first date, if there is an especially well-prepared absinthe, if there are shirts hanging in the sun, if there are soapsuds and shaving cream or toothpaste, if there are deceptively innocent membranes on children's eyes, if today there is intact new-fallen snow, if the emperor of Siam is reserving a herd of elephants for the viceroy or the governor, if there are cotton blossoms brushing against the chests of blacks sweating and cutting, if there is a woman in pain and misery capable of saying no, of getting up again, capable of not counting the coins, of not reckoning the immediate future, of not giving away a useless thing.

All this long thing, the impossibility of telling the story of the inappropriate moth-eaten, crooked, old wedding gown in a sentence three lines long. But it was all of that: dress, bathrobe, nightshirt, and shroud. For everyone, those who had preferred to take prudent refuge in ignorance and those who had chosen to form a displaced personal guard, recognizing its existence and proclaiming that to the extent possible we would protect the wedding dress that was getting older every day, hopelessly approaching the category of a rag, protecting the dress and what it enclosed, unknown, unforeseen.

The sterile, silent, contradictory but never hostile proposals of those of us old men who gathered in the Plaza or at the new Club building did not last long—less than three months, as already stated.

For smoothly, suddenly, so smoothly that afterward, when we found out, or when we began to forget, it seemed sudden to us, all the imaginable moribund white shades, more yellow every day, approaching the ultimate color of ash, grew inexorable, and then we accepted them as the truth.

For Moncha Insaurralde had locked herself in the basement of her house, having taken some (but not enough) Seconals, wearing the wedding gown that, in the veiled tranquility of the Santa Maria autumn, could serve her as a true skin around her thin body, her harmonious bones. And she lay down to die, tired of breathing.

Then it was that the doctor could contemplate, smell, confirm that the world he had before him, a world he continued to accept, was not based on tricks or sweet lies. The game, at least, was a clean game, properly respected by both parties: Godbrausen and himself.

There were distant, fanatical Insaurraldes who wished the dead woman had suffered an unforeseen heart attack. In any case, they succeeded: there would be no autopsy. That is why it may be that the doctor wavered between the obvious truth and the hypocrisy of posterity. He preferred, all at once, to give himself over to absurd love, to inexplicable loyalty, to some form of loyalty capable of creating misunderstandings. People almost always choose that way. He refused to open the windows, accepted the inopportune communion, the idea of breathing the same corrupted air, the same smell of stale grime, of the end. And finally, after so many years, he wrote, without the need to linger and think.

He was trembling with humility and justice, and a strange incomprehensible pride when, finally, he wrote the promised letter, the few words that said it all, the full name of the deceased: Maria Ramona Insaurralde Zamora. Place of death: Santa Maria, Second District. Sex: female. Race: white. Name of the country of birth: Santa Maria. Age at the time of death: 29. The death occurred the day of the month of the year at the hour and minute. Condition or illness that caused death: Brausen, Santa Maria, all of you, I myself.